Praise for Linda's First Novel, *Life a la Mode*

"In her zesty literary debut, Linda Lenhoff serves up a warm slice of twentysomething life laced with a satisfying blend of sugar and spice, saucy dialogue, and a sprinkling of sharply drawn secondary characters. Readers are sure to relish *Life a la Mode* and will likely be left craving seconds."

—Wendy Markham, author of *Slightly Settled*

"A surprise ending tops off Lenhoff's delightful novel and leaves readers satisfied and hopeful."

—San Mateo County Times

"A lighthearted romp... a very funny look at singles life in Manhattan. Readers will laugh loudly."

—The Midwest Book Review

"The satisfaction of a great slice of pie without any of the calories. *Life a la Mode* is sweet, rich, and tasty. Read and enjoy!"

—Lynne Hinton, bestselling author of *Friendship Cake*

LINDA LENHOFF

The Girl in the '67 Beetle

Laurel
Canyon
Press

First published by Laurel Canyon Press 2021

Book cover by Michael Everitt. Author's photo by Haley Nelson.

First edition

ISBN: 9780578911175

This book was professionally typeset on Reedsy. Find out more at reedsy.com

To Cindy Lambert

For her wonderful friendship

Contents

I

Part One

1

Goodwill to the Rescue

I am scanning the aisles of Trader Joe's, looking for something celebratory but inexpensive for dinner. It is my anniversary, and I realize I'm acting a little like a New Agey Hallmark card for a thirty-four-year-old celebrating the first anniversary of her divorce (and you just know the card would be too pink, with a girl holding a martini glass with too much martini in it). Still, I'm here anyhow. Trader Joe's is the grocery store of my younger self, where I came as a college student to buy very cheap wine (I still buy it) and big blocks of cheese (I've cut down on the cheese—dairy, you know). The store looks brand new, having undergone renovation this past year. A lot like me, but more fluorescent and way more noticeable. You can now find some form of chocolate at the end of almost every aisle. Something that makes me think they know I shop here, or there are a lot more women like me than I ever thought.

A crowd has gathered around the low-carb section, which thankfully isn't too large an area. I wouldn't want it to take space away from the chocolate, say, which I believe plays a more important role in one's healthfulness, mental at least. I will not trade my semisweet organic chocolate—a proven friend—for a trend that says bad things about pizza, another proven friend. But then, I've always been relatively thin. Not that the crowd around the low-carbs looks fat—this is Santa Monica, California, after all, not a heavyset town but weight-conscious nonetheless. I'm not sure I could get up in the morning knowing each day would be low-carb, let alone carb-free.

An older man is watching the low-carb folks, too. He looks at me, and we share a smile. He then accidentally turns and knocks over an entire rack of chocolate bars (the ones with the white wrappers and hazelnuts inside, a very good choice), and the whole group of low carb-ettes turns to see, with looks of longing on their determined faces. The older man looks slightly bemused. I wonder if he planned this.

"You're a tempter, is that it?" I ask, helping him pick up the bars. I put one in my basket. I don't care if it fell on the floor. It's wrapped.

"Who could resist?" he says, with a mischievous smile on his face. "Thanks for the help. I should buy you a chocolate bar," he says.

"Please, I'm over thirty," I joke. "You should buy me two."

"I don't think they'd approve," he says with a nod to the low-carbettes. They've all gone back to reading the confusing low-carb packaging with all the tiny print tucked under the fold. I can never make it past the first line of text. Food shouldn't come with so many instructions.

"Well, enjoy your not-good-for-you treats," I say.

"Dark chocolate is very good for you, I've heard," my older man says, waving a dark chocolate-with-cherries bar at me.

"I don't have a problem with milk chocolate," I say. "You could call it a personal health study I'm conducting. All the results aren't in yet, but so far, I'm finding I'm a lot happier when I see that the store has refilled the selection. I don't even necessarily need to buy one—it's just something about knowing they're here."

"In times of need," he says, completing my thoughts. No one's done that in a while. I laugh and wave, then head for wine. I know my needs so well. He waves back then goes to the premade frozen-dinner-with-a-flair section. Most of which serves one. I hit that section already. Trader Joe's can tell you a lot about a person.

After checking out, I pack up my car with my anniversary dinner, wine, and dessert (a rich, smooth chocolate sorbet, which fills so many needs at once). My older friend packs up his car as well, which is parked directly across from mine. Dog biscuits drop from his bag, and he picks them up. He certainly drops a lot. He looks up to see me and waves, unembarrassed. It must be nice to be a little older, beyond self-consciousness. He drives one of those classic round Volvos (from before they went boxy) that are usually falling apart, but his is in great shape. He points to my car and gives me a big okay sign. I throw my hair back, an "Of course this car is mine." It was a hand-me-down from Aunt Lucille, when I left behind the Audi Hooper had given me, a supposed trendy car he loved that actually just broke down all the time and spewed some kind of blue plume. This is my car now, as Aunt Lucille has given up driving. It's a 1967 powder blue Volkswagen Beetle convertible, in very good condition. *Cherry*, as my uncle used to say. The top is up, but somehow my hair still blows back when I drive. Maybe there's a leak in the roof, but I don't think so. It may be more of a feeling than an actual breeze, but it works for me. I wave good-bye again. We both get into our classic cars, if an old Volvo is a classic. Both cars have a plumpness that complements the other in almost a sensual way. We each have a curvy, chubby car that's a little out of date, but still looking good. And we know it.

* * *

What makes this night special: I get out a candle I bought at Trader Joe's, a long white taper (six for $1.99), and place it in a Depression glass candlestick holder Aunt Lucille has left behind for me. (Yes, she's lent me her condo, which I do pay for, as she's moved up to much newer senior housing two blocks from the beach.) The candlestick is heavy and deep green, more significant in weight than any of the glass candlestick holders I once owned, in my previous existence as an up-and-coming lawyer's wife, working woman, and not-very-together trendsetter. I place the candleholder in my hand a moment. It has the comforting weight of an old college textbook, something loved, something real. I light the candle.

My celebration dinner consists of a salty, prepackaged green mixture of Thai chicken and veggies. Hooper would not eat anything with sauces—only pure food, he used to say, meaning plain, unadorned. This made ordering Chinese unhappily impossible, a sign that maybe things do happen for a reason, divorce anyhow. I love really soupy Chinese food. Anything saucy makes me feel exotic, a little dangerous, and ready for a surprise. It makes me feel like someone else entirely.

I pour myself a glass of wine (white, not red, because this is about me). I love sweet white wine. This is my anti-establishment dinner, Thai food and wine, with a candlestick stuck in only one holder, not two, as was once required. I do realize, of course, that thousands of happy couples might be sitting down to exactly this same dinner (maybe without any candle at all)—that it would be perfectly fine for them, a happy occasion or at least a happily normal one. This stings my eyes for a moment, but after I let it sink in, I start to feel a little more included. I'm not really eating alone; I'm more or less happy to celebrate joining the normalcy of eating just what I want, at last.

It is my greatest pleasure to spoon out two pieces of chicken, wipe off the sauce, place them on one of Aunt Lucille's old china saucers, and give them to Lulu, my cat. On the table, yet. It's the height of decadence for me. She likes it, too.

Getting Lulu was the first thing I did after separating. I went to the shelter and found her all cooped up in a cage, a youngish, long-haired, maybe part Ragdoll cat with dark brown Siamese markings, the look on her face suggesting she thought she was royal, though not treated appropriately to her rank. In our year together, she has become even more regal, a full-blown mishmash of buff- and a variety of brown-colored long hair poking in all directions, and what used to be known in literature as a supercilious expression. She does not take kindly to combing unless she comes up to you and stabs you (okay, me) with two toes on her left paw. She's insistent but utterly loyal, dedicated to me and Friskies—pâté only, naturally. Hooper would have hated her at first sight. Turned out he was a man who disliked cats. I was so blind.

I drink quite a lot of the wine, listening to the stereo placed beside the dining table, so I can switch the stations round and round. This, I know, would drive someone else crazy, someone

I might have had to share my wine with, someone who would never have eaten a Thai prepackaged dinner in the first place. Someone gone now for a full and very long year. I switch from country music to rock to something where a guy is yelling. I nod along with him. You go, guy. After a minute, it occurs to me that it may be a woman. I nod harder. Then, when the yelling gets too annoying, I start switching the dial again. Lulu just looks at me. When I switch to a way-too-young boy group, she jumps off the table. Fine, see if you get dessert.

Ah, dessert. My chocolate sorbet. Who'd have thought it'd go so well with more sweet wine? I feel so sated. And I don't even need to eat the whole carton.

* * *

After dinner, in my somewhat trancelike state, I'm startled by the sound of large vehicles, tanks maybe, and although the image might be a little warlike, I find I feel very excited by their approach, that I've really been looking forward to this. I rise to greet the tanks, but instead find only the Goodwill truck. And two burly guys. I don't know why they're always burly, but I take great comfort in this fact. They have no tattoos, just so you know I'm not just being cliché about burly guys. And come to think of it, they've got very similar music blaring to the girl (or guy) screaming on the radio earlier. I guess it's a popular tune.

"You guys are working late," I tell them, with admiration in my voice. I've always envied people who drive big, noisy trucks. I don't think a lot of people know this about me.

"We've squeezed you in," says the first guy, whose voice is much higher than I would have thought, judging from his dark curly hair and Dodge Truck T-shirt. The shirt doesn't say anything in particular about Dodge trucks, but I guess he likes them. And I'm all for that. The other guy is shorter and wears a red T-shirt with a cute giant Panda on it and the San Diego Zoo written across the top. I have to admire a burly guy in a Panda bear T-shirt.

"It's all here," I say, pointing to my hallway and boxes of stuff that I packed up, the merchandise of marital bliss, if you believe the ads in glossy magazines, on TV, and everywhere else. If I knew you better, I'd beg you not to believe any of it.

The burlies take my boxes. They don't even strain lifting them, but I know the boxes are heavy. Weight being relative, of course, especially if you're the one who packed the contents, with great relief, too.

I open the last remaining box, which holds a fancy silver convection oven that was too tiny to cook very much in. Aunt Lucille has more of an industrial-size microwave that sounds like an airplane engine. I like a microwave that makes a statement. The ridiculous little silver box looks like a silver-plated Easy Bake Oven. (I could never get mine to work as a kid, come to think of it, and raw chocolate cake is just never as good as you hope.) I slip my hand inside my pocket and pull out a plain yet weighty golden ring, not inscribed—although at one time I begged for an inscription—and slip it inside the oven. I shut the little door and close up the box. It takes less than five seconds to complete this task, which for some reason I've counted out loud. One, two, three, four, five—all done.

I wave good-bye to the Goodwill boys. I don't ask for a receipt. I don't need one.

2

Portrait of an Artist (Photoshop Sometimes Required)

Working at Kids Press in Santa Monica, California, does not mean that I have to wear primary colors or polka dot jumpers, but it does have its perks, one of them being that if I did show up in primary colors or a polka dot jumper, no one would much care. I am the Co-Director of Artistic Endeavors, according to my boss, a cheerful entrepreneur named Nelson. My title is even printed on my business cards, which I always forget to carry, maybe because they're shaped like little artist's palettes. There is of course another Co-Director of Artistic Endeavors named Chris (short for Christopher, which he doesn't much like being called), who's about my age. I have heard him use his full title when he answers his phone, saying "This is Chris, Co-Director of Artistic Endeavors." Sometimes, he even adds, "What would you like to fingerpaint today?" He gets quite a few hang-ups, but maybe that's his intent. I usually tell people I'm the co-art director and leave it at that. I leave most of the phone answering to Chris, anyway. It's a thing with him.

"Ugh," I hear from the front of the office, meaning our administrative assistant and all-around super helpful person, Kelly, has arrived. She's about twenty-two and has blonde surfer girl looks she cannot stand about herself, which those of us whose blonde hair isn't quite so light and shiny anymore just can't understand. Kelly lives out in the Valley, and although it isn't that far if you're a bird flying directly—a big strong bird, say—it can take an age to get here on the cracked, hot freeway, given that every single other person in L.A. drives a car, too. The carpool lane should mean you can drive faster, but really it just means that there will be even more frustrated people late for work in your car, not that I have anything at all against conserving gasoline. Carpooling also means someone can hand you your coffee, although no one out here drives with two hands on the wheel, even highway patrol officers. They like Starbucks, too, it seems.

"I had a very pleasant bike ride to work," my co-director Chris says, loud enough for Kelly to hear, unless she's plugging her ears with her fingers, which I've seen her do. I don't blame her.

"All that clean ocean air," Chris says, bragging again. He lives near our Santa Monica office, but then, so do I.

If you haven't been to Santa Monica, you've still probably heard of it as an overpriced, always-sunny, please-let-me-live-here city. And it lives up to its reputation. I love my town. I grew up south of here toward Redondo Beach (yes, it's a fine beach town, too; I've never heard anyone say a bad thing about it). But I've just always wanted to live right where I do. You can feel the beach—it's in the air, the casual way people stroll, and the requisite need for sunglasses—all the way in toward

Westwood or so, but then it just starts to feel like L.A. Could be the smog. Okay, we get a little smog, too, but it's rare and only reminds us how truly lucky we are. We are all grateful. We are all repeating under our breath, *Thank goodness I live here*, practically every minute of every day. Even if we don't realize this about ourselves.

"The ocean is polluted," Kelly says. "There's no telling what you're breathing in living near it. At least the smog in the Valley is obvious."

"No luck finding an apartment out here, huh?" I ask her.

Kelly shakes her head. "The last one I looked at was $2,900 a month. For a studio."

"Indoor plumbing?" Chris asks.

"Barely," Kelly says, and I'm not sure I really want details.

I, of course, have my rented condo unit à la Aunt Lucille just a few blocks away, and Chris has a loft in Venice that he's spent eight years fixing up. His parents loaned him some money that he's still paying back. He doesn't really like talking about that, but his place is really cool and hip, with a trendy multi-fabric couch and a lot of tables made from recycled wood, though there's not all that much furniture, come to think of it. Co-Directors of Artistic Endeavors are not that well paid out here, if they are anywhere.

Our office, near 20th on Wilshire, is set in a weird part of town that's somehow older feeling. The area has been remodeled—just not recently. So you'll find shiny banks mixed with older buildings like ours (we're on the second floor), within easy reach of two taco shops, a GAP, a healthy foods store, two donut shops, several cafes, and a sporting goods store where you can ogle kayaks of enormous size and pretty colors—or at least Chris does. Not that any of us has bought one. And even if I did, I'm not sure how I would get one home with my Beetle. Chris drives a twenty-year-old beat-up Forerunner that could hold a family of Saint Bernards, not that we've tried it, but it's been suggested. He likes to haul strange materials after he dumpster dives, like most of us who like to make things. Thankfully, I can't do that much, as the Beetle demands a more minimalist lifestyle.

"You two are taking up two perfectly good rental spaces," Kelly says. "The least you could do is not look so peppy in the morning." It's true, it takes me only five minutes to get here by Beetle; twelve minutes if I walk. I'm a little north of here. (It only gets better as you go north, ask anyone. Or better yet, don't. People who live north of Montana Blvd. can be a little snobby.) But I like bringing the Beetle, just so it can get some exercise, which, for some reason, I feel is more important for the Beetle than for me. People in the office seem to like to see it, too, the cheery little bug.

"Kelly, it's not that we don't feel for you."

"It's just that you're young, and struggle is good for you," Chris finishes, although I don't think that's what I would have said. Not out loud, at least.

"Please," she says. "I'm twenty-two and living in my parents' garage."

"Not exactly garage," I say. I've seen the place. "You have a bay window." It's true, Kelly lives in a guest room above her parents' garage in their peaceful Sherman Oaks neighborhood. She has a bay window and more storage than my Santa Monica condo will ever have, no matter how many plastic purple space-saving boxes I buy at Target. They really don't save much space, anyhow.

"But it's my *parents'* bay window," she says, shuddering a

little, poor girl.

"Say no more," Chris says with the sympathetic nod of a thirty-five year old man with an outstanding loan from his parents. We both understand.

Kelly walks off to start the coffee, not that it will be her first cup, and not that it even comes close to Starbucks.

* * *

The bell rings. Now, it's not that we're strictly Pavlovian around here, but at a company that publishes children's books, it feels so right having a school bell ring and then assembling just where we're supposed. We don't walk in a single file line, though. If anything, there's a dash to the coffee room before assembling, and then a lot of bumping into one another, which may be just like third graders after all, minus the caffeination. We're not talking a little jingling bell, either. The Pacific Elementary school is across the street from our office, so at 8:30 a.m., we hear the morning bell, our signal to get to work. It's so ingrained—we really can't help ourselves. We get to work.

We are in an older building about twenty blocks from the famous beach, our office a sprawling and converted second floor that spans two storefronts below. Our offices are wall-less on the inside, sort of a groupwork idea before it got cool, but we do have some dividers between some desks, even if they're just those folding space dividers you would have bought at Pier One had it not gone bankrupt. Lots of plants around Kelly's desk, a few dying ones everywhere else. Actual windows that open. Try to find a place in metropolitan land where that's still true.

Our style is casual eclectic, we-like-it-here-if-you-don't please leave. Plus, we don't have all that many guests. Getting to work means going to our staff meeting, where we meet every day under the tutelage not so much of our leader, Nelson Davis, a darling, brown curly-haired, late fortyish person who's chubby in all the right places so that he would be the perfect Santa Claus, but not someone you'd be embarrassed to eat lunch with in a nice restaurant, which Nelson really does like to splurge on for us now and then. It's with Nelson at lunch that I tried my first focaccia. I didn't much like it, but Nelson is not the type of person who's afraid to finish someone else's meal. And he's not wheat-free. I find these qualities useful in a boss, especially when he's paying, which he always does.

But Nelson, despite being our fearless leader, having founded Kids Press fifteen years ago (I've been here for about ten), doesn't really like to lead meetings. He's more of the stare off into space and come up with the occasional brilliant idea type, for which no one can much fault him. We're in the black, after all, not to mention one of the last surviving independent children's publishers on the West Coast, or on any coast, in a beachy neighborhood with a juice bar and a two coffee houses down the street. Not one of us is complaining.

Which leaves the leading of our staff meetings to our editor in chief, Hannah Wallace, who won't really admit what her business card title is. Chris and I are constantly guessing, as Nelson would never give her something as mundane as Editor in Chief. We're thinking Creative Wordsmith in Execution, or at least Chris is. I think it's something like Executive Girl with Red Pen, but Hannah's not telling. She is in most ways no-nonsense and organized, and she really does use a red pen. She keeps a couple of them hidden on her at all times, or at least it seems like it. Hannah is tall and slim, but not in an obsessive way. She wears her auburn hair in a blunt cut. She calls herself fortyish, and leaves it at that. She is in charge at all times, a fact I find comforting.

Our meeting room is called the Staff Exploration Environment, but it's basically still a room with a long table—real maple, as Nelson hates laminates, but who doesn't—and several steel chairs that are modern, trendy, and pricey, and actually more comfortable than they look. I always figure I'll get a shiver from sitting down on the cold metal, but somehow, they're a little warmer than I expect. I've never understood metallurgy. Or maybe Hannah has Kelly come in and warm them up. It's not below Hannah to suggest this to Kelly, although it does seem a little obsessive. Nelson's chair has a red-and-white checked pillow on the seat. No one's ever mentioned it, as far as I know. Everyone has quirks, after all.

Chris and I bring our drinks into the room to join Hannah and Kelly, plus a woman named Robbi, who runs our foreign rights department, and a woman named Bobbi, who runs our sales department, or rather who is our sales department. That their names rhyme amuses Nelson no end and is no doubt why they were hired for a children's book publishing company. Nelson wishes all of our names rhymed, I happen to know.

The rest of our art department, two just out-of-school beginners named Jefferson and Gabriella, do not have to join the meetings, but instead get to answer the phones and, from the looks of things when we leave the meetings and rejoin them in the big art room, fold paper into intricate planes while complaining about art school. How I envy them, sometimes.

"Good morning, class," Nelson jokes. Kelly serves him a cup of coffee in his favorite mug, which has a Tweety Bird on it and is coveted by many in the office as one of the largest mugs ever created, although I find it a little too heavy. There is nothing sexist, by the way, in Kelly serving Nelson coffee, one because he really appreciates it, and two because Nelson's known for occasionally donning a waiter's apron and carrying a tray full of Starbucks around the office, handing us each a cup. I always tip him.

"Now, now," Hannah says. "Let's not make this any more fun that it has to be." She's fairly serious, as meetings can get a little silly with Nelson around, not to mention the rest of us. Chris is convinced that something must make her laugh, but he's yet to find it.

"I'm timing this with my new watch," Nelson says, showing it around.

"Ooh," Chris says, and I have to echo it. Hannah just clears her throat.

"Wow, major purchase," I say. I haven't made one in a while, if you don't count groceries, which are a major purchase in themselves, but not the kind you could time a meeting with.

"It comes with seven different faces and eight different bands," Nelson says.

"I'm not good at math," I say. "Just telling time is enough in a watch for me."

"It also tells the time in six different languages, and has an FM tuner," Nelson says.

"It's from one of those catalogs, isn't it?" Chris says. Chris is always perusing Nelson's catalogs with him, making notes. But he doesn't buy much, either. Catalogs, I've discovered, are to boys what *Vogue* is to girls. Neither publication has a lot to do with your actual life, is all.

"Does it beep at the end when you're done timing?" I ask. I

don't like beeping.

"You can have it play 'Rhapsody in Blue' or 'The Boogie Woogie Bugle Boy,' " Nelson answers. "There's no beeping whatsoever."

"We won't ask how much it costs," Hannah says, almost an order.

"Because you're the party pooper," Nelson says. "Okay, go!" He presses the watch's timer button. It starts to play that music from *Jeopardy* during which contestants consider their final answers. Hannah shoots Nelson a look, and he somehow manages to turn down the volume. I can still hear it a bit, though. It's kind of nice.

"Progress on the *Janey Wants a Truck* series?" Hannah asks.

"It's in final layout now," Chris says, and I nod. I love the Janey series. Now she wants to buy a truck and is considering a long bed with a net tailgate. In previous books, she tried construction work and archaeology. She liked them both.

"Progress on the *Why Bobby Doesn't Drink Milk* book?" Hannah asks. Nelson checks his watch. We're none of us too big on meetings. It should all be in the computer anyhow.

"The lactose-intolerant Bobby is responding nicely to a print check," I say. Bobby is a cute boy with red hair and freckles, somewhat bereft that he can't eat ice cream. All his friends share soy milk ice cream with him in the end, and not one of them complains about the funny aftertaste. I've been responsible for drawing Bobby in all his endeavors over the years. He's recovered from a broken arm and chicken pox, not to mention his parents' divorce. And now no ice cream. I feel for him.

Hannah continues down her list of projects. We each have a list, but Chris is busy looking at Nelson's watch, plus a catalog

Nelson has slipped him called Guys on the Move that shows electric stand-up scooters. Nelson wants one. I'm hoping if he gets one he won't fall and break something, but maybe I'm just thinking about the Bobby books too much. I haven't heard what Hannah's been talking about, and I admit it appears she's talking to herself. Plus, I've got the *Jeopardy* song running in my head. Over and over like no one can write down the right answer.

"Amy," Hannah addresses me, "the *Goldilocks* book?"

"Isn't that redundant," Chris answers. "Can't you just call it *Goldilocks*? All we do is books around here."

"We should branch out," Nelson says. Something besides just books."

"We do CDs to go with the books," Hannah says.

"Let's make the CDs in bright primary colors," Nelson says. I write down the idea. I like it.

"Those shiny silver ones are so old-fashioned," he says.

"I'm starting to feel old, with CDs becoming old-fashioned," I say.

"Age is a made-up construct," says young Kelly.

"Easy for you to say," Chris tells her. "You have no idea what an eight-track is, do you?"

Kelly shakes her head.

"Kids today," Nelson says.

"So, back to *Goldilocks*?" Hannah says.

It's my project. I'm supposed to devise a new Goldilocks, but honestly, how many times can you retell the same story?

"How many times can we retell the same story?" I ask out loud, not that many of us aren't thinking it anyhow.

"Till we get it right?" Chris asks.

"Till she has dark hair?" Nelson suggests. "Brawnylocks?"

"I don't think so," I say.

"Till she has no hair left from coloring it so much?" Chris says.

"But you got the text from the writer. It's all edited," Hannah says. "Doesn't it give you some ideas?"

I admit, I have been stuck once or twice before in my creative endeavors, but I don't admit it out loud.

"I think the story needs work," I say. Hannah huffs. Story is her department. Paints and (she believes) crayons are ours.

"I'd like Amy to take a stab at the story, too," Nelson says, and despite Hannah's grumbling, we know Nelson's will shall be done. It's the way it goes.

"What do I know about Goldilocks?" I ask. "My hair is fading." My gold isn't quite as golden as it once was.

"Go to the salon down the street," Kelly says. "Highlights start at thirty-two dollars."

"Live a little," Chris tells me. He already has blond hair, and I can't really see that it's done him all that much good.

"Maybe you should rewrite it," I tell Chris. "You're four shades up from me." It's not only our hairdressers who know for sure, after all. He shakes his head.

"Nah, you work on the new Goldilocks. Goldilocks for the new woman. Goldilocks rejoins the dating world," he says, winking excessively, although I think this is getting a little more personal than our usual children's book discussion.

"Goldilocks after the divorce," Nelson says. I open my mouth in surprise, to which he answers, "Why be indirect?"

"Would Goldilocks really get a divorce?" I say.

"Maybe from the big bad wolf," Chris says.

"Aren't we mixing metaphors, if not fairy tales?" I ask.

"But why would she have married him in the first place?"

Kelly asks.

"These things are a long story," I say.

"We can edit," Hannah pipes in, surreptitiously removing a red pen from her hair.

"Why dwell on the bad parts?" Nelson asks. "Let's have a Goldilocks not afraid to go out there and get what she needs."

"What has Goldilocks ever been afraid of?" I ask.

"Furniture, mostly," Chris says. "Imagine the damage she'd do at Ikea."

"That's right," says Kelly. "Didn't Goldilocks have a habit of breaking things?"

"And busting in where she's not wanted," said Chris.

"I do not do those things!" I say, feeling a little attacked on the character's behalf.

"Maybe a little destruction wouldn't hurt you, er, Goldilocks," Chris says with a wink.

"Goldilocks needs to put herself out there and make some discoveries," Nelson says. "For both herself and the good of humankind," Nelson says, and I'm not really sure who he's referring to. Fortunately, he pushes his timer button, and "The Boogie Woogie Bugle Boy" starts up. It's our cue that the meeting is over, we understand, even if it's the first time he's done this, and even though we're not exactly finished.

Back at my desk, which is partitioned next to Chris's and lined with a soothing and somehow almost edible sky blue flannel (not that there are really any sky blue foods, just that something about it makes me crave something soft and marshmallow-y), I pull out my Goldilocks drawings. Scribbles, doodles, what have yous. Needs work, I hear my art instructors saying, and not in the nicest way, either. As usual, they're right.

"New and improved Goldilocks," I say.

"*Goldilocks Gets Real*," Chris says from just beyond the partition. We sometimes brainstorm this way, or just tell jokes. He tells the jokes, mostly. "*Goldilocks Gets Some*," he adds, but quieter.

"*Goldilocks Saves the Word*."

"*Goldilocks Reaches for the Stars and Goes for the Gold*," he says.

"But she's already golden."

"*Goldilocks Brings Sparkle to the World*."

"Urg," I say, with a shudder.

"Come on, it's just a little glitter, a little sparkle to life. Isn't it time?"

"There's more to life than sparkle," I say.

I want a tale ready for today. But I open my art supply drawer and notice no glitter, no fuchsia, nothing hopeful at all. I've been gathering an earth-toned collection of pens, charcoals (and yes, crayons) over the year, and it's certainly lacking. There's nothing to catch your eye, spark your imagination, give you ideas. Just then, Chris reaches over the partition and allows a gentle sprinkle of golden flakes to fall my way.

"Goldilocks: The Girl Beneath the Glitter," Chris says suggestively. I softly blow glitter off my shoulders, although I leave a little on my arms, just to see if it'll have any effect. I realize I have missed having any kind of sparkle whatsoever, and if I'm honest, I do feel like I've broken a few things in my life.

3

Just Looking

I think it's a sign of our times that when we feel low or confused, unsure or unloved, we look for someplace warm and comforting, with soft colors and soothing music, and find ourselves time and again at Pottery Barn. At least, my pal Susan and I do.

"Shopping has gotten a bad name," Susan says. Susan is my bestie from college, though we don't use the term bestie because it's a little too cute, and Susan is a serious person. She has a serious face with a serious haircut—auburn tinted straight hair, excellent posture, and one of those fit bodies where everything's proportioned right. I think it's because she's tall. But she doesn't lord it over me or anything.

"It's true," I say. "I feel guilty shopping now. Even window shopping makes me look over my shoulder to make sure no one's watching. When did this happen?"

"It's all those TV shows where women in too much eye makeup are constantly shopping for shoes."

"I've never willingly gone into one of those pricey shoe

stores," I say.

"Boutiques," Susan corrects me.

"That's a polite word for them," I say. "What's wrong with DSW? What's wrong with grabbing your own size and putting shoes on yourself?" I ask.

"You just don't get what it means to be a modern woman," Susan says, raising her nose in the air. "A modern woman who spends money on shoes that hurt."

"I'd rather have a nice quilt," I say, looking at a nice quilt. It's five-hundred dollars, so I won't be buying it, either. But at least if I did, it wouldn't pinch my toes.

"You're sensible," Susan says, fingering the quilt, then making a horror movie face at the price tag. We both remember when Pottery Barn was fairly cheap. Progress isn't always for the best, although it's true the store doesn't reek of scented candles like it did when we were younger shoppers.

"Sensible," I say with a sneer, or at least with one in my voice.

"Sensible shoes," Susan says.

"I hate that term," I say. "It's one of those left-handed compliments, as if wearing something that won't give you bunions weren't a good thing." We both look at our shoes. Susan's wearing Nike's, which for some reason never fit me. I'm wearing brown boot moccasins that zip up the back and don't much feel like shoes at all. You can call them sensible if you want. At least they don't cost a lot.

"Why would anyone want this?" Asks Libby, who has accompanied us today. Libby, Susan's daughter, is a slender child even for a six-year-old, with very pale skin that will one day make her a popular girl, and dark blonde hair that will one day allow her to accompany us to the hairdresser for highlights, although she's sworn she never will. Libby's preschool teacher once described her as well-versed, and she wasn't kidding. Libby's looking at a large chair that appears to be made out of the kind of orange plastic they used to use on kids' slides, something that would make you happy just because it has no other purpose than to make you happy. The chair is square in a Flinstonian way that looks uncomfortable but prehistoric. Actually, it looks like something your average six-year-old might enjoy climbing into, but as Susan and I know, Libby is no average six-year-old. Just ask her.

"Try it, Lib."

"Give it a whirl, girl," Susan says.

"This is peer pressure, isn't it?" Libby asks us. "Because I don't see why I'd want to sit in a square chair."

"I'll try it," I say. I do try it. It's not as bad as I'd have thought, but a nice pillow wouldn't hurt.

"It's like a throne," Susan says.

"No jewels," Libby replies. Libby thinks of these things.

"It's not soft like I'd want a throne to be," I say. I've thought of this kind of thing before, but I don't go into it.

"What would Goldilocks say?" Susan asks me. She knows I have to rework the fairy tale. "Too orange?"

"Too bright," Libby says.

"Wouldn't Goldilocks like bright?" I ask her. I don't know how they get the color this intense or even if it's plastic or some other material. I somehow feel Libby should be the expert.

"I don't think Goldilocks would waste her money," says the always practical Libby.

"Would she be more into shoes?" I ask.

"Please," Libby says, with a grimace-y face I envy. I wish I could make a face like that in public without people looking

25

at me funny. It's one of the things I miss about childhood. "Enough about shoes," Libby says, moving away from the throne. Libby doesn't get the shoe thing, either, as she mostly likes rubber boots, even in summer. Especially in summer.

"Maybe you're just not the throne type," Susan tells her daughter. "Nothing wrong with that."

"Thank you," Libby says. "Comfort should be much more important than brightness," she adds, in that authoritative way first-graders tend to share. Not to mention in a tone very similar to her mother's.

"I agree," I say.

"Unless there's jewels," Libby adds.

Susan and I nod. The child has a point.

We wander to the bedding section.

"Now this is an entirely different story," Libby says. She's been speaking in paragraphs since she was three, so her diction doesn't surprise us any, although an older woman turns to look at her with something a little less enthusiastic than surprise on her face, as if good grammar combined with a clear opinion in a child were a bad thing. Susan just smiles at the woman proudly. We love Libby, confident enunciation and all. Even when her voice gets a little loud in public places.

Libby spots a tall bed dressed in rich purples surrounded by a dark purple curtain that hangs from the ceiling to make a turret-style drape, if you can make a turret from a drape.

"It looks like mosquito netting," Susan says. Purple isn't her color, and she's fussy, as she works in an art museum where the sections are differentiated by color. As in yes, there's a green room. The museum reopens soon with its new color coordination, and sneak peek reviews have been mixed, with some critics calling it too simplistic. I happen to know Susan thinks simple = good, as she hates a snooty museum. Snooty, to her, is a cuss word.

"I think mosquito netting is underrated," I tell her. I've always wanted some, especially in the summer.

"Target sells them for less," Susan says. We look at the purple drape, which is ninety-nine dollars for a twin size. Libby is wrapping herself up in it. lovingly.

"This costs ninety-nine dollars!" Susan tells her daughter.

"It's majestic," Libby says. Susan just shrugs. It's not on sale, so there's no way she's buying it.

"It beats those little video games the other kids want," I tell her, backing up Libby. Libby is my unofficial goddaughter, so I get to take her side. I even get to buy her the canopy drape if I want to, but I'll have to see if it's just a passing desire for her, not to mention whether it comes in another color.

"Time for gadgets, I think," Susan tells us, which means it's time to go next door to Williams-Sonoma, where we like to wander the gadget aisle in search of the thing we would most never use. This is how we spend a Saturday. It's important to have hobbies.

"Farewell, princess bed," Libby says, as if we're dragging her by her feet. Susan and I share a look.

"What would Goldilocks say?" I point my head back to the draped bedding.

"I think you just heard it," Susan says.

* * *

I spot him in Williams-Sonoma, over by the juicers. Libby is examining something that's supposed to peel garlic for you, which I have my doubts about. Also, it looks as if it could take

27

someone's eye out, which worries me, although not Susan. She has her eyes on a special pancake flipper.

"I believe this is covered in the material they use to insulate astronauts with," Susan says.

"How would you know that?" I say, keeping an eye on the juicer department.

"I read *Time* at the dentist."

"I read *The New Yorker* at the dentist," Libby says. "The cartoon captions," she admits. I'm relieved. I've noticed *The New Yorker*'s writing isn't what it once was. Plus there are pictures of bloodied embattled soldiers, not to mention beaten civilians in it now, which I think is highly inappropriate for reading when you're trying to prevent yourself from thinking about an impending buzzing drill in your mouth. I read *Highlights* at the dentist, myself. I can't get enough of those find the hidden pictures. And you rarely come across bad language or carnage.

Susan sees me staring at juicers across the store.

"You don't like pulp," she reminds me.

"I gave my juicer away," I say, looking proud of myself. "Along with my bread machine."

"Which bread machine?" I know she's teasing me. I received several when Hooper and I were married. I never used one of them.

"I've met that guy, sort of." I use my nose to point at the man, but not in an uppity way or anything.

"Impish," Susan says, but not in a mean way. I give her a look anyhow. She gives me a "What?" movement with her left eyebrow. She can raise just a third of her eyebrow for really meaningful glances.

"He's nice," I say. It's the man from Trader Joe's, the guy

with the Volvo who knocked over the carb bars. "He's funny."

"Older," Susan says. "Not senior yet, exactly, but still older."

"I guess." It's hard for me to tell about age. It's something about my having always been nearsighted, I think. Either that, or I just don't pay enough attention.

"Late fifties, sixty tops, maybe," Susan says. "Still, not too bad. And interested in staying young with vitamin C, judging from the way he's studying the juicers."

"Hey, I'm not looking for a man," I say, "or anything."

"Hey, you're not even looking for a juicer," Susan says. "I know."

Libby sneaks up next to us, silently pretending to peel garlic with her implement. I notice it has a jewel-like handle. I'm catching on.

"He's adorable," Libby whispers. I think she likes his size. Libby is not trusting of men who are too tall, a distrust I wish I'd developed as a child myself, as it might have prevented divorce, not to mention marriage. Hooper the ex is very tall, of course.

"Shh, she's just looking in the general juicer direction, not for anything in particular," Susan tells her daughter.

"Oh, right," Libby says. "Just go pretend you're really interested in making lemonade. Like for a small child you know."

I give her a look. The encouragement on both her and Susan's faces is identical and kind of *Twilight Zone*-y. "This is definitely peer pressure," I tell them both, leaving them behind with their gadgets. I notice them jump up and down a little as I walk off. The things you do for friends.

* * *

As I really am a proponent of the five-a-day fruit mentality, I have no problem surveying the juicers, even though there's a perfectly good Jamba Juice that I frequent down the street from the office. Not to mention that I had no idea there were so many options in juicers. One of them is enormous, as if you could juice a giant grapefruit on it. One of them looks like a blender anyhow, and this is where I find the guy from the classic Volvo, not that he's in it at the moment. He looks up at me in a way that no one has looked at me in quite a while, with a kind of serene happiness.

"I have a thing for small kitchen appliances," he says.

"I'm not sure you'd call this one small," I say. Really, it looks like it must weigh fifty pounds.

"Oh, it's industrial strength," my new friend says. "I'm just not sure where I'd store enough oranges to keep it busy."

I look at the price tag. It costs more than the quilt. "This juicer is twelve hundred dollars," I say, shocked and outraged, as if the makers of it were trying to personally offend me.

"The price does make your blood pressure rise, doesn't it?"

"Yes," I say, a little relieved that he might feel the same way. "Why does anyone need this?"

"It may be the kind of need that can't really be defined easily," he says, "let alone fulfilled. At least not without professional help. Some kind of anxiety-based need for those in the upper tax brackets. A desperate longing for oversized appliances."

"What do poorer folks with anxiety disorders do, then?" I ask. I'd like to know. Artists such as myself at children's publishing companies aren't exactly raking in the big bucks, not that I'd ever want this juicer.

"Ah, we regular folk," and here he sort of guides me by the arm in a way not at all alarming, "go in for this sort of thing." It's not all that surprising, as after all, he is a man and I'm a woman, that he's led me to the coffee grinders. I have a little experience with this sort of thing, as I'm a woman over 30.

"Oh, men and coffee grinders," I say. "What is the deal?"

"Okay then, you'll have to tell me," he says, gesturing about the store. "What's your Achilles heel? What's your secret Williams-Sonoma passion?"

"What makes you think I have one?" I ask. "I'm here with a friend." I gesture back to Susan and Libby, who are spying at us and quickly pretend they're not by hiding behind a giant red ceramic rooster.

"Sure," he says, "it's always 'I'm just here with a friend.' Fess up. I won't laugh unless you say cookie-cutters."

"Fine," I say, gesturing for him to follow. I point. "Griddles. It's pancake griddles. It's always been pancake griddles." I feel only a little defeated by my admission. Maybe a little relieved. Maybe even encouraged. He bends down to the griddle level and gives them a look and a long whistle. Not the construction worker kind of whistle. He's not whistling at me, but it kind of feels that way, yet is not offensive in the least.

He nods in approval and runs a finger over the smooth (not Teflon-y) griddle. "I'm Chester Anderson," he says.

"Amy Shepherd," I say. If I'd ever changed my name to Hooper's last name (the hard to pronounce Tomlinson), I might have had trouble rolling off the Shepherd again after all those years. So, there's something to be grateful for.

"I have no problem with pancakes and freshly ground coffee," Chester says.

"Well, I don't really have a griddle," I say.

"I don't really have a coffee grinder," Chester says. "I have a Starbucks."

"Your own personal one?" I ask. You never know. I've never actually met anyone who owns one, if they're owned by separate people. I'm not sure how the business world of java ownership works. I draw for a living, after all.

"No, but nearby," Chester says. "On Eighteenth."

"I work near that one. But I try to frequent the independent coffee store." I shrug.

"Oh, The Latte Lesson," Chester says.

"That's the one," I exclaim, happy that someone else knows my secret hideout, although I guess that makes it not so secret anymore. You can also take writing classes there or join a reading group, hence the "Lesson" part of the name.

"So, we live in the same neighborhood," Chester says. "Which I'd sort of guessed from the Trader Joe's incident."

"I'm not sure spilling a few candy bars constitutes an incident," I tell him.

"Unless you run them over with your cart," he says a little sheepishly. I guess he did do that.

"I don't think anyone eating one of those tasteless carb bars would much notice if it'd been run over," I say. Not a food bar fan.

"Not like pancakes," he says. We look at the griddles some more. I notice that Susan and Libby have now circled us and are watching me from behind a collection of French tablecloths. Libby has a matching napkin draped over her head for camouflage, as she's not much of a spy. She's more the tell-it-like-it-is type.

"Would you like to continue this critique of cultural food

phenomenon over, well, food?" Chester asks, not quite as smoothly as it sounds, and suddenly shy and not really looking at me.

"Oh," I say. I'm not sure being picked up in Williams-Sonoma was what I was going for, but then I'm not always the best judge of my motives, or even desires. Not that I know who is.

"Nothing fancy," he says. "Just to talk. Maybe even eat."

"Oh, I eat and talk sometimes, too," I say. Why not? True, he's older, and now that I notice it, a bit shorter than I am. But impish, yes, Susan is right. Impish in a good way, and clever and nice. A girl could do worse in a kitchen gadget store, even if it's by buying that useless looking garlic peeler. I just know Susan's going to get talked into it. It's jeweled, after all. Chester, on the other hand, is not bejeweled, or even accessorized. He's plain and simple, wearing a gray and graying sweater, and casual khakis. Sensible black tennies (and I don't think they're Nike's, which I like about him right off). His hair is brownish with gray around the edges, and sticking out in several places in a shaggy but oddly interesting way. Chester has a cute, unimposing appeal and a real energy coming from him. Plus, he seems fond of pancakes. As everyone knows, I've dated worse. I've married worse.

We exchange numbers and make a date. Susan pays for the implement headed for Libby's play kitchen, filled with sparkling wands originally intended for unidentifiable culinary uses. I don't think it'll ever peel garlic, but we can hope for the best, sometimes. It's not a bad haul for a Saturday, really.

4

How to Improve on a Classic

Maybe it's all this thinking about the three bears from the Goldilocks' story that makes me feel like I'm coming out of hibernation. Judging from fairy tales, I guess you never know what you'll find when you wake up one day, not that fairy tales are all that reliable, seems to me. But I do feel like I've been under a blanket of hibernation of some kind (mostly Aunt Lucile's lovely purple quilt, silk and sweet smelling), but I know it's time to wake up and get out a little. I imagine Goldilocks walking into my house, looking for something nice, running her fingers over the quilt. Did Goldilocks ever feel the need to hibernate, maybe after seeing the warmth of the bears' house, the smoothness of the beds and blankets? Did she just want to dive in and pull those covers over her head? Did she ever come to realize she needed to just plain wake up? Or was she not the type who doubts herself? Did she leave the bears' house with less confidence or more?

I may be overextending the metaphor. But my life needs tending to, no doubt. First, I killed several plants in Aunt

Lucille's garden. Plus, I've let what's known in my family as the "hell" drawer—you know, where you keep batteries and tape and thumbtacks that always stick you when you're looking for batteries and tape—well, I've let it go all to hell. It's a real mess, which isn't something the old me would have done. Or am I really just disorganized and messy at heart, and have felt really pressured not to be by a certain ex-husband?

I really do have to do something about the hell drawer. Besides, I think there may be Hershey's kisses in there, somewhere.

But, and I pride myself on this, there's one thing I haven't let slide, one thing I'm bound and determined to take care of (besides dear Lulu of course), and that's my inherited Beetle. It's a beautiful thing, the kind of car I think I've coveted since I was a small girl. I was the kind of girl to covet cars. Cars aren't just a boy thing, especially if you grow up here in Southern California. It's not exactly that you are what you drive, but it's pretty close to it. My bug is a '67 powder blue glorious creation, cared for mostly by Uncle Harry, late of Aunt Lucille, her dearly beloved. And I think the car was his dearly beloved thing, not that he wasn't crazy about Aunt Lucille. The bug's a convertible, as if it weren't perfect enough in its perfect roundness. *I live at the beach and drive a convertible*, I say to myself. I realize that to most women's magazines, it would sound better to say, "I live at the beach with a husband, two children, and a high-paying job, and drive a convertible," but really, I think that's just catering to overly high expectations. Plus, I've found the Beetle so much happier to see me, after a long day, than my former husband ever was. Not that I'm bitter, just that I'm learning. And anthropomorphizing, but what do you expect from someone who works in children's books?

Which leads me today to the mechanics' shop because my Beetle is coughing. It seems slow and feverish, wheezing at intersections, which is leading people to look my way even more than usual. (The bug gets a lot of looks in our direction—everyone loves a Beetle here in Santa Monica, it seems.)

The bug and I frequent a mechanic's garage that's notoriously small and neighborhood-y, and that Aunt Lucille swears by. It's one of those low cement buildings—cement color, if you know what I mean—that can really screams auto mechanic garage in a really California way, though for all I know, they look like this across the country. Inside, they have a huge coffee machine where they brew several kinds of Peet's coffees—complimentary. (Have I mentioned this is Santa Monica?) Plus they don't overcharge on auto work—urban mythbusters that they are. Aunt Lucille feels strongly about this, and on my salary, I'm happy to agree. And they, too, love the Beetle. Since Uncle Harry used to scream and yell— completely out of character—when he tried to try to fix it himself, I suspect that it's not that easy a car to work on. Anyplace that loves my Beetle, I love by default, or at least, I visit when maintenance is required.

The garage owner, whose actual name is Mac and who wears one of those little round name patches, greets me and my Beetle. He's got dark graying hair and wears different colored Swatch watches every time I visit. I sometimes wish we had a little uniform at Children's Press and could wear name tags and have a service that washes our clothes for us. It sounds like something Nelson would go for, too.

"Hi, Amy," Mac says. There are over twenty cars parked

around the tiny garage lot, and I know Mac has hundreds if not thousands of customers, but he knows my name, and Aunt Lucille's, and if the Beetle had a name, he'd know it too.

"How's our bug?" he asks. It's probably not like he sees that many '67s around here, although there are more than you'd think, us being coastal and all.

"The Beetle's been coughing funny," I say. I don't know much about engines, but no one here seems to hold it against me.

"We'll fix her up," Mac says, fondling the keys I've handed to him. They're original '67 keys and apparently have some sort of value of their own in the classic VW world. Even my push button radio and hubcaps have value, which seems funny to me. I wouldn't mind a nice CD player, not that I really drive very far. Just to the office, Trader Joe's, and, well, here. Maybe the Beetle needs more adventure in its life. Maybe I'm not being a daring enough Beetle owner, although I do keep the car waxed. I may be overly personifying, if not projecting, but it's a cute car, and my life is a little low on emotional attachment these days.

Mac regains my attention. "Is it a deep chesty cough?" he asks. "Or more a nagging dry cough?"

"Kind of nagging," I say. "People are starting to stare a little."

"You've got a baby blue convertible in cherry condition," Mac says. "A little staring won't hurt anyone," he adds, a little provocatively. He sends me off with a wave, and I head for my job. Several mechanics have surrounded the Beetle, leaving depressed Toyotas and Hondas in pieces around them. One guy begins polishing one of the bug's hubcaps. I've come to the right place.

* * *

Some people might think we do things a little oddly at Kids Press, especially if they saw a group of small children running around and the place like a day care center, although a really fun-looking one. When I was little, every once in a while my mother used to dress up in her best gabardine suit and leave me with a babysitter—a teenage girl who lived up the street and didn't mind sharing her *Teen Beat* with me. I learned a lot on those occasions. My mom would go off in search of fun, which in her case was what was known in those days as market research. My mom and a group of her friends and neighbors would head to a room at the local shopping center (which is now really fancy but wasn't back then), where they would critique a new brand of potato chips, paper towels, mops, or assorted Tupperware-like containers. We often got a few bags of these products to use for a month, and Mom got cash. Not a lot, but enough to keep her hot on the market research trail.

Ours is not my mother's market research, though. This afternoon at Kids Press, we're ready for what we call Kid Testing, which unlike the educational system of today does not involve standardized tests or anything where you're required to fill in a bubblelike shape with a number two pencil. Instead, we bring in kids from the elementary school across the street to read through our proposed books, look over our sketches, and generally mess up the place. Our electrical outlets are childproofed, and so are our desks. Chris has a cupboard that's padlocked, and I'm sure he has his reasons.

Leading the kids' team is my close friend Libby, who has tested so many of our projects that she has a junior-size director's chair here with her name on it. Libby's first-grade class comes in behind their teacher, Miralise Silva-Abramowitz, a woman I've come to know in my years here. Miralise was once engaged to a fellow we all liked named Steven Hale-Gonzalez, and she used to make up married names for herself that included a number of hyphens and several z's. It didn't work out, though, which was disappointing. I really wanted to design her stationery, and not just as a gag gift.

"Why exactly do we need another Goldilocks book?" Libby asks, seated in a room that has a twelve-by-twelve-foot polka dotted rug, which also makes for an interesting twister game, especially if you happen to enjoy falling over a lot. Libby's class of first-graders, in particular a small sampling of girls (as statisticians might say), sit around her. "Let's break it down," Libby says. Her dad's a lawyer, after all.

"I'm not sure it's a really grabbing topic," says Libby's friend Autumn, a girl of indescribably soft-looking bronze skin. I don't know what ethnicity she is—I'm never good at those things—but she's headed for commercials for skin-care products someday, if she doesn't become an architect (her first choice; second is taxidermy, and I haven't asked for details).

"It's a fairy tale," I answer, sitting cross-legged with the group of six girls, who are pouring over some sketches and the preliminary text for Goldilocks. "It's for littler kids," I say.

"Ohh," they all agree in unison. Littler kids. The way to a first-grader's heart and mind is by reminding them how mature they are, which in the case of these kids happens to be true. And they know it.

"What would we like the littler kids to take away from Goldilocks," Libby says. "Let's start from scratch."

"No offense," says Lolly, a little girl with three braids. It looks like a mistake, but I've been told it's her favorite hairdo.

Lolly goes her own way but is thoughtful about it.

"None taken," I say. "I've been wondering myself if we can take Goldilocks somewhere a little different while still leaving her lost in the forest."

"So to speak," Libby says.

I nod. "Anyway, the story is updated a little. She's in the national forest, sort of a state park, where she lives with her forest ranger family. She's adventurous and brave, not wimpy of course. And there's still bears."

"Sometimes a bear can be more than a bear," Libby suggests.

"How about another creature entirely?" asks Windy, a particularly small child who prefers stories about hamsters, I know.

"I think we want bears," I say.

"But why?" Windy asks. It's not a bad question. Sometimes a bear can be something entirely else, as some of us have learned.

"We're being too literal," Libby says. I think about this. "Well, it can be a bear in a way and still make you think it's something else, someone else."

"What is it Goldilocks wants from the bears?" Lolly asks. "And don't say a chair. I never get that thing about the chair."

"Who eats sitting down at a table anyhow?" asks Sophie. Both of her parents work late, although I think that can be said of almost all these kids. As I myself rarely sit down for a meal, I make a note of this. All the girls nod. And as we're all sitting on the floor, I have to figure kids don't really think that highly of chairs.

"Chairs rhymes with bears," says Jessie, the last in the circle to speak, always the most reserved.

"Does it have to rhyme?" Libby asks.

"Tell me it doesn't have to rhyme," Lolly says.

"It's so beneath even the youngest kid," Libby says.

"You forget," I tell her, "how much little kids love rhyming. It's important to their success as readers," I say.

"Real poetry doesn't need to rhyme," says Autumn. "I'm pretty sure," she adds. As I'm not entirely sure about this myself, we all just exchange nods for a moment.

"I'll make a note of it," I finally say. The girls seem to let go of their breath, relieved. We always feel better when at least one of us is right.

"Okay," I start again, "so we don't necessarily need chairs, and bears can be symbolic."

"Right," Libby says. "Bears as symbols, or metaphors."

"Is it metaphors or similes?" Windy says.

"We're studying that," Lolly says with a nod.

"I was sick that day," Windy says. I think I may have been out that day too. I can never keep the two straight, but then, I'm in the art department.

"What are the bears symbols of?" Jessie asks. "And just because we know what a metaphor is, don't expect a kinder-gartner to."

"True," Libby says. "But it won't hurt to expose them."

"True," Jessie agrees. "As long as we're all clear."

I really like these meetings.

"What are we exposing kindergartners to?" Sophie asks.

"Bears as symbols of other things in life," Libby explains. "Things that scare us, or are big, or different."

"You should really be writing this down," Lolly whispers to me, as I seem to have forgotten to take notes. She says this in the most helpful way, not snidely or anything.

"What will the bears look like, Amy?" asks Autumn. I show her a sketch of a brown bear, slightly traditional but not too threatening. The girls take a look, and all seem to sigh in unison.

"You may be limiting your imagination by focusing on just bears," suggests Lolly. "There really are no constraints."

"You may need to broaden your worldview entirely," Autumn tells me.

"So to speak," adds Libby says, making me suddenly feel as if I'm in group therapy, even though I outweigh the next largest member by at least fifty pounds. I'm not sure this really gives me the advantage, though.

* * *

Late afternoon takes me back to Mac's garage to get the Beetle, which is sitting in a place of honor before Mac's front door, waxed and polished and no doubt cured of its cough. I could just hug it, clean and shiny Beetle that it is. It seems happy to see me, too.

Standing just inside is one of the other mechanics, also smiling at the bug. I enter Mac's lobby, which has that auto garage smell despite its cleanliness, but it's a smell I kind of like, and it mixes well with the Peet's coffee brewing, although I wouldn't have guessed the scents would complement one another.

"So, you're the Girl in the '67 Beetle," says the mechanic, not really a question. He's not wearing a name patch, I notice. He's also fairly young with very thick dark hair, although I can't say why I'd notice this, except of course how could you miss it?

"I guess I am," I say.

"She's in very nice shape," says the dark-haired mechanic.

"Why are cars referred to as girls?" I say. "Or is it just my car?"

"No," he says, "you're the girl, she's the car. I don't think I've mixed that up." I'm not sure what he means, but he says it in a very interesting way.

"Did you work on the Beetle?" I ask.

"Yep," he says. "It's a great one. I've seen you drive around in the neighborhood."

"Kind of a noticeable car."

"Maybe," he says. "I like how you always use the turn signal."

"Oh," I say. "It has a great click-clack sound, the turn signal. I guess I like it." I make a click-clack sound with my tongue. It's really one of a kind, although I guess all Beetles made that sound. He probably knows this already, and I can't really think who else would much care besides a mechanic, or someone else who has no real romantic life and loves his or her car. I still think it's healthy sublimation, though. I stop making the sound. "Don't you find it hard to work on? I've always heard it is."

"We love your car here," he says. "I'm afraid I can't let you say bad things about her. Plus, a little hard work can be rewarding."

"Um, where's Mac?" I ask. I feel a little funny all of a sudden knowing this attractive person has had his hands inside my car.

"I can ring you up," he says. I hand him my card, which he studies. "Oh, so it's Amy," he says, reading my name.

"Yes," I admit, starting to flirt a little maybe, as it's the end of the day and this person seems fond of my car, even if he may still be what Susan would call school age. Twenties maybe.

Not even late twenties. Safe to flirt with. It's good to know a mechanic when your car is older than you are, even if it looks better in the morning than you do.

"Ben," he says. It takes me a minute to figure out what he means, but then I'm trying to sign the receipt for what seems a very low amount to fix anything originally built in 1967. Fixing the VCR would cost more, which is why I never fixed it. It went to Goodwill.

"Oh," I say. "But you don't wear a name patch." Twenty-three, maybe.

"I put on a fresh shirt," he says, looking at me, then at the Beetle. He is awfully clean.

"I hope the Beetle didn't wreck your shirt," I say. Uncle Harry used to be a mess after trying to take the bug apart.

"It's the price we pay," he says. "Your car should be running great, but don't forget to bring her in for a checkup and an oil change pretty soon. We need to keep an eye on her." He's not looking at the car at all when he says this. There's at least an eleven-year age difference, if you're the type who enjoys adding and subtracting. I've never been.

He finally hands me the receipt and my classic key. "Did you want to change the oil today?" I ask.

"Already taken care of," Ben says. He actually walks me out to the Beetle and opens its door. Closing it, he gives the side a nice pat. A cute boy likes my car. I feel about sixteen, but of course at sixteen, I drove an aging gray Toyota sedan that was higher on the left side than the right, although it wasn't due to anything I'd done to it.

"Bye, Ben," I say. "Thanks for fixing up the Beetle."

"Bye Girl in the '67 Beetle," Ben says.

"I should get a name patch that says that," I say.

"It's written all over your face," he says, looking at my face, which, pale as I am, I believe is turning red.

He watches us drive off into a not at all bad looking Santa Monica sunset, my Beetle and I, both of us feeling nicely tuned up. I've never understood why anyone would go to a dealership. The service here is really something.

5

Bingo

"**T**his place hasn't been here very long," Chester tells me, "but I've become something of a regular." He says this close to my ear, so I can hear over the heavy drumbeat music I think may have been called hypno-something twenty years ago.

We've met in an odd indoor playground of sorts, a nightclub meets Bingo parlor called Play It, where music blasts and neon spotlights flicker. People of all shapes, ages, and levels of tattoo-ness surround little tables, on which they play the games of my childhood. Bingo, of course, then there's the Operation table over there on the left by the row of plastic tarantulas, and to my right, the Game of Life beneath a giant blown-up Jupiter, and isn't that Battleship where those young women (dressed in trendy fatigues) are high-fiving one another beside the aquarium filled with superballs? It's all surprising, shocking even, yet somehow alluring in a really primal way. I want to be twelve and live here.

"What would you like to play?" Chester asks, suggestively,

except for that he rubs his hands together excitedly like a twelve-year-old. He points out a Candyland game in progress played by two twenty-somethings in purple lipstick, both of whom have large pinkish-purple drinks in front of them, the color of the sugar plum fairy. One of the post-teens may be a boy, but that hardly matters.

"I have no idea," I reply. "I've never seen anything like this." Is this what the dating world has become? And what took it so long? I may be completely ready for this.

A look at Chester reminds me that he is smallish. (The term elfin comes to mind, yet that's unfair, although I do love gnomes, not that gnome applies to Chester.) He has curly brown nearing gray hair and still that indeterminate age of something over forty or maybe even fifty approaching sixty, something a little older than the ideal date for someone my age. Not that it isn't going really well so far, and I've barely come through the door. He wears khaki pants and a wrinkled dark blue shirt beneath a charcoal sports jacket that might be the kind of corduroy you really want to run your hands over, but you never know what may happen when you run your hands over someone else's jacket.

I'm wearing a black long-sleeve T with a relatively long and nearly outdated slim dark purple skirt, which would be a good match with the post-teens' lipstick. Not that anyone else would compare the two I suspect, as they're way too engrossed in great lollipop adventures and such. I'm not wearing heels with Chester due to his height, but then again, I wouldn't anyway. I see a young woman in high-heeled boots that have fake goldfish in them. I appreciate that they're fake, not to mention painted with long eyelashes.

We go deeper into the room, which smells like bubblegum

and rum, which is not nearly as sickly sweet as you might think. I wonder if you can smell grenadine, too? I kind of do.

"I thought gambling wasn't legal here," I say, the words *party-pooper* echoing in my ears in a voice not unlike Susan's. I'll have to bring her here. And if only my goddaughter Libby were old enough.

"Oh, it's not gambling per se," says Chester. "Although you can win a piercing. Maybe two."

"Oh," I say. "Do you have to accept the prize?"

"No, no, maybe just a little temporary henna tattoo.... Would you like a large frothy drink and a game of Mystery Date?"

I actually get goosebumps at this question. Thank goodness for long sleeves.

Mystery Date. I had one, although it predated me by quite a lot. Come to think of it, maybe it was Aunt Lucille's. Still, I had one. So yes, I want the drink and the game.

"And Magic Eight Ball for later," Chester says.

I can't stop smiling. I wonder if they have Rockem' Sockem' Robots, and whether it's appropriate for a first date.

"There's Twister, of course," Chester says, but then as if reading my mind adds, "but maybe after we get to know each other."

My heart races a little from memories of Twister and junior high, and a boy named Mark with the loveliest straight blond hair and one of those spaces between his teeth known unromantically as a midline diastema. Some things you remember from twelve. "Wow," is all I can reply.

"Although, nobody's a stranger for long with Twister," he says, with a smile that's not bad at all (no midline diastema, but still). The idea of Twister with rum makes me smile. I haven't been out in a while. I had no idea dating had become fun.

Just then, bells go off and pink and blue lights flash even faster, as we hear "We have a winner at table four" and a cheer among a couple in their fifties wearing Hawaiian shirts decorated with red parakeets. Seems they've won matching navel piercings, or temporary tattoos that say "I heart Tinkerbell." We don't wait around to see which they'll choose.

The Bingo cage rattles along with the hypno-sounds, a percussive feat I wouldn't have thought of before as anything more than grating noise. We settle into a game surrounded by a man and a woman with his-and-her blue-streaked hair and giant lime green peace sign rings on their wedding fingers. Plastic ones. The rings look like they came out of a gumball machine, and also like you'd be really happy to get one with your gumball, or even instead of the gumball. The lime green in here takes on a magical sheen, and I feel as if I can smell lime Jell-O. I wonder if the rings are scented.

"On Friday nights, you can win the rings," Chester says, watching me stare. "They're exclusively designed for Play It," he adds. "On Thursday nights, they sometimes award purple berets, not that I come every night or anything."

"I think it's amazing," I say. "And in a good way." I've been having fun all this time, and not just because I just won a date with the cutest mystery guy, in the board game anyhow.

"It's been a while since I've been anywhere like this," I tell Chester. "Maybe since summer camp, not including the rum."

"There's something about the place that makes it impossible to feel sad, or lonely, or anything but alive in a truly evocative way," Chester says. "Even when they play Madonna songs."

I nod. "I'm not a fan of hers, either, not that I have anything against her," I say. "I admit to being amused by her outfits, I just don't think that anyone over thirty should have to listen to her anymore."

"It's like we've earned that right," Chester says, agreeing. "Although she's good when you're playing Tiddlywinks, surprisingly."

"This is a real eye-opening experience," I say. "I haven't, um, dated in a while."

"Oh, you can easily forget you're dating in a place like this," Chester says, sharing my relief. "That's one of its best features. That and the all-you-can-eat pork rinds for three ninety-nine. Not that I indulge."

"Good. I'm sort of a pork rind nonbeliever myself."

"You can get red vines, which, when paired with a daiquiri, really brighten up an evening."

We enjoy an order of Pop Rocks with our fruity drinks, which are called Pearl Frost Gloss, as if created by Revlon. Revlon and Bacardi. When you add a Pop Rock, it bubbles and makes a sizzling sound. Like a magic potion, and it's pink too.

I can't tell you how comfortable I feel here, sitting with a slightly shorter man at a Mystery Date table, both of us unafraid to drink a pink beverage in public. I'm not sure what this says about either of us, but I am hoping to get to Chutes and Ladders, or at least cheer for someone else. I've always been attracted to the ladders.

Later on, after playing two rounds of Mystery Date, two Bingos, Battleship, and a round of Clue (it was Miss Scarlet in the library, with a revolver, as if you couldn't have guessed), we enter an area called the Conversation Pit, a darkened living room–like space where you can sit at checkerboard-topped tables, and I guess, talk, or at least hear yourself think, and eat enough to recover from the Pearl Frost Gloss. We order chicken potpies and settle in over our chess pieces, which are from the old *Bullwinkle* show. Rocky is the king. Natasha is queen. Two Bullwinkles serve as knights. The pawns are pure Boris.

"I could live here," I tell Chester. "All these games. Actually, it is a little like where I work, at Kids Press. What about you?"

"I teach Philosophy. College. It's not that different from here, some days. Around finals, you know."

"Existential stuff?" I ask. It's layman's terms, but probably still correct.

"No, no," Chester says waving the invisible stench of existentialism away from our order of curly fries. "I teach logic. It's all games, all the time."

"Like my job, but with more math?"

"Logic is just numbers plus questions without answers, that's all." Chester says. "How like life. Or the Game of Life."

"Questions without answers may be too technical for a first date," I say, then wonder if I shouldn't have said first date. Am I dating? That's the kind of existential question I really hate.

"Okay, then maybe something more personal," Chester says.

"Hmm, I already know what car you drive."

"Then how about the bigger questions of life," he says, blowing on his potpie.

"Not religion, politics, or, hmm, I've forgotten what the other thing you're not supposed to discuss anymore is," I say. I thought there was a third.

"Income," Chester says.

"Oh yeah," I say. I feel like a winner.

"No, no," he says, "the big questions, like, 'Why am I still available?'"

"Oh."

"You must be wondering," Chester says, sort of jokingly. I wonder if he wonders this about me. I guess there is some explaining to do, as we are both clearly over thirty (in my case) and fifty (probably?) in his case.

"So, why are you, available, I mean, a man of your obvious abilities to scope out unusual gaming rooms and frothy drinks?" I ask.

"All of my best qualities are things I learned from my late wife," Chester says.

"Oh," I say. "Oh." I pause. Oh gee. "That's a really nice answer. Sad, but nice."

"It's my epiphany. It came to me about a year after she died. Emily," he says. "I have rejoined the living and embraced my inner knowledge and ability to amuse."

"That is big," I say.

"And my favorite color is maroon," he says.

"Well, there you go," I say. What more is there, anyway? "I'm going through a lime green phase," I tell him. That's about the extent of my epiphanies lately, although I don't add this. I don't add that I've recently thrown out unimportant kitchen machinery, although it comes to mind.

"And now, Amy, why is a fascinating and stunning person such as yourself, though lacking in Battleship skills, available? Or have you gone underground witness-protection style with a new top-secret identity? You can tell me in a place like this. Many of the people here look as if they're on at least their second identities, if not several most-wanted lists."

"I'm divorced," I say. "Joining the ranks of the hundreds of thousands, or the three in five, or whatever it is."

"Free to embrace the aisles of Trader Joe's with no burdens, no expectations at all, just a certain willingness to experiment."

"And how," I say, swallowing a bite of fry. "If you melt the three for a three seventy-nine dark chocolate bars over the wheat-free waffles, the results are really worth the fight for a parking space," I say. I have experimented. And it's led me here, where I feel lighter than I have in weeks.

A girl with green hair shouts out "Jenga!" then we hear a crash. We all stop to applaud.

Chester resumes. "If you cook the frozen eggplant parmigiana for thirty seconds less than instructed, then place it on a bed of organic fresh spinach, sprinkle with a pinch of crumbled goat cheese, then stick it all back in the microwave for twenty-two seconds, it's better than restaurant food. If you add a cheap Merlot, and drink a few glasses," he says.

It sounds good to me. Sad, again, but good.

"And it's far better with two," Chester says, making second date suggestions, I think. "Not that I can't make a fresh dinner. I know my arugulas from my baby spring mixes."

"Oh, and I'm up on the mushroom varieties, like trumpet versus cremini versus minokes versus shitakes," I add. Hooper-the-ex wouldn't allow any mushrooms anywhere, anytime.

"You should really try sauteing them in the Spanish olive oil. The Italian is overrated."

"Huh," I say. "Cooking seems to have become popular again."

"Cooking's become what we talk about, instead of the weather."

"It's all the rage," I say. "As if it never went out of style. Kind of like Bingo, and walking around the block, and those little troll dolls over there." I see some in the corner—I'm not sure if they're a display or prizes. One has lavender hair—I realize six-year-old Libby would like one. She'd like this whole place, minus the junky music and guys with piercings in their cheeks. I wonder if you can rent this place out for parties, maybe play a nice James Taylor album in the background, or if you want to be funny, some Wham, maybe.

A waitress walks by, carrying a dessert tray from the seventies: large hot fudge sundae, banana split, meringue topped pies, creamy frosted cakes. We both watch her go by with huge smiles on our faces.

"And thank goodness people are eating big desserts again!" Chester exclaims. He's thin, so he can probably pack away a fluffy dessert now and then without it being a big deal, but then, so can I.

"All those years when you weren't supposed to order dessert," I say, with a shake of my head. Even I knew about that trend.

"Or were forced to share one," he says.

"Oh my God. Or one for the whole table." Many a time on my nights out with the ex-Hooper, as I've come to think of him, those were the rules. Four people, one dessert. Why live?

"Oh, those days when people would shake their heads at you, or mutter about cholesterol."

"Carbs," I say, making a *pffft* sound. "I hate when someone uses that word in public, usually in a perfectly nice restaurant. Who wants to hear an ugly thing like *carbs* when you're sitting beside elegantly swirled mousse?" I don't know what has happened to etiquette.

"Let's order strawberry shortcake, then go play Strawberry Shortcake Dance Dance Revolution," Chester suggests, and I have nothing at all to object to, although I do hope the dance mat isn't scented.

I wonder briefly whether I'm ready for Trader Joe's trumpet mushrooms sauteed in Spanish oil, for two, with a bottle of whatever's not too cheap, but not so overpriced it feels like it's from outside California. Maybe something with a pretty monarch butterfly on the label, or a hand-drawn silhouette, as opposed to something that looks like Clipart. I'm dating. I'm on a date and (yet) happy. Or at least not unhappy. The thoughts float through my mind, but maybe what I feel is more like a general excitement not related to dating or romance, but instead to brightly colored games, rolling the dice, slushy spirits, and the promise of shortcake. Or is it more? Is it possible that Twister might really be in my future? I stop worrying about it and try my luck.

* * *

There's something really thrilling about having sex with someone that you've just had the best evening with in a long, long, time. Especially after you've been drinking steadily and playing games that something deep within you just instinctively loves, a part of you that's mesmerized by the fairies of Candyland, the Rudolph-red nose on the Operation patient, the clackety sounds of a Bingo cage, the smooth texture of the Twister mat.

So yes, we made it to Twister.

After that, back in my own home, it's just not as embarrassing to remove my clothes in front of somebody as I remember it being. I'm free, I'm Twisty, I'm a little inebriated—I've had actual fun involving several senses. And it's about time.

It happens as if in a dream. Okay, no, that's not true, but it does flit through my mind for a second, how this seems to be happening to someone else whose life is way more fun, and yet I have no problem joining in. I want sex, and I want chocolate, and I want to run out tomorrow and buy a Mystery Date game we can play at girls' night, and I want to start having a girls' night. I want to invent my own game for girls' night and buy a disco ball. But first, I want out of my clothes.

Chester seems to feel exactly the same way.

"Wow, what a great T-shirt," he says to me, kissing me just at that spot on my neck midway between shoulder and jaw. (Find yours, it's pretty sensitive, no about an inch lower, see it kind of tickles, is that a muscle in there? Sorry, it doesn't matter. Just get someone to kiss you there, fast.). He has tripped over my cat and landed with his mouth just there, which although a little less than balletic, is working out nicely. We kiss. I can still kiss. Good God, I wondered for a while if I could. I'm not bad.

We kiss for a while on my couch, Aunt Lucile's couch. I love this couch. It is at the moment all I want from a couch, as it has me on it being kissed. Chester knows how to kiss. He knows how to have a really fun first date, and he knows how to kiss.

I can kiss all I want in my own apartment with my own favorite couch, despite Lulu the cat sitting on the back of it staring at me, her fur ruffed up in an almost Elizabethan collar, as if she was just brushed by servants.

"I've always liked cats," Chester says sweetly. I'm startled by a man saying this, so much so that my mouth opens, which leads to even better things. Cornelius Hooper the third (how ridiculous, I know, I know) would have hated Lulu and all her kind. *Don't think about this now, Amy. Don't think with your mouth full.*

A man on my couch removes my black T-shirt. It comes off over my head much easier than I would have thought. *Get back into it, Amy (the kissing, not the shirt).*

"I so wished it had been strip Twister," Chester says.

"It is now," I say. I may invest in a Twister game. I'm in this thing. It doesn't take much.

Chester is not exactly muscular, but he's not too skinny (for a slight person), a little bony in the shoulders, but the eyes are good. His lips are great. I sense exclamation points coming on.

I lead Chester to my bedroom. It has been over a year since any male has been on a bed with me like this, or in any other way of course. Way over a year. I practically pull this elfin person on top of me, and I'm not an aggressive girl. I'm just pretty Twistered at the moment.

"It was the Battleship win that really got you excited," Chester says.

"But you won," I say.

"Yes. I sank your Battleship," he says.

"Filthy talk," I say. "I like it."

"In the bedroom with Colonel Mustard," he says. "So to speak."

"I can be Miss Scarlet when I want to be," I say. I feel sexy, like a 1950s movie star. Scantily clad, too. What was in those frothy drinks?

I admit to not being all that curious about Chester's body, or I would admit it, but I've stopped talking. Sometimes, you don't need to see everything. There's no reason to dawdle. Just roll the dice, land on Boardwalk, collect free parking. I start by passing Go.

This is actually fun, it occurs to me till I stop thinking and just be. It's all about me here, tonight—Chester needs little encouragement or attention, both of which he's lavishing on me in ways I'm too embarrassed to describe any further.

"I'll just call you slinky," he says.

I slinky all over, several times.

* * *

I'm not even all that embarrassed when "it" is over, when we start to extract our hand from the appropriate places, kind of like when you have to get off the Twister board in the end. It is that last tumble over on top of one another in Twister that so often takes your breath away. And makes you want to play again.

Chester begins to braid a few small strands of my hair, as our bodies determine whether that's enough playtime for one night.

"I also really like you naked," he tells me, sheer honesty in his voice. It's been so long since I've felt so complimented. I think I even blush, although it's a little late in the game.

"Thank you. What an adventurous evening," I say. I'm out of thoughts, really and pretty happy about it.

"I'm always the last to leave a party," he says. "I'm bad at picking up social signs. So, just tell me when to go, no problem."

"Oh," I say. I don't know what the current thing is in dating these days. Do people stay overnight? Do they leave quickly? I guess I should have picked up that *Cosmopolitan* at the dentist's office. Or maybe *Glamour*. Even *AARP magazine* probably knows more than I do.

"I'm not much of a sleeper," he says. "Three or four hours a night works. But I'm happy to do Sudoku while you sleep."

It's a picture in my mind: Naked, older Chester with a pen and Sudoku pad at 3 a.m. Somehow, I choose just to think about it rather than try it out.

"I'm not great at sharing this bed," I say, which is true. Ask Lulu the cat, who often goes tumbling onto the floor when I roll. Now that I've had a year to myself and can roll at will, I realize I may not be ready to share yet. Also, people turning pages in bed keeps me up. That scratchy sound.

Chester leaves sweetly, with a chaste kiss on the lips then a giggle, the same way he did earlier in the night, that time he tried to put his hand on green just below a body part of mine he seems to like. And he succeeded.

6

A Bug by Any Other Name

Refreshed, I head to the office the next morning early, which means I have the place to myself, a nonfat mocha from The Latte Lesson to cleanse my system. My theory is that strong chocolate-spiked coffee will do almost no end of good for you—so forget about those thick gross green drinks. I also want some kind of treat for myself, for getting out there, for trying something new, taking a chance, okay maybe even a big chance. I want to reward myself for doing something outside of my comfort zone—well, a few things, judging by memories of last night that keep coming back as I sip. That was me, I giggle to myself. About time, I hear someone's voice saying, maybe Aunt Lucille's. Maybe Susan's. Maybe mine.

I arrive at the office early to try my hand at Goldilocks.

"Looks like Goldilocks had quite a makeover," my co-art director Chris says. He's looking at me as he says it, which makes me wonder if I forgot to put on underwear, if that somehow shows, or if he just somehow knows. I've left my less than golden blond hair with the couple of little braids in it that Chester made, but I thought that was about the worst thing anyone might say about my appearance this morning, out loud at least.

"A little early in the morning for insults, especially if you didn't bring any muffins."

"Touchy," Chris says. He looks less than well-rested himself, but at least his blond hair is well combed. "It's just that I wanted to let you know that Goldilocks was once an old woman."

"What?" I ask, not even sure I want clarification. Do I look that awful?

"I've been looking into it for you. Call me a research assistant. In the eighteen-hundreds, in the *Story of the Three Bears,* Goldilocks, at first, was a nasty old woman who broke into the bears' house."

"Who told you that?" I ask.

"Wikipedia," Chris says, waving a printout at me.

"That only means it may or may not be true," I say. I refuse to give up my doubts about Wikipedia. I believe the truth is out there, but that it shouldn't be quite that easy to find.

"Yep, first she was a scary-nasty-craggy old crone, then later she morphed into a young girl, with varying shades of hair color, finally Clairol-ing up to Goldilocks herself." And yes, he's looking at my hair. I feel a blush coming on, as if you could tell I'd had sex by looking at my hair. Yes, I still blush. It's not as cute as it sounds, especially over 30.

"Why are you telling me this? I'm comfortable with my hair an off shade of nothing in particular and refuse to identify with the old craggy woman, if that's what you're going for. Besides, I don't steal. Buddhist precept number five, or six maybe—I didn't finish the class."

"No, look at this." He waves warm printed paper at me—I can feel it's fresh out of the printer, which I love. "It's fascinating. From a mean old biddy to a blonde if greedy cherub, all in a couple of centuries. You've come a long way, baby, so to speak," Chris says.

"Well, baby," I say back, since it's the only proper response to the word *baby* headed in your direction. "Let's examine this. An old woman scares three bears. I'm not sure it's the kind of estrogen-positive tale we want to spin here." I can't think of anything positive it says about women at all. "Not to mention entirely the wrong demographic. Although it is interesting that the bears weren't always the scary part," I say. An old woman breaking in on some bears. I can't think of anything good that says about humanity. "I guess she'd be brave, though."

"This lady gets out once in a while. You could say she's not afraid to mix it up. She's not afraid of anything."

"And how's this supposed to help me with my story?"

"I would think it's helpful to know that Goldilocks has been made over before."

"I thought you were commenting on my appearance or something,".

"Who says I'm not? The braids are cute, though. Trending."

"I've never been trending a day in my life."

"I would just think," Chris says, "that it's freeing to know that such a makeover is possible."

He comes over and points to the fading fabric of my blouse, which has been washed till it's super comfortable. Then he points to my braids, which I can feel are uneven and messy. My not quite blonde shoulder-length hair responds very little to smoothing and barely tolerates the braids, although I may be projecting.

"They do give off that certain glow of youth," Chris says, pulling on each to straighten them.

"I'm not sure my Goldilocks will have braids."

"Maybe she won't need them. Maybe she'll be brave and let her hair all the way down."

"This is an awfully metaphorical Goldilocks were talking about, plus I think the entirely wrong storybook."

"Don't you get it? She can be anyone she wants," Chris says, handing over the Wiki printout pages. "Goldilocks. Sounds like an alias anyway, doesn't it?"

"She does deserve a real name."

"A couple of them," Chris adds.

"Hah."

"Maybe even a hyphen. Goldi Morganstern-Lochs. Goldi Lewis-Stevensen." Chris says.

"Goldenrod Applebaum-Lochsenball. Hyphenated."

"She sounds like a three-dimensional character if I've ever heard one," Chris says. "Not just a homewrecker, a chair breaker, a food stealer. A character in search of something. Maybe herself. Maybe something beyond that. Tough. Rugged. Kick-Ass Goldi."

"Okay, okay, I get it already. Goldilocks gets a life."

"A hyphen is a terrible thing to waste," Chris says.

Chris reparts my hair by moving one of my braids to the other side, which doesn't bother me. I go back to the drawing board again, literally.

* * *

We all sit at our conference room table, eating from a large bowl that holds pastel-colored M&Ms, which Nelson found on sale after Easter. After-holiday candy sales have really become something to look forward to at this point in my life. Holidays seem mostly for kids; adults light up the day after, which you can witness by visiting the candy aisle at Target the morning of December 26. I happen to know that Safeway also puts candy on sale: no pushing, no shoving. And hardly anybody's there in the mornings before work. Hardly anyone I know.

Anyhow, Nelson stocks up, having realized long ago that M&M's have a significant shelf life, which is one of the great things about life.

"I've also purchased a good supply of new toothbrushes for you all, which you'll find under the bathroom sinks," Nelson says. "And that bright blue toothpaste we can't get enough of!"

I love my boss. I wish everyone felt this way.

"You know," Chris says, "M&M's aren't really bad for you."

"Define really bad," says our young assistant/receptionist/youth representative Kelly, who is (actually) cutting a lavender peanut M&M in half with a thin knife. We all stop to watch her do it. I didn't know it was possible. I think it's one of those fancy ceramic knives.

Chris takes her other half (yes, the bigger one). "Really bad would be things with food coloring in a more neon shade," he says. "Pastels are better for you."

"And it has peanuts," Nelson says, "which none of you is allergic to and which are part of the protein section of your food groups. You can't have too much protein."

"Oh, I think you can," says Robbi our foreign rights sales-person. "Or too many of the wrong proteins." She eats five at once, a thin woman who enjoys her candy despite criticizing it.

"I think they're pretty," I say. "Calories shouldn't count when something's really pretty."

"How I've always felt about tiramisu," Chris says.

"Exactly," Nelson adds, then looks dreamily out the window, whispering, "tiramisu...." I recognize that look. I'm hoping some will appear after lunch. Kelly can slice it as thinly as she wants; it won't stop us from enjoying it. Chris, I happen to know from experience, would be willing to eat it off the floor.

"I have an announcement," says the imposing figure of our editor in chief, Hannah, really at many times the only adult acting like an adult at Kids Press. I've noticed her resisting the candy.

"Here ya' go," Nelson says, rolling her two light blue M&M's, which begin to roll in different directions. Hannah stops them with the palms of her hand, as if swatting a fly against the table. Still, Chris will eat them smashed to smithereens. We all know it. (I would, too, but only Chris knows this. I hope.)

"I have to leave," Hannah says.

"Oh, I don't see it on the schedule," says Kelly, who actually tries to keep a schedule for all of us. Nelson's often just has hours blocked out for "playtime." It's good to be king.

"What I mean is I have to leave Kids Press," Hannah says.

We all inhale at once, as if we've been told to. As if Hannah had raised her red pencil and led us in the opening aria of an opera, one where you just know everyone's going to suffer or die, but definitely suffer.

"You can't want to leave us," Nelson says. "No one could want to leave us." Nelson looks at us all. To say that Hannah runs this place is an understatement of her abilities and intense level of concentration in an often-times chaotic mess of a workplace.

"I have to. My husband's been transferred to Houston."

"It's hot in Houston, and you have to wear a big cowboy hat," Nelson says. "We'll hire him here instead."

"He's a brain surgeon," Hannah says.

"You say that like I wouldn't have a use for him," Nelson says. "It's over a hundred degrees there daily, Hannah—heat like you've never felt before."

"Maybe you want to speak to Nelson privately?" asks Robbi.

"Yeah," says Nelson, who has grabbed a red rubber ball from the center of the table and is hanging on to it, sort of blankie style, not that I would ever use the word blankie or any baby talk around Libby, or any other child. I reserve terms like blankie more for someone like Nelson, who does have a blankie in his office.

"There's no need for secrecy," Hannah says. "This way, you all know and can begin making whatever adjustments will be needed."

"But we don't want you to go," Nelson says. I think about never seeing a red scribble from Hannah again, and while that has a certain appeal, I know someone else's red scribbles would be so much harsher. And sometimes she uses a pink glitter pen, which makes me more receptive to her edits.

"That's nice, but irrelevant," Hannah adds, marking something red in her notes. We all sit quietly, a little chastised. Hannah looks back up, "But nice."

Kelly runs to the fridge and gets us each a juice box. "I don't like apple," Nelson says quietly, so I trade him my lemonade.

"Sales are down, I'm sorry to report," says Bobbi, our accountant and sales director.

"Yes," Hannah says, "it's time to deal with that, too."

"This is a really bad meeting," Nelson says.

Kelly leans in to me and whispers, "Do we have any cookies?" I think the question is rhetorical, since we almost have one of those large bags of Mother's animal cookies. Pink and white. I nod at her. She runs fast and reappears like a superhero with the cookies. Fortunately, the kitchen is actually right next to the conference room. Small building.

We grab pink elephants and other irregular shapes. The pink ones always go first, but such is life.

"Nelson," Hannah says sternly. "I would have had this conversation with you in private, but I have had this conversation with you in private and you've stuck your fingers in your ears. I think it's time we get serious about our options."

We look at her, our mouths open with pink and white cookie crumbs falling out. Nelson pretends his little bear cookie is walking on the table and refuses to look up.

"There have been valuable offers made, Nelson, offers of investment or complete buyout."

A camel falls from Chris' mouth and bangs the table. Hannah shoots him a dirty look.

"I had no idea," I say.

"You all live in a bubble," Hannah tells us. "No offense. A safe primary-colored bubble. Don't you read the newspapers?"

"I don't read a newspaper," Chris says.

Nelson raises his juice box toward Chris, and they clink, although it's mostly symbolic, as juice cartons don't make much noise when you tap them together. Maybe a little squish sound.

"I don't want to sell," Nelson says petulantly. No one likes the direction this meeting has taken. Even the art assistants out in the front have stopped flying their paper airplanes around the room (we can usually hear them crashing around out there). We are a sad group of children's publishers.

"I think you should reexamine the offers, Nelson. The one from MyBug is very good."

"What's my bug?" Chris asks.

"And who would want one?" I ask.

"Bugs are big sellers, as a concept," Hannah says.

"There's a bug in the front closet," Kelly says. "Been there for days. I was hoping someone else would get it out of there."

"Is it brown with extremely long legs?" I ask.

"Yeah."

"Yeah, I was hoping someone else would deal with it, too," I add.

"Jeez," Chris heads for the front closet. We don't approve of killing bugs, and Chris often has to take them outside for us.

"Don't squish it," Kelly says.

"MyBug is not that kind of bug," Hannah says, exasperated. "Although the one in the closet is near the umbrellas, to the right," she says.

"My Bug is a company that wants to buy us and destroy book publishing as we know it," Nelson says. I grab my notepad and hug it, as if that will help protect our future in any way.

"No, no, no," Hannah says. "It's quite innovative."

"Uh-oh," Chris says. Nelson nods his head wildly.

"Change is bad," Nelson says.

"I want you to meet with them," Hannah says. "We'll invite them over for some nice treats, and we'll introduce ourselves. I think you'll be surprised."

"No more printed books?" I ask. I want to run to a drawing table, fast, before the notion of a drawing table becomes obsolete. Chris and I may be the last book designers to still use them, as he figured out a great way to prop up our monitors so they won't angle toward the downward slope of the desk. Everything's balanced on toddler size Lego bricks. It's fun and functional, and you can roll milk balls in and out of the Legos.

"My Bug has developed a small electronic reading device that brings books to life in a new way," Hannah says. And she's not even reading from a brochure.

"They've brainwashed you," Nelson says.

"You can hold the Bug in your hand and read from it. You can project the images on the wall, on your TV or computer, on your ceiling! Bedtime stories on your own ceiling! You can't argue with that," Hannah says.

She's right.

"Readers can add images from their own lives. Put their pets in the story. Change the ending. Redesign the setting. Add unicorns. They can make their own endings for our Bobby series, make him well again, introduce him to a whole new family. This device gives 'The Neverending Story' new meaning," Hannah says.

I think about my Bobby series, poor Bobby who can't eat ice cream and has divorced parents and suffers through every childhood illness in print, for the world to see. What child would even want to project Bobby in his current state (lactose intolerant) onto his or her ceiling?

"But you can't feel the printed page," Nelson says.

"Yeah we all really need to get over that," Hannah says. Hannah (of indeterminate age, maybe forty-six or so) has worked all her life in book publishing. Her home is full of books and magazines (but neatly arranged, like a large cataloging system).

"You're over it?" I ask her.

"I am evolving," Hannah says. "I recommend it."

"There's no evolving in Houston," Nelson says. "They're as evolved as they're going to get."

"You need to meet these guys with MyBug, all of you. Otherwise, forget being bought out. We'll just have to shut down. And then tell me, what will happen to Bobby?"

"It's that serious?" I ask. It's news to me, but then we really are sheltered here.

"I can show you spreadsheets," Hannah says, "but they'll make you cry." Bobbi and Robbi both nod in agreement. Bobbi looks like she might cry any second. Even Kelly, who isn't more than twenty-two, is starting to look a little obsolete.

"My Bug," Nelson says, and not in a very nice way.

"I'll set up the meeting for next week," says Hannah.

"Exterminate," Chris says in a robot-y voice under his breath, and I'm not sure I get the reference entirely but still kind of know what he means.

7

When the Punch Is Real

My former college roommate, Susan, aka Libby's mom (she often wears a name tag that says Libby's Mom, even when she's just going to the grocery store), also happens to be the curator of a smallish museum in Los Angeles known for being not only slightly out of the way but slightly out of the ordinary. It's called Chroma, as of this week, having changed its name from L.A.'s Craftmakers Museum, which confused everyone, as there is also a Museum of Craft and Folk Art, which has a better budget and idyllic location in Beverly Hills amongst rich and famous purveyors. Chroma stands alone in Venice, California, a cool, cool town everyone wants to visit, but the museum is in a somewhat skuzzy area, surrounded by a tattoo parlor on one side and a pool hall that plays all Def Leopard on the other, so you have to be a bit brave to stop by. The museum has been in the red for some time, and not a pretty shade of it.

So, bring on Chroma, a name so hip it implies they'll be serving fancy sliders or the freshest of sushi, which they will,

71

in the Chroma Bar. I have no problem with a museum that has its own café, especially when you can get cookies there. (You know they'll be warm and oozing dark chocolate, not to mention way overpriced.)

Tonight is the grand reopening, renaming, and unveiling, as all the artwork and some new pieces are now arranged by colors: Colors meant to lure you into a specific mood, and keep you there. If you feel the need to surround yourself with blue, you can visit Indigo (or as the museum's new brochure says, Embrace Indigo). Chroma claims the various shades of blue in the artwork will bring you into a state of awareness, truth, and serenity. I like blue, but this is asking a lot from something hanging on the wall, or maybe I need to stay a lot longer than I normally do. Maybe they should set up cots instead of the typical leather reproduction Barcelona chairs here and there.

The walls are all a slightly different shade of white that complements the main color, so that the yellow room (called Rays) has white walls with just a hint of orange in them. (Susan claims the shade is called Sunlight, and it's not available commercially.) You probably wouldn't notice this slight hint of sun if your best friend wasn't the curator and hadn't been laughing with you about this for weeks. The walls help emphasize the blues/yellows/what-have-yous featured in each piece of art, whether it's a painting, a sculpture, or something in between, a sort of modern art piece that defies description and that looks a little like a three-year-old might have made it, if you ask Libby at least. And you can ask Libby, who is dressed as a mini curator tonight, with special name tag and a flapper-y looking dress that features every single shade of color in the museum. And she still looks adorable in it. The multi-jeweled (and costume) tiara on her head doesn't hurt the effect—and is one of the prettier pieces of art in the place by far. Though I keep this to myself.

But enough about the gleaming space and identity problems of a design-y small studio that no doubt one day will make a great space for more tattoo artists. Or maybe Zumba. Tonight, I have decided to bring Chester with me, as I'm not really expecting to see lots of people I know, and Susan has already seen him. Not that I'm embarrassed about him, just that I'm not the date-in-public type. And of course until recently, I was barely the date-at-all type. Since our splashy first date, Chester has suggested several activities that sounded equally unusual if not flat-out weird. There was video bowling night, where on a large screen above the lanes you can watch an action movie (last week's was *IronMan*). In Dolby. With flashing lights. It sounded a little migraine inducing to me. Also of interest was The Salsa Taste Test at a local community college, where you get to chip and dip to your heart's delight for four hours. I'm not really that fussy a girl, but I don't think I can eat my weight in salsa (for four hours), so I passed on that idea, as I did with Croquet at the Hollywood Cemetery Night (just no, thanks), the Bakersfield Rodeo (with try-it yourself roping on ponies), and the skate marathon fundraiser for Easter Seals (ice skating from 3 p.m. till midnight, last couple standing gets an extra $1,000 added to their donation), which I suggested might be okay in the summertime. I have consented to going to the movies (twice), dinner (twice), and plain out sex (once; on the other date, Chester begged off with allergies: He'd gone to the rodeo the day before and was suffering from hay exposure). The movies were way overrated; the sex was four-star and surprising, but then, four stars usually are.

Instead of being just another unknown face in a crowd of

generous and anonymous-to-me donors, as I'd expected, I find that I know nearly every person in this room. Susan must have somehow got hold of my email list. I'll have to remind myself that sharing isn't always a good thing, once you're done being a kindergartner, at least.

For here are all my workmates, family members, and friends from the past. And here I am with Chester, who as usual, seems just delighted with life and where this moment has brought him. There's free champagne, which neither of us is about to turn down, although free is a relative term in a room brimming with consequences like this one is.

I don't know who to hide from first, so for whatever reason, I don't hide at all. I decide to act like I'm the kind of person who belongs in this room.

"This place is amazing," Chester says, holding his champagne glass gently in his hand in a way that suggests he's gone to a zillion museum events, and maybe he has. He does get out.

"It's all redesigned," I say, "with space for you to ensconce yourself in colors and moods, and apparently, every single person you know."

"What a selling point," Chester says, ready for anything. It does rub off on me a little, so I greet my Aunt Lucille with a deeply felt kiss on the cheek.

"There you are!" says my aunt. And there she is: The woman who rescued me after my divorce, turned over her perfectly located condo, some comfy furniture, the blue VW bug of my dreams. Aunt Lucille moved into a semi-retirement kind of place with no regrets. They get great cable service and have two pools to choose from. The people there are more active than I am by far. Aunt Lucille swims fast. Often with white-haired men trying to catch her, though none has, I happen to know.

My Aunt Lucille is, I think, the aunt many people wish for. Grand looking, but utterly down to earth. A really nice shade of gray hair (yes it's tinted toward blonde, everyone's doing it, nothing wrong with it) pulled back elegantly. Her clothes drape her, like the ones from Chico, but much nicer quality. She could be one of their models. Aunt Lucille has never worn heels and strictly advises against it. She's all imposing till she smiles, and then it's all over. Everyone loves my Aunt Lucille.

"Don't we know each other?" Chester asks Aunt Lucille.

"Oh," I say, thinking this is a request for an introduction, which I really need to snap into. "Aunt Lucille, this is Chester Anderson. He teaches philosophy and drives a classic car, too," I say. "Chester, my Aunt Lucille Garber."

But they're already hugging. "Oh, it's been years!" Aunt Lucille says.

Oh, they actually do know each other.

"Well, it's just a pleasure to see you Mrs. Garber. You look completely unchanged!" Chester says, practically bowing at her feet.

"Chester Anderson! Amy, Chester was one of my piano students oh so long ago—and I don't want anyone mentioning how long ago, thank you very much," says Aunt Lucile.

"I still don't practice my scales," Chester admits, cheeks a little red.

"Oh, you were an excellent student!"

Chester turns to me. "I admit, I had quite the crush on your aunt!"

"Oh," I say, as non-judgmentally as possible. Oh. Eew. I'm feeling creeped out a little but am not sure why. I notice that a couple of Chester's teeth are graying. I tell myself it's not like me to be so shallow, so surface. In spirit, Chester acts way younger than I do much of the time. He rode the rodeo ponies, he mentioned. A braver man than I by far.

"All my students loved me," Aunt Lucille says. "Especially the boys."

"Your aunt is a treasure," Chester adds.

"Isn't this a treat," says another voice I know, this time my co-art director/office mate Chris, who I could swear has just had his hair lightened (again, not that I'm judging; I just take notice of these things). He's at least two shades lighter than me. I feel suddenly a little drab. "Hello, Aunt Lucille!"

"Hello, Chris, darling," says my aunt. They've met many times.

"I'm Amy's partner ... in art," Chris says as introduction to Chester.

"This is Chester," I tell Chris, and Susan who has just joined us, and Kelly our receptionist, and Nelson Davis (my boss), and our sales and rights directors Bobbi and Robbi. I notice Chris' hair is lighter than theirs, too, which makes me feel a little better, although I'm not sure why. Jefferson and Gabriella, our art interns, wave, too. I am surrounded by my literal circle of friends. Or maybe I should say cornered. I am the unwilling center of attention.

Chester, though, is delighted with everyone, every color of artwork, every mood, which makes me remember why I brought him. He's something of a joy to have around, when I stop worrying, which happens on occasion.

Aunt Lucille practically pulls out a man who's been hidden behind her, or maybe he's just approaching and I couldn't see him through the forest of friends. Thank goodness it's someone I don't know, although I don't recall ever having felt this way before.

"May I introduce Jeremy Pitcher, my dentist," Aunt Lucile says. Jeremy makes a little bow. He's around my age, brown hair, taller than Aunt Lucille. (She's as tall as she is imposing; and believe me, she can be imposing.)

"Hello," Jeremy says to all around. He hands Aunt Lucille a cup of blue punch, although I didn't know we were allowed to have drinks in this part of the gallery, and I don't know what makes the drink blue. Chester shakes Jeremy's hand warmly, then Jeremy just kind of waves to the rest of us, although Libby, my goddaughter and the greatest person on earth, has joined us, and shakes Jeremy's hand heartily. He just kind of lets it happen with a light little laugh that makes him seem a bit nerdy, but not in an awful way or anything.

"I know you from the health club on Olympic, right?" Chester asks Jeremy.

"That's right," Jeremy replies. "I go three times a week. Whether I want to or not."

"Thought I knew you," Chester says. It's fairly official: Chester now knows everyone in the room.

"Jeremy's mom and I are old pals," Aunt Lucille says. "Old!" she directs this to Libby, who laughs along with Aunt Lucille. Chester laughs with them. Jeremy looks a little like he's come to the wrong party, and he sips the blue juice. I watch for his reaction: He only raises his eyebrows quickly for a second, leaving me to wonder about him a little more. I think he likes it. Maybe it's spiked.

We break into smaller groups, thankfully, Chris engaging dentist Jeremy in talk about teeth whitening; Chester admiring Aunt Lucille's outfit (deep green, kind of like a queen's robe, but more comfortable looking); the office folks in their own worlds. And then the worst thing happens.

I notice it first in a look on Libby's face. She drops her mouth open as if someone were stealing a painting, or a sculpture had just come to life and is attacking a visitor. I reach for her to offer comfort: Whatever it is can't be that bad.

"Look what the cat dragged it," Susan says, and not very softly.

Hooper Anneas Tomlinson the third (my ex) approaches, trailing behind Robert Coles, Susan's husband (another lawyer, but a much better guy, I've always thought and which later turned out to be so true). Robert has bad taste in friends, I have to think, and I know Susan agrees. We all go back a long way, one of those long ways that's so way back, it's hard to admit the fault in your friends. Unless one of them recently divorced you, recently being a relative term.

I so don't want to do this.

Even Robert doesn't seem thrilled that Hooper's here. Maybe he didn't bring him. Hooper's not below (or above) just walking in with someone.

"Blue punch," I say to Chester, grabbing his arm and tugging him in the direction of the punch, which I'm assuming is in the blue room. He looks at Hooper approaching, then turns back to me.

Chester takes my cue. "Who can resist blue punch?" asks Chester. He doesn't exactly look like a knight in shining armor but nails it anyhow.

The punch tastes like grape juice. I don't know why it isn't purple, and another night, I might really wonder what kind of additives are in it. Although this is Venice, California—it almost has to be organic punch.

"I thought maybe more blueberry-ish," Chester says, clearly

trying to bring up a safe, nontoxic, nonthreatening, mindless topic.

I try to bring my thoughts back to punch. Dear punch. Who doesn't love punch? The elixir of kindergarten parties, back when the world was innocent.

"I admit," I say, taking a deep breath then sipping my punch. "I thought it might be a little fizzy." My blood pressure is returning to its normal state of low, calm, healthy.

"Oh," Chester says, "ginger ale punch. Mock punch," he says critically, a hand on my shoulder gently. I could love a man who knows how to calm me down like this. "Although I was a little hoping for Kool-Aid, just because it's so not PC," he says.

We sip again. "A little like Otter Pops!" Chester says excitedly.

An uninvited voice joins in. "Amy, there you are, good to get away from the crowd, don't blame you," says my ex-husband. Okay, he looks good. I'll get that out of the way. Reddish brown hair, not a trace of gray yet. (He's 36—could it still be natural brown? Not that I care.) His suit is incredibly unwrinkled. The thought crosses my mind that perhaps he has a troop of elves who follow him around with a clothes steamer, although this is unkind to elves. Maybe the punch is spiked after all.

"Hello, Hooper," I try to say in the tone that heavyset guy on Seinfeld used to say "Hello, Jerry," with condemnation in his voice. I think it comes out more of a whisper, though.

"Hooper Tomlinson," he says as introduction to Chester. He does not even offer to shake Chester's hand, which strikes me as the most insulting thing I have ever seen. And yes, this punch sure feels spiked.

"Oh, I'm not familiar with your work," Chester says. What a

guy.

"Amy is my ex-wife," Hooper has the nerve to say.

"And yet she has many, many charming qualities," Chester adds. He is much smaller than Hooper in every way—slightness, stature. Who cares?

"I was hoping we could talk," Hooper says, trying to steer me away from Chester and my world, air and water and sustenance, and all happy things.

"We don't want to spoil the mood," Chester tries, "which I think in this room is supposed to be blueberry-esque."

"It's just that I've been taking these Buddhist classes and need to tell you the truth," H.A.T. says. (When Susan uses the acronym, it has quite a bite to it.)

"What?" I ask the least Buddhist person I have ever known.

"I had a vasectomy," H.A.T. says.

"Ah," says Chester. "And clearly you're still under the anesthetic..."

"Uh," I say, trying to wave away the statement. I start shaking my head from side to side like I'm trying to get water out of my ears.

"Years ago," H.A.T. says. "I never told you."

I am mouth agape, a sentence I never thought would apply to me, and I have been surprised plenty in my life. Yes, you can guess: I thought we couldn't have kids. I guess he had a doctor lie to me about his, um, resources, for lack of a cruder word. I am utterly agape.

Cuss words I'd like to use float in my vision like migraine warnings. They might be.

"I feel better telling you," the actual bastard actually says.

"But we were just about to dance," Chester says, and somehow, being slight and using some sort of sleight of hand, and moving fast and gracefully (Fred Astaire comes to mind, and he always seemed older than the girl, too, right?), Chester guides me away in a flowing, completely natural gesture that veils just how clever it is, if you're not watching closely, that is.

Not to mention I don't know if there's dancing allowed here.

In a gesture far less assuming than you'd think and with such great care you'd almost be practically smitten, Chester brings a small hand to my chin and very gently shuts my mouth. You would have to fall for him, even if just for the moment, wouldn't you?

We head off toward the eggplant room (purple with a touch of pumpernickel, if that's a color, sleekly elegant, makes you feel very upper class, or maybe just plain big-headed). It's such a rich, dense color that if I threw up on it right now, I bet it wouldn't much show.

"I don't think there's dancing," I say. I feel a little purple myself.

"There's always dancing," Chester says, spinning me off into the fresh air just outside the room, where I want to immediately forget there is a man called H.A.T. who has messed up my life, a man I thought I'd gotten rid of for good.

"Smell that L.A. air," Chester suggests. We're in Venice, so it's cleaner than it sounds. It smells a little of puppies, although I don't know why. Puppies at the beach. It couldn't smell better. I love puppies. I'll have to ask Susan about that punch. Could I have imagined this whole scene? (Except the puppy smell, I hope.)

Chester leads me to his super round car, lowering the windows (by hand cranking) so we get to breathe in deeply. I picture golden retriever puppies. It's very important to replace unhappy memories with pictures that will make you glad you're alive. Cuddling sleepy puppies wrapped in pink blankets, with their just-bathed puppy smell. He puts on a CD of Lyle Lovett—an early one with ponies and wide front porches, and fiddlers who know what they're doing.

Chester takes us to the ballroom dancing place on Olympic, which I've never been inside before. It's a gaudy building outside in some architectural manner that seems to require a lot of turrets—though like most things it's a façade. Inside, we step across a red-carpeted lobby into a dance floor and side tables filled with ladies in long sparkling gowns and elegant gloves. A few men are dressed this way too, no judgment. Here we can instantly tango or just pretend to. We can dance well or badly or just for fun. No one criticizes. No one gives you mystery ingredient punch. It's a straight vodka, bourbon, gin kind of place. No one's going to sneak up and try to ruin your night. No one tries to tear your heart out. No one asks anything of you at all. You are here to glide, to smile, to feel securely held. You can toast to it. You can spin and dip. You can even sit it out if you want to. But you won't want to.

Thank you, my personal Fred Astaire, for this fairy tale ending to the night. Let's just face the music and dance.

II

Part Two

8

New Kids on the Block

Monday morning, I run over a rock. I think it was a rock, and not a small one, and I'm glad at least that it has not flown up and hit the windshield. I'm pretty sure it was something of the granite nature, since it made a huge thud, then four banging sounds as it bounced around the bottom of the car, very much like a pinball machine, but without the bells. And certainly no prize. Now the car's rattling. I don't blame it a bit.

I don't mess with the blue Beetle. I may not take great care of my hair or fingernails or toes. I really can't be bothered with the toes—I've just never seen the point, and sandals make me trip, so I stick to closed-toe flats. I fell really badly wearing flip-flops on Lincoln Boulevard one time and finally got where I was going with a bloody left leg. It was horror movie ugly. Thankfully, no one got pictures—no one I know at least. Sometimes, my T-shirts get holes around the shoulders, but that just adds to the beachy feel, I like to think. But I believe it's my job to watch out for the Beetle. I am the only creature standing between it running for eternity (or at least a little while longer) and being condemned to spare parts. I've really come to identify with the Beetle, even though I think overall it may not be a good idea to fall in love with a car. I don't know if it's the kind of love you can put your hopes for the future into, but for now there it is. I will go the distance for the bug.

Which fortunately of course isn't that far to go: I drive the rattling Beetle over to Mac's mechanic shop on Pico, not far from the office. And seemingly waiting for me at the gate is that young mechanic. Ben. For a second it looks as if he's holding two cups of Starbucks coffee, one for me, until I realize he really is holding two cups of coffee. Maybe he heard the rattle coming down the street. It is a particularly offensive sound, especially if you're fond of VWs.

Ben greets me, almost with a kind of salute. "The Girl in the '67 Beetle."

I nod as the car makes hideous grinding sounds.

"Ouch," Ben says.

"I know. I ran over a rock I think." I say. "I'm so sorry."

"Tell it to the Beetle," Ben says. He offers me a coffee. It could all be a dream as there's cream and sugar in it, and a sprinkle of vanilla. It's certainly not a bad dream at all.

"I have an extra," he says with a shrug. As it was not a great weekend for me, I'm not about to ask questions, and the vanilla smells really good.

Ben directs me to a parking space, so I park and jump out and nearly grab the coffee, or maybe it just feels that way because there's something about this really good-looking guy. Twenties? Is twenties a guy or a kid? I'm going with guy, since I'm not about to look it up in Urban Dictionary. I don't think Webster's would be particularly helpful, as it wouldn't be able to see the slight dimple on his left side. They're so good on the left side.

I really need the coffee.

"Thank goodness you're here," I say, although it's way more intimate than I meant, but then I am upset about the car and the rock. The Beetle even rattles while it's not moving, just sitting there with the engine on, which worries me. I take the cup.

"Thank you," I say.

"Sounds like a bad morning," Ben says.

"I'm terrified something terrible has happened to the Beetle," I say somewhat redundantly. "The noise is louder than the static on the radio." It's the original radio, which isn't quite as cool as it sounds.

"It just wants to be noticed," Ben says, looking directly at me.

"I have to go to work," I say, when it seems like someone should say something.

"Well, we'll look after her. Take care of all her needs," Ben says, patting the Beetle's round fender. Hmm. "Where do you work?"

"Oh, I'm in children's publishing. Illustration, although I'm also writing a new book on Goldilocks," I say, though I've no idea why.

"I'm familiar with it," Ben says.

"We want kind of an updated version because—" and then I can't think why I'm writing a new book on Goldilocks at all. Complete blank...

"Because it hasn't been done right?"

"Yeah, maybe. Maybe the definitive Goldilocks happy ending is still waiting out there."

"I think you're right. I've been studying this."

"Ah, children's lit scholar?"

"No, it's all about the stars. One of my many fields of interest. You know, the Goldilocks Planet theory."

"I have no idea what that is. There's a theory?"

"There's a theory," Ben says. "You should definitely know about it. But I asked where you work because I can bring the Beetle by later, if you like. It's a new taxi-ing service we're developing. Since your credit card is on file and all." I am a regular, or at least the Beetle is.

"I'm just up on Wilshire at sixth. Kids Press."

"Near the Latte Lesson," Ben says. He does like his coffee. "A place of great learning. I've seen you there."

This young guy has noticed me at the Latte Lesson cafe. I'm starting to not know what the oddest part of this morning is.

"Okay," I say, not sure what I'm agreeing to, exactly.

"Fred will call with your details," Ben says. Fred, I've learned, works in the back office part of the garage. I've yet to meet Fred. He has a high, unusual voice, which sometimes makes me wonder if Fred is a real person at all, or if maybe they take turns pretending to be Fred. Maybe Fred is an amalgam of them all. There are worse things, and sometimes you do have to amuse yourself at work, especially if you run out of coffee.

"Would you like a ride now?"

"I think a long walk to clear my head is in order." I hand him my car keys, although for a second it feels as if I'm giving him something much more personal.

"Original VW keys," Ben says, admiringly. "A real find." Hmm. I thank him again for the coffee and wander up toward the office.

* * *

Back at the office, it looks like a local Boy Scouts group is visiting, although the boys look a little old to be Boy Scouts, but not by much. They're loud enough, though. There are five of them in our office, not in uniform or anything, but each has that scraggly, scrawny look of boys not yet fully grown. Torn T-shirts with half-washed-off slogans on them. Frayed pants with holes. Some wearing caps. Several of them look away when I walk in the door. I guess they're a roomful of shy Boy Scouts. Just another day.

"Welcome," Chris says, taking me aside where we can stare at our visitors, who are in ebullient conversation with Nelson. Nelson seems to be greatly amused by them, and vice versa. One of the boys has the same ha-ha laugh as Nelson, which is plain weird. The thought, *Getting on like a house on fire*, crosses my mind, but I let it go. Nelson is the biggest kid of all, of course—not so much tall as, well, the embodiment of grown-up boyhood delight. He's explaining wildly with his hands as one of them explains wildly with his hands and nods profusely, a rhythmic balance not unlike rubbing your head and patting your stomach at the same time. These guys have their own proprietary rhythm, which you wouldn't guess at all from the Pokémon shirts. They're on their way to the conference room, such as it is.

"Did someone's mom drop them off or something?" I ask Chris quietly. Several boys drag loose ratty shoelaces behind their sneakers, which do not even seem to be name brand. Although I like this about them, actually. They're too old to be our target audience of kids for a marketing group. They're too young for just about anything else.

Although looks can be deceiving where age is concerned, as I'm coming to understand.

Kelly, our office assistant, looks like she's trying to instill a little law and order, but her wild gesturing isn't working.: These guys seem to be almost climbing the walls, stumbling over chairs. They are in perpetual motion. Kind of like kindergartners. Certainly nowhere near as well behaved as Libby's first-grade classmates.

"Guys, let's go," says one who seems to be their leader. They all wear name tags (like all our guests, who are usually primary school age and often put the name tags on their nose). His name is Steve G. He is tall with dark hair and an expression that goes from clownish to dead serious in a way that I kind of envy. He commands respect yet looks as if he might put a whoopee cushion under your seat without the slightest hesitation. (And yes, we do have whoopee cushions in the closet, for silly days and third-graders.)

"Steve, Steve, Steve, Steve," the others chant not exactly football-team style, but with true respect. Or like a mantra. It does seem to calm them a little. One of them tries to grab a juice box off of Kelly's tray, to which she can only reply, "Boys!"

Actually, these guys may be in just the right place.

They also grab at the bowls of potato chips in the center of the table as if they haven't been fed at all today. We serve the healthy kind of chips (not really made of potato, but kids are often taken aback when you ask them if they'd like a hemp chip). Two of the boys have nice manners and punch at the messy ones. I finally notice that one kid just looks above it all. Serious. Kelly sits next to him, as it seems a relatively safe spot. It looks like even the good greasy kind of chips wouldn't tempt this guy.

Chris holds a chair out for me and I sit, although he doesn't usually act this way. Two of the guys' faces actually turn into large O's with their mouths, as if they've never seen such a thing. No doubt what Chris had in mind.

"Kids these days," says 35-ish Chris. Even Kelly looks worlds older than these guys, and she's not. Hannah, down to her last couple of weeks or months, not that she has given us a specific date for leaving, walks in, sits down, and slams her tablet on the table as if gathering everyone's attention. A couple of the boys jump in fear, or at least surprise. One comes over to sit next to her, which makes Hannah move to the side for a minute in response. Then it becomes clear: He really just wants to look at her tablet. (It's a new model.)

Our young artists, Jefferson and Gabriella, sit behind the main table in chairs against the wall, looking as if it's very hard for them to keep a straight face.

Steve claps his hands: "Let's get this party started!"

Hannah replies formally, "Welcome to Kids Press."

Nelson, our leader, comes running in with something that looks very much like cherry pie around his mouth. Kelly quickly hands him a napkin. (There's always a large stash in the center of the table, as we have kids visit here, and Nelson, who can take on the whole first grade in terms of his need for cleanup.)

"Hi guys," Nelson says. "Yes, we're Kids Press, and I'm Nelson Davis. I started all this," he motions around to the primary colored walls filled with posters of kids' books, many of them featuring smiling kids' faces, except Bobby, from the *Bobby Suffers the Latest Calamity Series,* who is always in some sort of pain, be it mental or physical, and therefore only smiles slightly once in a while, when relieved of some problem or quandary. Next up for Bobby, a housing crises, as his mom must move to a new city for her job. We really ought to have given Bobby some siblings to torture, as all the Bobby tragedies are getting to be a bit much. Bobby has more of a soft, hopeful look on his face than an out-and-out smile. And he's still a big seller. Go figure.

"Well, we're most of My Bug here," says the Steve one. "Although there are a few guys we left behind who do some programming and stuff, who don't really fit into meeting situations all that well."

"Ha-ha," snickers one guy, Nathan P., who is juggling juice boxes at the moment.

"Have you no women working at your company?" asks Hannah..

"We are so totally open to the idea of women joining us," says Paul J, who speaks very fast and has the look of someone who cannot tell a joke, or maybe someone who tells bad ones on purpose.

"Absolutely," says Joel K., kind of a tall, quiet one who has read each side of his juice box, maybe even more than once.

Chris giggles audibly next to me. Kelly looks at a loss for what notes to take down on her laptop, which the tall boy next to her, Michael R, keeps adjusting for her, though I doubt she's asked him to.

"Thank you for letting us look at your company, first of all," says Nathan. The others mumble their "oh, yeah," "really," "neat," except for the tall Michael guy next to Kelly, who whispers something to her about screen resolution. I think I detect a Swiss German accent. He has that serious European look along with little eyeglasses that are too cool to be American. Kelly does not seem interested.

"First off," says the leader Steve, "we have developed My

Bug from a little idea we had in a college dorm one day while watching *Spider-Man*..."

"And laughing hysterically at the improbabilities—" Nathan adds.

"True," Steve evaluates for the group. "We were a couple years younger then." I roll my eyes at Chris, who rolls back.

"We've taken it from a little idea to a real product with enormous potential," Steve continues, bringing out what I guess is a My Bug. Each boy has one, in different colors: ROYGBIV (two boys hold up two, if you're wondering about the math). Steve has the red and blue, which I somehow get the feeling are the major players here.

"Ooh," Kelly admits, looking at Swiss Michael's violet one. He hesitates with a grimace a second, then hands it over to her. Kelly stops taking notes for a moment. Serious Michael crosses his arms over his chest, then begins to point at the violet object, which is smooth plastic, about four inches across and three wide, with rounded edges that give it a cuteness, an allure that kind of reminds me of something.

"Cool," says Nelson, who is admiring a green one. Green is his color. I wonder if they knew this about him. The tall Joel hands me a blue one. The My Bugs seem to multiply: The boys start pulling them from nearly all of their pockets, and these guys have a lot of pockets. Cargo pants all around.

Joel places it in my hands as if it's a living thing, something that needs care if not feeding, although it doesn't seem breakable in the slightest.

"Hmph," says Hannah, who has an orange one in front of her she's yet to touch. Nelson has two green ones and is bouncing in his chair like he's had too much sugar. Kelly moves his juice box just out of reach. It's the natural kind, but still.

Each boy leans this way and that, showing us what My Bugs do. And even I would have to admit that the colors on the screen are just this side of remarkable.

"Wow," Chris says.

"Right?" Steve says. "Okay, so yes, as you can see, mostly now it's games, it's true," Steve says.

"Games can be good companions for some children, don't forget," says the bespectacled Paul, who is now working three in front of him (and two in front of Nelson), with the kind of concentration you see in movies where kids are sitting around the room staring at their SAT or another equally alarming exam. I suspect he'd get upset if someone moved one of his Bugs right now, but I really kind of want to.

Steve begins. "The thing is,"

"Right," Paul says.

"We love books. We're all intense readers here."

"Oh, yeah," the boys echo.

"We worship books," Nathan P adds.

"So, it's nice for you to entertain the idea of joining us," Steve says.

Serious Swiss Michael makes a gesture with his hands, kind of like a mushroom cloud, and makes a sound like *phhhh*, but he nods profusely, as if this were all a good thing.

"Exactly," Steve says. "Books on the My Bug. Interactive books, games with books, books with games—"

"Games, books, numerological tasks, right-brain challenges, mind-crunching problems, brain-twisters," Nathan says.

"It's so possible," Paul says. "It's a snap to create them."

"A very good snap," adds the tall Joel with a smile. "Challenges are important to kids."

"And books aren't?" I say. Okay, that just slipped out.

"Books are," Steve says.

"Didn't we say that?" asks serious Swiss Michael.

"Yes, it's true," Steve says, not for the first or second time. "But we can do more than give a boy a book to hold in his hands..."

"Or a girl," Paul says, and the guys are quick to nod and say "sure, sure" a lot.

"We could take all your books," Steve says.

"Easy!" Paul says with a snap.

"Put them on My Bug. Let kids decide how they end, what pictures they want to see, how they'd change the pictures if they were illustrators, how they'd change anything, everything," Steve says, moving his hands now in as if he were shaping a mountain of Play-Doh, which we have a crate of in the closet. I wonder what he's making in his mind.

"Independent art projects," Nathan says.

"Right?" Paul says. They're nodding like crazy. The My Bugs are communicating with us. Chris has his making little bop-bop sounds, and he seems deeply engaged with a game where sheep are multiplying in front of him. Or cloning. Hanna's Bug hiccups, and I can't see why. Nathan's croaks like a frog, a really cute little tree frog, not a toad sound that might make you run the other direction. Gabriella's and Jefferson's seem to be locked in some kind of battle, and our interns look as if they have no idea where they are, and don't care. Kelly's is quiet, but the screen keeps changing colors. Mine has produced a drawing game and doesn't seem concerned that I use the wrong colors and have accidentally gone outside the lines. I've just colored in a purple and fuchsia planet Earth, and I got extra points.

"And the shape," Nelson says, handling one as if he were on LSD and it was hypnotizing him, although I don't know why drugs should come to mind at a time like this. Mostly, I suspect he's just had a lot of juice.

But I let it slip out. "It's nice," I say, running my hands along the sides, admiring that there aren't any sharp edges, not really any edges at all. "It reminds me of something."

"Really, what?" Nathan P asks. Several of the boys stop their games to lean in. They want to know. They take this thing seriously.

"I don't know," I say.

"Right," Steve says, bringing back everyone's attention to the fun and games. "We could take something you're working on, and capture it, amplify it, bring it to life for the reader, the new student, the new young thinker who wants to engage, but in his own special way."

"Or her," Paul says. Murmurs of agreement from the boys.

Kelly has put down her notebook entirely and is now sitting very closely next to the studious Swiss boy, who has stopped acknowledging anyone else at the table.

I look to Chris, who also seems to be taking it all in, looking from face to face, bemused. I open my mouth to say something to him, but nothing comes out.

"So, what are you working on, for instance," asks the tall Joel at my side.

"Me?"

"Oh, tell them about Goldi," Chris taunts me.

"No, not Goldilocks, I don't imagine you'd be interested," I say.

"Oh, the Goldilocks Planet," Nathan says. "Really hot topic."

"Yes," Steve agrees. Joel smiles at me as if I've done well.

"What?" I ask.

"The Goldilocks Planet," Paul says. "The paradigm, the concept. You know." They all begin making that cloudlike shape with their hands again, nodding, and I'm lost as to how these guys could be interested in a girl's search for the right chair, or lamp, or conversational tactic with bears, or whatever my book is going to be about.

"We basically do not understand what you're talking about," Chris says.

"Oh, right," Steve says.

"The Goldilocks Project," Nathan begins. "Aka the Goldilocks Planet, depending on who you talk to—"

"Or which scientific journal you read," Joel says.

"All-of-Them," Paul says faster than humans are meant to talk, then laughs as if he makes this joke all the time. It garners a couple of ha!s from the guys, and one high-five, despite that they have to lean way over people to do this. Boys.

"Right," Steve says.

Nathan picks up: "Out there, somewhere, are planets that so closely resemble the Earth, that have the qualities we need for life, that they are potential other Earths."

"I think you're the second person to tell me about this to today," I say, remembering Ben's comments about Goldilocks and the stars. And that I need to know. Am I the last person to hear about this? "What does this have to do with Goldilocks?"

"You know," Nathan says, "To be another Earth, it needs to have just the right amount of water, just the right amount of nitrogen. Not too much, not too little. Just right. Goldilocks planets."

"Not too far from the sun, not too close to the sun, just right," says Joel. Other boys nod more, one finishes his juice box noisily, then smashes it and aims for the trash. He misses. Hannah puts in in the can for him, looking as if she might kill someone, not that she lets go of her orange Bug in her other hand. Hannah would make a great principal of an elementary school. Maybe even a military school.

"Yes," says Steve, "it's exactly the kind of book that's right for us, just what we'd hoped for, and here you are, already at work on it."

"Here you are," Chris says softly to me, the woman whose last idea for Goldilocks had her shopping at Sharper Image, although she could be shopping for telescopes, for all I know.

"With My Bug," Nathan says, "you can go beyond the page. You can offer research the kids could delve into, in language they can understand; bios about those scientists studying the project; illustrations of the ideal Goldilocks planet out there somewhere, beautiful, sustainable, just right."

"Or close enough," Paul says. The guys say "sure, sure."

"Pages and pages of information, details, games, you could never afford to print in book form, but you can store in My Bug, a shape, a device, a creature kids keep close at hand," Nathan P says.

"Yes, it's win-win," Steve says.

"It's win-win-win," Paul says, "Actually, it's win-infinity-win." He means it.

Nelson has looked up from his Bugs, and just looks from guy to guy. From fellow nerd to nerd. His device giggles, and he looks as if he's in love. Nelson in love is mankind at his best self. Or hers.

"The Beetle," I say. I lean over to Chris and gesture around the soft curves of his toy with a few warm feelings of my own. "It reminds me of the Beetle," I say. "My Beetle."

"Ah-ha," say the guys. "Yep, good, sure."

"Ringo, right?" Nathan P asks genuinely.

9

Your Planet or Mine?

After a good lunch of cranberry, rice, and kale salad from the cold foods section of the Latte Lesson—this selection is way better than the jalapeno, garlic, quinoa, and kale salad, which gives me vivid monster-movie dreams—I feel as if I'm awakening from some kind of sleeping pill or glass of wine, or two. Not only am I dropping things, I feel slightly uncertain about everything, a little fearful, a little grumpy, and I notice that Chris is acting this way as well. He has spilled his water bottle twice and called it a Dingledorf. Or maybe he was calling himself that. Either way, he couldn't have meant it as a compliment. And he doesn't usually use language out of *Snow White*. Chris is out of character.

We spent the morning playing with My Bugs and were won over. Utterly and completely. (Probably not Hannah, just out of stubbornness, but she wants this merger anyhow.) Could it be we were hypnotized, though? Brainwashed? That the toys appealed to some part of our mind that requires constant attention and interaction from small devices? I'm starting to question my own thoughts, wondering if they've been tickled too much by technology in ways that neuroscientists have yet to examine but that are pretty subversive anyhow.

"Wait. I love books," I say. "Leafing through pages. Running my fingers over the paper. Good paper, recycled paper, I don't care what kind of paper."

This is sort of a lie. I hate books printed on cheap paper. I'm just afraid to say so. I'm afraid of the Bugs. I even feel itchy from the name.

"You're just upset because you feel you're betraying everything you believe in," Chris says, angrily but not accusingly, as if he feels the same way. I guess he was referring to himself as the Dingledorf.

I run my hands over the books at my desk, on the little powder blue shelf I like to admire. "Oh, my God," I realize. "Think what those guys could do to Bobby." I envision poor, tortured Bobby, who has been broken and injured. I picture him trapped in a video game, under attack by diseases that have yet to be discovered and that undoubtedly have no cure. He's having trouble walking; he's exhibiting facial tics and a stutter. "Who will protect Bobby if not us?"

"Bobby goes viral," Chris says. "Is there a world where this could possibly be a good thing?"

Nelson stays in his office area playing with My Bugs all day. Every few minutes, he asks Kelly to bring him a new one, then he grabs his phone and records himself saying something quietly.

"Nelson's getting ideas," I whisper.

Chris snatches a Bobby book and shields Bobby's eyes. "Don't look."

"Given technological plus medical progress," Chris says, "it's possible that Bobby's future may become ... open ended," he says, making an aghast yet facetious face.

"Ha-ha," I say, having heard it all morning.

At around 5:45 p.m., a bell rings at the school across the street. We've no idea why: Wouldn't all students be home by now? Is it a reminder for teachers to go and eat, or is it just something they can't get the bell system to stop doing? For us, it is a kind of closure thing: Start wrapping up (if you haven't already, and we do get pretty caught up in our work around here), start thinking about dinner, start thinking about your personal life, such as it is. Start saying good-bye to the comforting lull of the workday, no matter how busy/worried/stressed you were: All of those things are really just a comfort, a cause to rejoice. I know where I will be every day and what I have to do, and that I'm producing books (real books, for real kids who hold real books). Okay, so I love my job.

I notice Kelly standing by the window, twirling her long blonde hair through her fingers. Gabriella, with the shiniest of long black hair, joins Kelly and places both her hands against the windows. (Fingerprints don't phase us; we invite kids here.) They are whispering.

"What are you girls gawking at?" Hannah says unamused, although maybe this is her way of showing amusement, who really knows.

"It's a who," Kelly says.

"Yeah," agrees Gabriella, "and he's driving Amy's Beetle."

"What?" Chris asks. "Who? Who's driving the Beetle? You let someone drive the Beetle?"

"Must be serious," Hannah says with no smile, although she's starting to twirl her hair a little as she looks out the window (short brown bob, not much to twirl, but you'd be surprised what one look at a good-looking guy can do to a woman with a bob).

"Wait a minute," I say, then rush over to the window. "Oh, that's my mechanic."

"Wow, you have a mechanic?" asks Kelly, in the way that suggests I've risen a whole bunch in her estimation.

Ben is downstairs with the Beetle, rubbing it with the softest looking cloth, although he's not in his work gear anymore. Nice jeans and a button-down blue shirt. Not tucked in. It makes a difference. It makes for a silhouette that really impresses the three or four people staring at you through a window. The Beetle looks good, too.

"Nice going, Goldi," Chris says to me.

I wave my hands through the air, wiping clean his dirty etch-a-sketch of a mind. "He's bringing me my car."

"Good service," Hannah says in a surprisingly filthy way.

"Uh-huh," Kelly says, mouth open.

I push them all away from the window.

"He's coming in!" Gabriella whispers to Kelly, who runs back to her desk.

"Suddenly such a good receptionist," Hannah says.

"Welcoming," Chris adds.

"Oh, shut up," I tell them, surreptitiously checking my face in the mirror I keep in my drawer. Okay, it's a Cinderella hand mirror. That really shouldn't matter at the moment though. Except that the Cinderella on the back looks so much prettier than I do. Mirrors are not our friends. Neither is Cinderella, who really isn't the brightest princess in the kingdom. Plus, talk about a bad self-image. I'm not sure Cinderella's face ought to be anywhere near a mirror.

"Your prince is here," Hannah says, looking my way.

"Talk about fairest in the land," Gabriella says under her breath.

Well, my coachman arrives, anyhow. Ben walks into the office as casually as most people walk into the coffee shop. (I'm always a little excited by coffee shops, what with the scents of chocolate and coffee and sweet things, plus the neat music, but I figure that it's just me that walks in and breathes deeply with her eyes closed for a couple seconds.)

"Welcome to Kids Press," says Kelly. Has she unbuttoned a button on her blouse?

I can't believe I'm capable of having such a thought.

C'mon Amy, you were young once, too. You were alive once too.

"Hi," Ben says. "I have Amy's car." Gabriella joins Kelly at the desk as if she had any reason at all to be standing there. She's carrying her iPad as if she's about to draw something Michelangelo-like that couldn't wait.

"This is really getting very good," Chris says from behind me. He grabs at my mirror and checks his own hair.

I grab my purse and wander over to the front desk. *Everyone else is doing it,* I hear Aunt Lucille say with a bit of urgency in her voice.

"Hi, Ben," I say, as if he's here every day.

"Hi, Amy," he says, as if he's here every day.

Kelly can't get any words out, though she attempts a few syllables.

Ben picks up a pastel blue My Bug from Kelly's desk, turns it over, holds it up to the light, then puts it down. For some reason, watching him is a little mesmerizing.

"Um, it's just a thing," Kelly says.

"Yeah," Ben agrees.

"My office mates, Kelly, Gabrielle, Chris," I say, since Chris is now lurking nearby as well. "This is Ben. He works on the Beetle." Ben waves.

"I have everything for you downstairs," Ben says perfectly normally, but Chris snickers, so I lead Ben outside quickly.

"Nice office," Ben says. What do you do here exactly?"

"Design and illustration, sometimes a little writing."

"Ah, right. You're revising Goldilocks. The Goldilocks Planet. I've been thinking a lot about that."

"Why does everyone suddenly know about the Goldilocks Planet but me?"

"There was a report on it on NPR last week."

"Oh." We don't play NPR in the office unless someone is being investigated, which Chris always enjoys, often narrating the guilty party's downfall. We usually listen to children's music, which may be why we're so behind the times. Not that good piccolo music ever hurt anyone, when you can find good piccolo music, that is.

"Plus, you know," Ben continues, "once you hear about something, you start hearing about it everywhere."

"There's probably a name for that phenomena."

"Probably something like the 'Occurrence of Minor Phenomenal Repetition,'" Ben says. "Or maybe just, 'The Internet.'"

I laugh.

"I have an idea. Are you up for a little drive? A small adventure? Nothing that would be inappropriate for a school night or anything," he says, handing me the paperwork from my Beetle's day in the shop, which I have no need to look at right now because I'm beginning to stare at his hair rudely. And the rest of him. He's a terribly cute person.

He opens the passenger door for me. I swear to God.

"Oh, I don't have school nights," I say, though then I realize this doesn't leave me much of an out for not going. Plus of course, the bell across the street rings for no reason other than that some god of dating may be watching. Does this mean I'm going out with Ben? "You must be busy."

"Please, I think you'll like it. Plus, it's semi-work-related. Less pressure that way."

"So, not a real date or anything," I say, although I don't know why. I'm old enough not to have to spell anything out for anyone, as I expect this younger guy is well aware.

"More of an investigative outing with educational benefits in a '67 Beetle," Ben says easily, as if he's used to such talk. I can see Kelly still watching from the window. She'd be way in the car by now, if she were me. I get in (*before I'm too old*—it crosses my mind).

"And I do have school nights," Ben adds, starting up the car so easily, it's as if they're in a relationship or something.

"You have school nights?"

"I take classes at Santa Monica City College. A few nights. I'm in no hurry to graduate. I already have the job of my dreams," he says, patting the dashboard lightly. "And I love taking classes."

"What do you take?"

"Hmm. Languages, Shakespeare, Astronomy," says this guy who is too young to be true. I mean, too good.

And I have to say, Ben can shift gears smoothly. Though I don't say it out loud. At least, I hope I didn't.

"I keep signing up for yoga classes," I reply, nervous, since I haven't touched anything Shakespearean in well over a decade. I sit there counting the years on my fingers. Oh, it's fourteen years. I try not to picture where Ben was fourteen years ago, but I'm thinking it involved skateboards. Or maybe a Big Wheel.

"Yoga," Ben says, "hmm, not so much."

"Yeah. I go for a while then have to drop out because the other students start to correct the way I'm standing, or leaning, or stretching. Even if I stay in the back and don't smile. They always come after me." I think for a few seconds. "I realize I sound a little paranoid, but these women in their sleeveless tops are really bossy."

"Oh, I believe you. I'll stick to the gym. No one cares what I'm doing."

Okay, I'll admit I picture him at the gym and look away quickly.

"I like to exercise in private," I say.

"I get that, Girl in the '67 Beetle."

I look down at the passenger seat to hide my face and smile. This is a fine passenger seat. I rarely get to sit here. My hair is blowing because the windows don't close all the way. A Beetle is all about the perfection of its slight imperfections. They're what make it a classic. Maybe it's what makes all of us classic, not that I've noticed any imperfections in my driver, slight or otherwise.

The Beetle runs incredibly smoothly. We don't even need to turn on the radio to cover up any clicking or clacking.

"The Beetle sounds good," I say. I look around at the other cars on the road, Hondas and Chevys and Toyotas, a lot of Hyundais. Every single driver smiles at me. And this is L.A. at traffic hour. I may be dreaming.

Ben turns on the AM radio and finds jazz playing. I don't know how.

* * *

We end up at the Griffith Park Observatory, and if you're from L.A., you know you loved it there when you were eight, and if you're not from here, you would have loved this place when you were eight. And you'd love it now because it is a patch of perfection in a city that's vast yet often claustrophobic with smog or traffic, and all-around a little selfish, not too keen on sharing the best of itself with others. The observatory is the opposite of selfish, though. It's just there to be looked at and admired by everyone, explored and discovered. The building stands open-armed, somewhat blushing in the early sunset. It's a classic, too.

That timeless white planetarium dome behind the center of the building. Two smaller domes at each side, the strange somewhat haunting Astronomers Monument in front, concrete and imposing. I know the names of all six astronomers featured, but I keep it to myself, so as not to seem like a snob. An L.A. snob (yes, the worst kind). Let visions of the movie *La La Land* float through your mind. But it's right in front of you in the fading light, tucked into the L.A. mountains, which aren't large but are still comforting. Although we're not that high up in altitude, the air is so much better here than in any single other place in the city. There's greenery and flowers nearly all year, even in the dry of a desert summer. This place is magic for all ages. Sure, Disneyland gets all the attention, but the observatory is the true star in the Los Angeles universe. Look it up.

Plus, Leonard Nimoy has a theater named after him here. And there's a Café at The End of the Universe. There is nothing bad to say about this place.

And of course it's been redone a bit inside since I was eight, but it still looks pretty much the same outside, with its smooth surfaces that you just want to walk up and start running your fingers along, feeling the cool of it. Like most of us I suspect, I haven't been here in far too long because I live here, so I seldom visit. There's some kind of weird L.A. logic about this. We know the observatory is there. We know we love it. But we never go there.

I practically lead Ben inside to the Foucault Pendulum because I find its sweep, sweep, sweep gesture magnetic and hypnotizing. I'm happy to stand with others and wait till the pendulum topples a peg as it rotates with the Earth. In fact, just try to drag me away. I can feel Ben smiling and wait for the peg, and the little cheer that always goes up among the crowd, even when they're mostly eight. You need to be part of this kind of thing when you live here, and maybe even more so when you don't.

Pendulum success reached and noted, Ben takes my arm and leads me to the almost romantically lit Wilder Hall of the Eye to the Beyond the Visible display. I don't know who Wilder was, but I'm envious. This darkened but huge area is lit by the a stunning room-size digital display of the sky. Glowing radio waves lead us mysteriously around the galaxy to the threatening but alluring black hole, but we don't get too close.

Not that I'm likely to jump into anything, it occurs to me.

"I thought it might help you get into the Goldilocks Planet mood," Ben says, but not in a suggestive way. This is science, after all, but with really intimate lighting. It sets a nice mood indeed. I look at the gamma-ray window, bright blue, red and yellow, pixelated and almost looking like it's made of Legos, but I don't need to share this. Something to show Libby, though, and soon. Although in some ways, this place seems like it'd be wasted on kids. This room, at least. Or maybe it's just this feeling I'm having.

"It's kind of magical," I say. Ben nods his approval and takes me over to the X-ray window, spooky, solar wind meeting solar flare in a pre–*Star Trek* kind of way, eerie and pretty.

"I can see why scientists really love this," I say.

"Imagine discovering your own planet. One that's just right or at least similar enough to Earth so we could live there if we needed to. One that can help us save this planet. You'd have to find just the right levels of oxygen, the perfect amount of water. The warmth of the sun. It would be using science for the ultimate good, and all that. That's the Goldilocks principle."

"It beats looking for a good chair, like the old Goldilocks." I don't say it beats looking for the right bed, though, because anyone who has ever looked for a new mattress knows how difficult that is. Though yes, the science is different for a whole planet.

"Any Goldilocks would have to be happy," I continue. "But more than just happy. What a discovery. Finding a whole planet, saving a whole planet."

"Imagine the calculations," Ben says.

"Um, not so much for me."

"Oh, I like math," he says, as if he's an utterly perfect human being.

We take in the room. Man, this place is date heaven. Were I ever to really take up dating again, of course.

"This is helping me with ideas for my book. It doesn't have to be silly or about breaking chairs or being rude to bears." The rhyme is accidental. I so didn't mean to.

I hold my breath, but Ben doesn't comment, thankfully.

"Finding the right bed," I add, though it comes out sounding kind of raunchy and far different from the innocent fairy tale. If fairy tales are even innocent.

"I don't know," Ben says. "It may all come down to finding a place to sleep in the broader sense. Existentially speaking. Maybe Goldilocks has just been too literal-minded."

I check his face to see if there's any sign of an accusing look, any judgment at all, but he still looks pretty much perfect. Maybe Goldilocks has been too literal minded. Way too literal minded.

"So, Goldilocks Explores the Galaxy," I say.

"Goldilocks Reaches for the Stars."

"Goldilocks Looks Outside the Universe," I say. "So to speak."

"Whatever gets her out of the forest."

I have to say, he looks really good in deep blue lighting.

In front of Eye of the Radio Sky, a swirly blue, green, and red version of Earth that's light on realism but heavy on let's just say atmosphere, Ben kisses me lightly, not too hard, but just hard enough. I hope very much that I kiss him back exactly the same way. Then a la Goldilocks' new job, we experiment a little, change stances, move hands (there are no eight-year-olds present by the way), expand our horizons. I close my eyes on the next kiss, and the neon colors continue to float around, and then some.

Ben stops, his voice quiet. "Did you know that the lead scientist on the Goldilocks Project is a woman?"

10

Read All About It

From the *L.A. Times*:
New Chroma Museum Adds Colorful Controversy to Venice Beach
by Jane Rosenberg

Sometimes it feels like all-inclusive L.A. slaps you in the face with its anything- goes, your-artwork-or-mine, put-it-up-on-the-wall and see-if-it-sticks attitude. Why not have an art museum where the exhibits are color-coded, the rooms chromatically coordinated to fulfill your inner need for rainbow hues, enliven your mind with migraine-informing neons or Hello Kitty-esque pastels that might soothe the average (or even above-average) four-year-old? Why not? Because if we don't have some standards, pretty soon, there'll be dog poop exhibits. I know, there already are, but we don't have to like it. We don't have to bow in gratitude to an Indigo room and a Day-Glo room, just because the hip couple next to us wearing Prada are. Just because it's Venice, and anarchy is king, and you're allowed to skate through the museum (between the hours of 4 and 6 p.m.; skate rentals $15). Is it art if you can do a pirouette on skates in front of it? Is it art if you can't?

These are the questions for L.A. and the wider museum world beyond, which often looks to us to see just what's wacky and wonderless (and laughable). We know that. Our response? Much of the time, we laugh first. Stick it in your face and see if you can swallow it, we say, you impoverished minds so far outside the land of dreams and hopes and several major art schools. Is this just a goofball, could-be-a-museum if you're high, or if just want a nice lunch (lunch prices start at $32, an all-new high for organic beef, and it's not like the hamburger is framed in gold or anything)? If this is just a joke shop of a gallery, then let's all laugh and enjoy it, until it closes in the inevitable six plus weeks it will take for everyone to have gotten a last laugh (at least until the next bring-it-down-to-the-populous museum failure comes along). That's at a steep $24 admission ticket price (plus $10 for the optional headset guide, which will instruct you how to breathe properly in the midst of the Forest Green Forest, and what mantra to try when you find yourself in Chartreuse City). On second thought, the narrated journey offers the biggest laughs around, so splurge and accessorize your ears with the fuchsia muffs. Afterward, you can get your ears or whatever pierced down the block at Ear, Nose, and Beyond, just to extend your inner shrieking to the audible sphere beyond, sharing your reaction with the masses huddled before the museum's Crayola colored walls. The Chroma Museum is really nothing but a washout.

(Rating: 1/2 star for sophomoric lunacy, plus a nice view of "Painted Peculiarities," a mural on the sidewalk outside of Prosaic Toys, the phallus-filled stationery store across the street from the museum.)

"Ouch," I say, when I read this in the office. Though as since my best friend, Susan, is the museum's curator, I might need to think of a harsher term.

"Of course, Susan will read this with a grain of salt," Chris says. "Probably the satisfyingly pink Hawaiian salt. Don't worry, art world people are thick-skinned."

"I hope so. It's not very nice."

"No one reads the paper anymore," Chris says, switching to his computer. "Oh, wait—"

"What?"

"The online version? Four-hundred and fifty-one comments..." Chris says, then starts making a sound that can only be called chortling, a laugh no one really likes to hear and no woman wants to hear herself make, either.

Snickering works, too, but reminds me of chocolate, obviously. And it's only 9 a.m.

"No one reads comments anymore," I say.

"Seems like no one hesitates to write comments, anymore. These are scathing. Colorful, actually, in keeping with Chroma Museum's theme."

"Susan's above all this and has a PhD in contemporary American artwork."

"As opposed to that pre-Biblical American artwork?"

"She's a serious art researcher who just happens not to have a problem admiring the lighter side of life."

"Plus the neon side."

"Geez, it's not like she built the place."

"I'm not criticizing. "I design contemporary fire truck drawings for the post millennial generation. I've got nothing to prove."

"Yeah, me neither," I say, thinking about my Goldilocks project. The very name, when you break it down, Gold-i-locks, with its Barbie imagery and cruelty to bears, doesn't scream 21st century. The contemporary Goldilocks—that's who I need to develop. A Goldilocks who goes beyond the somewhat crackpot imagery. The Goldilocks who dreams, who dares. I'm kidding myself, I realize: Goldilocks and I have plenty to prove, whether we choose to turn off the comments or not.

* * *

"Class, please welcome Libby's mom, Susan Bottoms-Coles," says our friend and Libby's first-grade teacher, Miralise Silva-Abramowitz.

Maybe to add insult to injury (or is it vice versa), Susan is the special guest mid-morning at Libby's class, and I, as godmother (and friend of Miralise's and Susan's anyhow, not to mention that I work across the street) have been invited to listen in. It's a chance not only for Susan to enjoy the day with her first-grader but for the kids to learn about a modern working woman/mom/museum curator/coolest person I know. I would have loved such an opportunity as a first-grader, but mostly we played with sand buckets and tried to convince the mom helpers that we knew how to read without their help, whether we did or not. None of my friends' moms had such a cool job—if I even knew about their jobs.

As the gods of coincidence/gods who like to mess with your day would have it, though, the morning has not gotten off to the greatest start, unless you're immune to criticism in the city's largest paper.

After the greetings and introductions, Miralise begins. "To prepare for your visit, Ms. Bottoms-Cole, we've all looked over the article in the *L.A. Times* this morning." Each child takes out his/her/their Xerox of the article fresh off the morning's newspaper, as if it were a good thing.

"I Xeroxed it before I read it, I'm afraid," Miralise says to Susan and me apologetically, "but still, it could help with a lively discussion! Ms. Bottoms-Coles, would you say a little about who you are and what you do?"

Susan begins. "Well, I'm very happy to be here, and of course you all recognize me as Libby's mom. I'm also the curator of the revamped museum called Chroma, which means I help assemble and take care of the art."

"This article was really nasty, to get right to it," says Lolly, Libby's friend with three braids (most of the time, though I've also seen her with five). I think Lolly's a little outside the box, or her mom is, although it looks as if Lolly does her own braiding.

"Now, Lolly, let Ms. Bottoms-Coles finish," says their teacher.

"I studied art history along with modern technique and mural art at the University of California, Los Angeles. I've worked for a few major art collections and museums in my ten-plus years since college. And I'm proud of the new museum."

"Is journalism dead?" asks six-year-old Windy. "That's what my mom said."

"I've always liked your mom," Susan says. I have to nod.

"Can we go see one of the dog poop exhibits?" asks a little boy with an earring. I don't think it's pierced, but it makes a statement.

"Todd," says Miralise, "we'll do no such thing."

"Please?" Todd adds.

"Art is somewhat subjective," Susan begins.

"Art is my favorite subject," says Autumn.

"Good," Susan says. "And subjective means that people see it differently. Any one piece of art can be seen as good, bad, happy, sad, colorful, inspiring, or whatever. It's how feel when you see it, the thoughts it inspires in you."

"Toby's paintings look like a mudslide," says a boy with a name tag that reads Rafi. "All of them look like mudslides."

"I was doing a series," Toby says unfazed. "A study."

"Of mud," Rafi says.

"Kids," Miralise says. "It's important to respect other people's artwork."

"They're mud paintings," Rafi says. "My dog could do that."

"My cat could do it better," says a girl named Lisette.

"The point," Susan continues, "might be more to enjoy what you can from each piece, and if one artwork doesn't speak to you, perhaps you're not the audience it was intended for, or perhaps you just don't care for it at this time in your life. Tastes change as you get older."

"Does that newspaper writer hate you or something," asks Libby's shy friend Jessie. Libby, I notice, has not spoken at all and seems to refuse to look up.

"I doubt that she hates me or even knows who I am, just because she's questioned what feels like every tiny bit of my reason for being," Susan says.

I whisper to Susan. "Too much info?"

"Well I won't say I'm unscathed," she says. Libby looks more interested now.

"Don't let the media hound you," Sophie says.

"Well, why shouldn't they?" Susan seems to turn around in

117

her thinking. "I work at a museum based on color coordination. This is not your mother's art museum!" she says.

"It has really good cookies, Mom," Libby says.

"True," I say.

"And the blue room is nice. Hardly anyone's ever there, so it's quiet." Libby means this as a compliment.

"You can really think clearly in there," I add.

"I agree," Miralise says. "The artwork lets you be, in that room, as opposed to say the tangerine room, where let's say things get a little more insistent, if not mind-bending."

"The Tangerine Tango Triangle," Susan says morosely of the little alcove of orange. "I did not name it! I really had very little say. I've tried to arrange the exhibits as best I could. It's hard to find a job as a museum curator these days."

"It's the economy," says little Windy.

"Recession-ism," Toby adds, with difficulty.

"Are the other people there nice?" asks a boy named Michaelic. Maybe the child's a girl. Not that it matters, of course.

"Not really," Susan admits.

"My mom runs a resume-writing service," Trixie says. I know Trixie from lots of readings we've held here. She wears a tie every day, albeit a different one.

"She does a good job," Miralise says.

"Hey," I say, "it's just one review. Should it really call into question everything a person stands for?"

"If it doesn't, what will?" Susan asks.

"I thought the writer used too many adjectives anyway," says Sophie.

"And alliteration," agrees Lolly. "Like, geez." The kids all add uh-huhs.

"She's probably sleeping with the boss," says Todd.

"That's not appropriate," says teacher Miralise. These kids are six. They surprise me constantly. Some of the boys are nudging one another, but most just look confused, blessedly.

"Journalists play an important role in free speech," Miralise says. "As we covered last month in our section on the Constitution."

"I guess," Libby says.

"Be true to your feelings, Ms. Bottoms-Coles," little Windy adds.

"Yeah," Rafi says. "Yeah." The kids all nod encouragingly. Especially Libby.

"As someone who works as an artist," I say, "I have an idea for how we can make these reviews more useful."

"Great!" Miralise says.

"Let's fold them into airplanes and see how they fly," I suggest. The kids are all for it, so Susan, Miralise, and I help them use their words, or in this case, someone else's, to make art.

"After," Windy says quietly, "there's cupcakes!"

I love these kids.

When we're done, Miralise takes us to lunch at The Latte Lesson.

"I couldn't be more sorry," she begins, turning to Susan. "I didn't look at it, obviously, before I printed them. I mean, how could anyone object to a blue room, whether you call it indigo or midnight?"

"Good question," Susan says. "But it's not like she's wrong. The museum is a little stupid. What does this say about me? Am I a joke if my workplace is a joke?"

"I suspect men don't worry about this as much," Miralise

says. "Though I could be gender-generalizing."

"Well don't ask me," I say. "I liked the tangerine triangle. It has a cool window seat where you can look out at an orange hummingbird feeder. Not something you see often enough at an art museum," I say.

"Everyone's so serious these days," Miralise adds.

Susan enunciates for effect: "Tangy. Tango. Triangle."

"Stop saying it like it's a bad thing," I add. "My office has a room with padded walls where kids can play and not get hurt," I say. "Art directors, too. It could start a whole new trend in workplace architecture."

"My office has water paints you can eat," Miralise says. "After all, if they don't want the kids to eat it, they shouldn't make it smell like taffy. And taste like it," she mumbles.

"Oh, I still prefer chewing on number two pencils," I say.

"Old habits die hard," Susan says. "I still sniff pink erasers."

"It's not like it's hurting anyone. It's just a colorful museum. Even if only one person enjoys it, isn't it worthwhile?"

"Yeah," says Miralise. "What's the number requirement here. If ten people like it, is it a success? If four people find it interesting, if seven people thought it made for a decent afternoon, and twelve people simply cannot live without those warm chocolate chip cookies, isn't that enough? What's the simple story problem here, anyway?" she asks like a primary school teacher.

"It makes me feel stupid being there," Susan says. "Under-valued. Embarrassed."

"Well that tops any story problem," Miralise says. "Off to LinkedIn jobs premium for you."

"Who would hire someone who directs a museum with a stairway designated as Sparkly Silver Stairway number two?"

Now, there's a question.

"You just talk about the areas you're proud of," Miralise says. "Just like when you do speed dating."

We look at Miralise, our eyebrows raised.

"Just like when I do speed dating," she adds. "Job hunting is about the same when it comes to sense of dread, not to mention embellishment. Well, maybe not quite as bad as speed dating."

"And the outfits are different, I suspect." I say. I haven't speed dated. I don't really have a high-speed function, or the clothes for it.

"I can't job hunt," Susan says. "I'm nearly 35. I have crow's feet. I have ..." she whispers, "greys."

"Hey, if it's not a color-themed museum," Miralise says, "who'll care?"

She may have a point. Even Susan nods.

"Can't we talk about something besides work?" Susan asks.

"As if anyone here has any interesting dating stories," Miralise says. Though clearly, she hasn't given up.

"Well," I say. "I have a young mechanic."

"Talk about a transition sentence, that sounds like a good start," Miralise says. "Wait, what about the old guy?" Susan asks.

"Chester is not an old guy."

"Fifty?" asks Miralise.

"Maybe higher," Susan says.

"Eeek," says Miralise.

"He's very sweet."

"True," Susan says. "You've done worse."

"But wait, didn't you say young something?" Miralise adds. "I didn't hear anything after young. As if it matters."

"My mechanic. His name is Ben. He takes care of the VW

Beetle."

"And then some?" asks Miralise. She's never shy.

"We kind of had a date to the Griffith Park Observatory."

"Was it kind of good?" asks Susan.

"What's with the kind of? I hear that all day in first grade," says the first-grade teacher. "I require far more adult-level adjectives and some plain-old dirty adverbs, if you don't mind."

"It was pretty lovely," I say.

"Now we're talking," says Miralise.

"And keep talking," says Susan. "I'm old and married."

"Almost 35," I say.

"Soon enough."

"He's cute. He's young. He seems to have a thing for my Beetle."

"So to speak?" asks Miralise.

"What is it with you?" I ask her. "I'm not even sure it was a date."

"So, you didn't sleep with this one?" asks Susan. "No judgment, just utter disappointment."

"Would that have made it a date?" I ask. "Wait, don't answer that. So, no, I didn't sleep with him."

"Good," they both say.

"He just kissed me at the observatory in front of galaxies far, far away." I say.

"I love that!" Miralise says.

"But you slept with the older guy," Susan adds.

"Chester," I say. "Yes. And I'm not going to count the times out for you, so don't ask."

"No math at lunch," says the first-grade teacher.

"I'm not judging!" Susan insists. "It's just, if you're going to sleep with the older one, well, why not try out the younger one? It's not math, exactly, right?" she asks Miralise.

"Oh, it's so much better than math," Miralise says. "If I remember correctly."

"So, now there's two guys," Susan says. "A simple equation."

"I'm not objecting to the addition problem," Miralise says. "Addition is fine in dating. It's subtraction that always seems to cause the problems."

"Story problems, in my case," I say, thinking of my divorce, remembering just how many steps were involved, not to mention how many lawyers it took.

"Yeah," Miralise says. "Too many story problems in a relationship always equal a rotten result. Take my advice," she says. "Avoid fractions, too. Somebody always gets the short end."

I don't know what she means, but it sounds reasonable to me.

11

Goldilocks Goes Gen Z, or Is It X?

Mirror, mirror on the wall, I hear ringing through my ears, even though that's not the fairy tale I'm working on at the moment. I'm not the kind of girl who has to look in a mirror as she passes by. Rather, I probably could stand to look in a mirror more often, but it just doesn't thrill me. And I'm not about to buy "hair product," fancy words for cream rinse, a term I still use on occasion and get stares for. It's still cream rinse, whatever you want to call it. But this Monday morning, when I glance at myself in the bathroom mirror, I notice my hair looks a little brighter. Have I been out in the sun? Maybe I'm just getting a migraine. Maybe that's the sparkle I see. Not that I'm complaining. But for whatever reason, I feel a little more sparkly this morning, not that I've ever used this adjective about myself before. I barely even add a little mascara and feel good to go. It's not a bad feeling at all. You go, Gold-i-locks, or at least, Gold-ish-locks.

I've been mulling over the Goldilocks story, hoping that if I go to bed thinking about it, I'll have the answer by morning.

Well, maybe some morning. I'm thinking about the planets, making discoveries, working with something a little more solid than the right tables and chairs, the most comfy bed (though lots can be said about a comfy bed, and I doubt even scientists can get a good night's sleep on something that's too hard or too soft). Still, my Goldilocks needs to think big. She needs to think outside the (Ikea) box. She's the lead scientist of the Goldilocks Planet Project. She needs to save the Earth, not decorate it with Swedish textiles and modular chairs, beds with white comforters and drawers underneath. Hold the Swedish meatballs, too: Our Goldi's got a PhD, I decide, and she knows how to use it. She's got to encounter more than chairs and bears, rhyme be damned.

I get myself ready for work a little early, saving time by not staring in the mirror saying, 'If only, If only...' I feel ready for decision making, taking charge. Like I could go out and discover a planet of my own today. I'm feeling pretty Mary Tyler Moore taking the world by storm, pretty Gilmore Girls on a day they drank a lot of coffee and ate a lot of pie, pretty Zooey Deschanel just about any day she appears on a screen as she's the only person you can look at. Pretty (much) me, Amy Shepherd, today but more so. Line up your planets, universe. I'm about to give you a good, decisive look over.

I don't know what's come over me, but I sense it's long overdue.

I drive my cool, cool Beetle to The Latte Lesson, ready to manually transmission my way through the day with the wind in my hair.

The Latte Lesson isn't Starbucks. When you walk in, it screams "I am not Starbucks," by displaying no merchandise for sale and having a homey, pretty interior with periwinkle walls and local artwork—usually colorful acrylic and water-color paintings, sometimes even by schoolchildren. Sometimes even by schoolchildren I know. Yes, there are twinkle lights, but not all matchy-matchy. Different sizes of white lights twinkle here and there. The Latte Lesson actually plays a tape (I suppose it's Spotify or something) of café sounds, so there's always the friendly sounds of coffee steaming from machines and whipped cream zipping out of containers, plus a pleasant piano-tinkling music on the tape. Pandora maybe. It's so soft that it doesn't distract. The lighting is brighter than Starbucks: This is not chain café, the interior says. We belong here, the Latte Lesson proclaims. We are Santa Monica. Here is our coffee. You can't even see the prices of the artwork, I happen to know. You have to ask.

Not one cup matches another, for that matter. You can request your favorite mug (I happen to like the ones with llamas) or fancy china teacup. If you really want it to feel homey, you can request a chipped teacup. They think of everything here.

I'm not expecting anyone I know so early at the café. I want to sit with a big latte (I don't even care if it's skinny this morning), and sketch Dr. Goldilocks. Or do I prefer Professor Goldilocks? Professor Goldish-Locks? Hmm. I'm going to give her cool nerdy glasses like the brave girls wear, like Zooey Deschanel. And kick-ass boots (no heels). The better to kick the big-boy bear scientists in the butt with, figuratively speaking.

Not sure what's got me so pro-protagonist this morning. Some days you just feel good. Not like you need the latte—not like you're treating yourself to the coffee, more like you're treating it to you. Come on and join me on my day, pretty cup of coffee. Let's do this thing together.

I get my latte, turn, and see Aunt Lucille with her friend, the dentist. The my-age dentist. Watching me. I didn't know I had an audience. I'm not the audience type, really, especially at eight in the morning, despite looking my absolute best for this time of day and driving a kick-ass car, and finally getting a grip on Goldilocks, so to speak.

"Hi, Amy!" Aunt Lucille greets me loudly (for this time of day). I'll admit I'm not big on a lot of talk in the a.m. Lulu's meowing is always plenty of noise for me, and she's a Ragdoll who mostly whispers.

"Join us!" Aunt Lucille practically invites the whole neighborhood.

Now, I'm always happy to see Aunt Lucille. I have my priorities straight. Family before work (preferably coffee before family, but still). Aunt Lucille is my biggest supporter, which is saying something when you have friends like Susan (and Libby) on your side. I'd love my aunt even if she weren't family. Everyone does. She's the longtime advice columnist for the *Santa Monica Daily Press*. She has an audience of thousands, and she's not in the least old-fashioned (and uses all the correct terms for body parts, if you know what I mean). The dentist beside her, for example, seems very pleased to be doting on her, morning light reflecting kindly on his auburn hair and just-shaved face. He's actually not at all hard to look at, even at 8 a.m.

The name tag clipped on his pocket that says Dr. Jeremy could be seen as endearing or a little much, were you the kind of person who can make such distinctions at 8 a.m. I am not. I'm just noting it. I can be judgy about it later, if I want. Yes, I have a J in my personality type. I know it's a fault—J for judgment-y. I can't ever remember my other letters. This one, though is just so obvious.

"Hi," I say, kissing Aunt Lucille on the cheek with real feeling. Why do aunts always smell so good, anyway? Aunt Lucille's blondish gray hair is pulled back neatly again. She's beautiful, handsome even, in that aging Helen Mirren way, but far less scary. No nonsense, too, despite her sort of coincidentally being at my favorite coffee spot this morning with an eligible professional.

"You remember Jeremy?" Aunt Lucille says, pointing at her dentist, who salutes me with his coffee cup. He's very good looking, now that I really get to turn and stair, hair cut short but well, not like he's in the military or anything, but with just enough hair across to front to see that it lands nicely across his forehead and might even curl if you let it. Like it might curl just enough to wrap around your finger, if you wanted to. I think I'm getting way ahead of myself, though.

"Of course. Hi."

"Jeremy Pitcher," the DDS says, reintroducing himself with his last name, which I do appreciate as who can ever remember something like that? (Answer: Certainly not me.)

I'm not too sure what to say, as I'd been hoping to gaze into my latte with real hope for inspiration, kind of like a crystal ball.

"You guys are out early," I say. When in doubt, state the obvious.

"At my age, early is 4 a.m.," Aunt Lucille says. "Anytime after sunrise is perfect for a latte or two."

"I have to agree," Jeremy says. He's drinking from a large mug with a Scottie dog on it, though I don't know if it was by request. Jeremy has a little froth on his face, which Aunt Lucille wipes away. I'm the only one who looks a little surprised by this gesture, but she does pull it off. There is grace in aging, maybe even power; don't let the Clairol commercials tell you otherwise.

"So, what's on the agenda of a busy publishing exec today?" Aunt Lucille asks.

"Ha, beats me," I say. "But I'm sketching and outlining a new kids' book. It's about space and planets. Discoveries."

"No dragons?" Dr. Jeremy asks. "My patients are so into dragons these days."

"Oh, you're a pediatric dentist?"

"I like to think I'm a family dentist. I'm up on kids' teeth, adults' teeth. Sometimes I clean my cat's teeth, but I don't think that counts." A guy with a cat. Hmm.

"Lulu I'm sure could use a teeth cleaning," I say.

"Daughter?" Jeremy asks.

"Ragdoll," I answer.

"Orange Tabby, Sam," he says. This is how cat people introduce themselves. We've now learned one another's vital statistics.

"You both love your cats, don't you?" Aunt Lucille says. She volunteers at the local SPCA but tends to slather her attention on the big dogs. Not that there's anything wrong with that.

"I'm a puppy person, can't deny it. Dogs feel like more of a social activity," she says. "You can meet people while walking them."

"Yes, people with dogs," I say.

"Cat people have to make more of an effort to meet one another," Jeremy says. "But it's worth it," he adds, looking at me in an interesting way, as if I might have even more than one cat. Or maybe I'm projecting.

His watch makes a little alarm noise, the kind of sound that insists you have a life to get back to. I, in contrast, usually forget to wear a watch, not that I don't have a job I meant to get to early, just that my job often involves coloring within the lines, rather than asking people to open wide, which I consider a good thing. My watch, wherever it is, doesn't have an alarm.

His beeps again.

"Did someone's crown just fall out?" Aunt Lucille asks.

"Probably just a cavity or two. If it's a dental emergency, my watch plays the music from *Jaws*. It gets your attention," he says. He gives me a shrug. "Dentist humor."

"Wow, we don't have our own jokes for graphic design," I say. Although maybe that was one. I think I've heard there's some font humor going around. Not sure the jokes would translate, though.

"Nice to see you again," he says, getting up. "And you, Ms. Excellent Flosser," he says to Aunt Lucille. She beams a bit, but I find it a little TMI for this hour. Flossing seems so personal. I do know my own dental hygienist considers it a godly quality and talks about it nonstop, though. But still.

After he leaves, Aunt Lucille just keeps smiling. When I glare at her, she says, "What? I like a medical man. Of course, he's way too young for me. But you, on the other hand..."

"I have a dentist. Lorraine Izenman. Former classmate. I'm very loyal."

"No reason in the world not to have a back-up dentist. For emergencies." Aunt Lucille just smiles at me, a know-it-all-smile in that saintly aunt way she has that says she's so happy to be able to help and Amy, shut up at the same time.

Then she lets out a sigh.

"Is something wrong?" I ask. "Are you alright?"

Aunt Lucille let's out an "Oh, well." She is seventy. All sorts of things can go wrong all of a sudden when you reach that age. Kind of like with the Beetle, but more serious. And then, the Beetle has its own good doctor.

I wipe away a quick image of Ben and focus, a little angry that my mind would wander at a time like this. (Men. Or maybe boys.)

"I'm perfectly fine. I may be the best me ever!"

"Good." I say.

"But—" I feel my breath catch, and Aunt Lucille shakes her head at my worries.

"It's not that. It's my housing situation."

"Oh, problem?"

"There are just too many old people there!" she says of her senior living condo complex. "I'm not old-old. I'm older; that's fine. I'm gray and a little bit beyond tree pose, let's say. More like leaning tree pose."

"I hear ya on that."

"Lost her leaves tree pose. Too old to bother with tree pose," she says. "Though balance is everything, so I do bother."

I nod. "Plank pose?"

"Don't be ridiculous," she says, pretty much the same way I feel about it. Give me a good long walk rather than pretending to be a cobra in public any day.

"You know I love the swimming pool, but I can get that at the Y."

Aunt Lucille is an avid swimmer. She leaves high school swim teamers in the dust.

"Plus, the costs are rising. I'm wondering if you might be willing to part with the old condo," she says. I moved into Aunt Lucille's place after the divorce. I pay a modest rent on prime real estate in Santa Monica, as they say, which is mostly prime real estate anyhow. I could walk to work if I didn't mind arriving sweaty, or if I were sure no one else would.

I'm downcast at the thought of moving. I've finally started to think of the place as mine, as the home where I'm moving forward, becoming the new me, occasionally even sparkling. But I can't tell my aunt this. And it well be all in my mind. I feel horrible that maybe I've been keeping Aunt Lucille from the life she deserves, whether it includes a pool in the building or not.

I don't think I'm a great niece, and I'm not sure which letter of my personality to blame for it. I have been so self-obsessed. I feel my eyes start to sting up, and I could happily crawl into the bug right now and cry, but I'm not going to because Aunt Lucille deserves better.

"Of course you can have the condo back. It's yours. I'm incredibly grateful to have had it for this time."

"Well, I passed it on to you," she says. "I'm just asking how you feel about it."

I take a deep breath and resolve to fall apart later. I'm good at this. I don't know about you, but it's simple: When in doubt, even heavy doubt, joke about it.

See if it doesn't work every time.

"For you," I say, "I'd happily move. But only for you. Don't be giving this apartment to anyone else, like your dentist or anything."

"I happen to know he has a lovely townhome in Marina Del Rey. Right on the water. And no one to share it with."

"You know this, huh?"

"I'm inquisitive. I ask for details. I like to hear stories."

"You're a social advice columnist," I say.

"Comes with the territory. He also happens to have a boat,

nothing gaudy, a very practical, sturdy boat on the Marina that many would envy."

"I see."

"And no one to share it with."

"You said that."

"It bears repeating," she says. "He's shy and needs bringing out."

"Is that why you brought him out here this morning?"

"Of course! I'm very loyal to my dentist," she says. "And to my niece, who has a good job and a fine Beetle. But no one to share it with."

I raise my shoulders and shrug. I may be losing a home, which hasn't sunk in yet, but with Aunt Lucille's hope, I may be gaining a new medical professional even if in she's suggesting I keep him around for other purposes. And there's no question this is what she's suggesting.

* * *

When I reach the office, no longer early at all, there's a buzz in the air—literally.

"What's that strange noise?" I ask Kelly.

"There's something wrong with the Bugs," she says.

Of course at first thought, I start looking around me for literal creepy-crawly bugs. I'm not super squeamish, but really, does anyone like the thought of bugs buzzing around?

"Eew?" I ask, looking around.

"No, the My Bugs," Kelly says, and of course she means the little handheld toys. She shows me a green one, the one given to her by one of the Bug guys (the names are all blending together). The Bug is making a deep, well, buglike noise, like a

133

very slow, very large, very scary cricket. A cricket throwing up. "Vuu-Ahh," it creaks, slowly.

"The Bugs are sick," Chris says.

"Are they dangerous," I ask. "I mean, are they shorting out or spewing something?"

"The Bugs are croaking," Kelly says, looking at her green one sadly.

I head with Chris into Nelson's office. He's got several on his desk, orange, purple, pink, blue. They're all squawking like very sick frogs.

"Turn them off," I say.

"They are off," Nelson says, a little frightened.

"Can you recharge them or whatever," I ask, though surely someone has thought of this.

Chris takes one and starts banging it against Nelson's desk, of which Nelson does not approve.

"My Bug!" Nelson yells.

Chris keeps hitting it against the desk, but it still croaks. "We changed the batteries," Chris says. "Nothing."

"Or just more of the same," Kelly explains.

So, Chris does what I've been hoping he wouldn't. He tosses one on the ground and tries stepping on it.

Nelson screams.

The Bug continues to drone, although maybe a little softer now.

"Seemed worth a try," Chris says.

Kelly gathers them up in a box. "Bring me your Bugs!" she calls. We all scatter to gather ours. I find mine in a drawer. It's not croaking, but it's kind of humming softly.

"Mine's not dead yet," I tell Kelly, but she just shakes her head and takes it. Jefferson and Gabby from art bring theirs over, holding them upside down in their palm, kind of like a dead mouse or something.

Chris hums Taps.

"How is that helpful?" I ask Chris.

Jefferson whispers, "Exterminate!"

Nerds laugh.

Nelson is near tears. "I can barely stand it. I don't know how I could become so attached so quickly, but I am," he says. "My purple Bug! It's more than a toy. It's like a pet, or a little friend. A little pet friend that plays with me!"

Nelson sounds about four years old, but maybe that's why he's so successful. There is something lovable about the Bugs, which maybe are misnamed, or maybe I'm just being too girly about it.

"Now what do we do with them?" Kelly asks. She covers the box and puts them in the front closet, but we can still just barely hear them.

"That's disturbing," Chris says. "Like the place is infested."

"Invasion of the bug snatchers," Jefferson says.

Chris grabs the box and takes it outside, where we have a small balcony with a tiny half-size table. He leaves it there and returns.

"Back at one with nature," Chris says, shutting the sliding glass door.

"On the balcony," Jefferson says, "no one can hear you scream."

Creepy.

"Emergency meeting now," Hannah, our editor in chief/person often in charge says.

"Us, too?" Jefferson asks.

Gabby looks doubtful.

Hannah barely gives them a look of acknowledgment. "Children should be seen and not heard," she says to our young artists. They're rarely invited anywhere. I suspect they have more fun without us all in the art department. I know I would. Anyone who's worked for more than a few years knows meetings are overrated.

Nelson sits in his regular seat with a display of plastic parts in front of him. Blue plastic, spilling out small mechanical parts. Chris sits next to him wielding a pretty large hammer.

"Autopsy!" Chris shouts, putting down the hammer. Nelson might cry, but something about all the small parts on the table enthralls both of them.

"It's not bigger on the inside," Chris says, a reference to more nerd stuff. He says this a lot. Robbi and Bobbi both look in, and when Hannah sees Jefferson lurking beyond the door, she says, "Fine." He comes running in to play with the parts.

"Boys," Hannah says.

"I don't think it's gender determined," Chris says. "The desire to put it back together."

"My desire is to sweep it up and toss it," Hannah says, "and you don't exactly see me wearing glittery hair ribbons."

"Doesn't mean we wouldn't be amused by it," Chris says.

Chris wears glittery hair ribbons sometimes. He's given a few to Libby, but there are a few he won't part with.

"We have to think about finding another buyer," Hannah says. Just then, one of the broken parts makes a chirp. Almost birdlike.

"It's alive!" Nelson exclaims.

"Just not in the way you'd hope," Chris says.

"Or in a way that you could play with if you were a child," Hannah says.

"I'm not so sure," Nelson says. He begins to try to put the pieces back together.

"It's not supposed to be a jigsaw puzzle," Hannah says.

"Oh, think outside the box a little," Nelson says, starting to color coordinate the pieces. We all help, except Hannah of course.

"Like Humpty Dumpty," I suggest. We go for fairy tales around here, so anything's possible.

"It's broken. Made in China broken," Hannah says.

"Not that anyone's making prejudicial comments about another country," Chris says. "I've seen you eat wontons, you know."

The piece stops chirping. Chris hammers it, but nothing positive comes of this. I can't imagine he thought it would.

"We need to call the Bug Boys," Kelly says.

"Do we have to call them the Bug Boys?" Chris asks no one in particular.

"Don't tell them about the hammering," I say.

"I wouldn't," Kelly says.

"I'm sure they can fix this," Nelson says. "They're young."

Chris holds up two blue pieces. "Maybe we can get these to reproduce?"

"I don't think it works that way with electronic bugs," I say.

"But you don't know for sure, right?" Chris asks.

"Let's glue all the pieces together and see what we get?" says young artist Jefferson.

"Whatever we get isn't going to save a publishing company," Hannah says.

A piece of Nelson's green bug makes a sound that only can be described as *Pfft*, in agreement.

The bugs have been silenced.

12

Dating Your Dentist, or Someone Else's

I t's not lost on me that Jeremy is the third man I've gone out with in only a few months, this after dating, well let's see, no one, for a year. No one. Then of course there's being married for ten years, which I don't count as dating. Dates with your husband aren't really dates so much as just a time-and-place outing, although if that's my outlook, no wonder it wasn't a happy marriage. Hooper called them dates. He scheduled them three weeks in advance and canceled pretty regularly. No wonder it wasn't a happy marriage.

Jeremy called me that night after the impromptu coffee meeting at The Latte Lesson, impromptu on my part at least. He has planned a fairly routine date (not a very positive term to start out with, Amy), suggesting dinner at an Italian place, then a walk along the Third Street Promenade. I know the restaurant fairly well as it's in the neighborhood. But familiar is good. Familiar is our friend on a first date (not like I'm an expert). Familiar means you already know the food is good and where the bathrooms are, that there's a bookstore or Anthropologie nearby you can pop into afterward when conversation runs low. There's always something you can pick up and talk about at the bookstore: a latest bestseller, something trendy but controversial, even if you don't agree about it. Whether to say you don't agree about it is also interesting, telling really. Will he be the kind of guy brave enough to criticize? Will his critiques be meaningful, shallow, esoteric? Does he read at all? Yes, bookstores. They should be required dating destinations.

Another first date.

"What do you wear to a restaurant you've been to forty-five times but want this time to be special?" I ask Susan over the phone.

"Why are you down on this date? He seemed nice looking."

"I'm not down. He is nice looking. He's a dentist." I know the last thing is a non sequitur.

"You're such a snob. If someone doesn't have a creative job, what does it matter? He's a professional. Teeth are crucial. He's providing an invaluable service."

"You make me sound desperate. And I'm not snobby. I met a mechanic I like, after all." Whoops. Did I just say that?

"Yeah what's up with him, where's he tonight, have you slept with him yet?"

"He's just a nice guy. A nice young guy. The guy who works on my Beetle."

With nice dark hair and a muscular build, I do not tell her.

"Well, a guy who knows the insides of your beloved car..."

"That sounds dirty and a little disgusting," I say.

"Not so much to me. I like someone detail-minded."

"Thank you for not saying Good With Tools."

"It's implied," she says. "How young again?"

"Twentysomething. Still takes college courses and is cute

enough to no doubt date any young blonde woman within the Santa Monica county lines, and beyond." *Like Kelly, our receptionist,* I don't say. I remember the way she looked at him. I wonder if I looked at him this way, too. I can't believe I could still produce that kind of wistful facial expression.

I glance in the mirror. A skeptical face stares back.

"You may not be as old as you think. And you're in the right regional demographic. Look on the bright side."

"Regional demographic?"

"Woman on the West Side," she says.

"Sounds like a bad romance novel."

"Hell, I'd read it," says my married friend.

But enough about Ben, though I have thought about what I'm wearing in terms of, let's say, would I wear it on a date with Ben? Would I wear the same thing on a date with Ben that I'd wear with Jeremy? With Chester? Does it say less about me that I might be dressing thinking about what a guy will think? Does it say less of me that I'm thinking about what three different guys would think?

Plus, what runs through my mind is: *What would Goldilocks do?*

Or do I really care more about how I want to look for myself. And was that a date with Ben at the planetarium? What did I wear that night, again?

Stop it, Amy. You know you're going to wear whatever you like best. Period. I hope.

That's what Dr. Goldi Locks would do. Dress for herself. Wear what she wants while finding the planet of her dreams, or something more reality-based. To find a good, kind, warm planet. In her honor, I wear my favorite gauzy shirt, which is dusty pink with embroidery around the shoulders. It goes well with some jeans that are super comfortable even though they're not this year's style, which according to the Sundance Catalog (I don't know why I receive it—oh yeah, it's addressed to Aunt Lucille) are straight jeans with rips in them. Cuffed awkwardly like you did when you were eight, and that didn't look good on you when you were eight, though really, no one cared what you wore back then, including you. And they wouldn't look good on me now, for that matter.

* * *

We meet for dinner at a restaurant on the Third Street Promenade, which is close to nearly everything else in Santa Monica. I leave the Beetle in the public parking lot—lot 5 is my favorite, although Hooper used to try to find valet parking wherever we went. (Do not think of the ex-husband before a date, I tell myself. It can't come to any good.)

I don't know why my brain is extra nervous, but my hands dropped each and every piece of makeup I used. (Okay, just lipstick and mascara, but several times each.). I've had dates with Chester, and I didn't run too much through my head beforehand. Or maybe I just felt like Chester wasn't a real eligible date. Although how much more real does dating get than taking off your clothes? I'm not sure I want to know the answer to that. Chester's being a little older somehow put me at ease, like, This is not an appropriate lifetime mate, so don't worry and just go with it, and throw your bra across the room, or something. And maybe the same, or the opposite, goes with Ben. With Ben, it was like, Just hop in the car and see where it goes (literally). And don't remove anything. Not even the top of your convertible.

But this is meeting a guy my age that others (i.e., Aunt Lucille, and who knows, maybe the world at large) feel is an appropriate person for me. He's a solid citizen. He's a dentist. I don't know why I don't find that profession more exciting, but I'm sorry, it's a little bit of a turn-off to me. Dentist, hands in others' mouths, drills. I guess it's self-explanatory, this bias, and I'm probably not alone in this. Fillings, spit, that draining thing that makes the whoosh noise—it all makes me shiver, and not in a good way.

Still, Jeremy's meeting me at an upscale (meaning pricey) Italian restaurant, not a risky game parlor or an adventurous evening under the stars by Foucault's pendulum. Which only makes it clearer that this is a Date. This is not a deodorant-optional, feel-free-to-forget your earrings evening. I will be expected to actively participate in my own experience. I will have to eat in front of someone I don't know (who regularly sees people with food in their teeth, but don't think about that, Amy).

We meet at Trastevere, a rustic spot with Tuscan-like tile on the floors and high ceilings sporting tall red walls that give the place a little extra spaciousness, even though you can't sit up there of course. The tables are a little more crowded together that you might like (remember, pricey Santa Monica real estate), but the lighting is nice, with a square glass candle on the table to play with, which by the way isn't a good idea when you're nervous because you (I) can start a fire, and have. Plus the restaurant spices things up by using two tablecloths: a red one covered by a white one, but so you can still see both colors. It's white tablecloth fancy, as people used to say, but more so. Trastevere stands proudly on the Third Street Promenade, which used to be a casual if not crummy space

142

when I was very small but has turned into a lovely, Italianesque-if-not-cobbled and trafficless road for strolling and meeting with friends, or shopping and hoping to find friends. The restaurant has a nice outdoor section where I like to eat and the more crowded interior with that kind of question-marked ambiance that says you might either be on a date, or you might be with your elderly aunt (for instance), or both. So, although no, I'm not expecting Aunt Lucile, there she is, and it makes me laugh (in a good way). I feel relieved, albeit confused.

"Hi, Amy," Jeremy says, shaking my hand. I'm not one of those women big on shaking hands, but I don't mention it. He means it in a nice way, I can tell. And it's clear he's not a germaphobe, which makes one of us.

"Hi Jeremy, hi Aunt Lucille!" I'm suddenly holiday-level excited to see her, or maybe it's a really bad case of date anxiety. Amazing how similar the two are.

"He made me join you!" Aunt Lucille says. Her graying blonde hair is pulled back in one of those super smooth ponytails that look so nice. And her silk blouse is pink, a prettier shade than mine, three or four numbers up on the Pantone scale. She has matching earrings. (I stuck with my usual tiny gold hoops, as although my ears are pierced, I hate changing earrings and usually wait till one falls out naturally.)

"Well," Jeremy says, a little more relaxed than I remember him being, after he makes sure I'm seated comfortably. (Gentleman alert!) "When I found out Lucille had no plans for the evening, it just felt wrong not to invite her." The gallantry of this gesture makes my eyes sting for a moment. Hooper only wanted to see Aunt Lucille on holidays (if then). Not that anyone's thinking about her ex-husband right now.

But here's the thing in case you're wondering: I met Hooper

143

in college, though he has a couple years on me. And my parents passed away not long after in a small plane crash that not one of us talks about because it's too stupid and too painful. I have Aunt Lucille, and my late Uncle Harry, who helped me through. I turned to Hooper. It's an excuse; it explains why I was so blind to his faults. He's a good fake. I've been told all this makes me seem a little distanced sometimes, as if I'm afraid to take a chance. Okay, so it's Aunt Lucille who's said it, and Aunt Lucille, columnist to those who live by the sea, is usually right. Though now is not the time to dwell, and tonight isn't about me. But this is always in the background for me, twinkly lights notwithstanding.

The waitress arrives and does not introduce herself, which is a thing at this restaurant. It's not meant to be unfriendly but more to show respect to the businessperson crowd. It's like the staff know most diners don't really care who their waiter is, or they feel we shouldn't care. I still find it weird, but then again, I rarely offer up to waitresses "my name is Amy."

She offers us the wine list and asks if we're ready for drinks. Jeremy orders what he calls "this nice bottle of Merlot and the Giant App" off the list, and I suddenly hope he's not a wine snob. I hate having a beverage evaluated by anyone fussy. We should just drink and enjoy. I'm not going to think about who I may have known that was a wine snob. I'm not thinking about him. I'm on a date, you know. With my aunt. And her dentist.

"Though Merlot's not great for your teeth," he says. Aunt Lucille and I laugh gently, although I'm not sure we're supposed to. Red (wine) flag.

Jeremy seems to sense his mistake. "So, Lucille tells me you're an artist. That must be so gratifying."

"I illustrate for a children's publisher. Not exactly art with a capital A."

Jeremy hushes me. "We have some lovely children's books in our waiting room. It seems to me that beautiful pictures are really the key."

"Amy also writes some of the books. Like a new Goldilocks," Aunt Lucille says.

"Oh, a big favorite," Jeremy says. I don't know if he's referring to his littlest patients or himself. Probably the kids, though he's looking at my hair, which yes, I have highlighted a little recently just because I felt like it one day. Not for anyone else or because everyone's doing it. I also want a purple streak, and despite my age, it's next on the list, and no one's going to talk me out of it. Not that anyone really cares enough to do that right now. I sense Aunt Lucille would really embrace the idea and might go for one of her own. Pink, probably.

Jeremy's looking at my hair in a way that suggests approval, by the way. His is auburn, plain and simple and nice. No detectable highlights.

Am I the shallow kind of woman who worries about a man's hair color?

Maybe *worries* is too strong a word. As an artist, I like to think it's important to take note of the color. I'm very good at fooling myself.

I taste my wine, careful not to let it sit on my front teeth. Dating, can't beat it.

After we order pasta dishes, Jeremy and Aunt Lucille chat about children's books, a good, safe, first date topic. Not that they're on a date, exactly.

"I just could never get into the graphic novels. Comic books," Jeremy says. "The teens seem wild for them. And they're backwards."

"It's a Japanese thing," I say.

"Oh, I know," he continues. "They love to tell me the storylines and about the characters, and it's all very inventive," he says. "I guess as long as they're reading...but some of those books don't have much in the way of words." He shrugs his shoulders, baffled, but not bothered. Shaken, but not stirred?

"How do they tell you the stories when you're working on their teeth?" I ask. I have always wanted to ask a dentist this sort of thing.

"It's part of the process," he says. "To gain trust, and also because I really enjoy spending time with my patients, I've incorporated a certain amount of stop-and-talk time. It's not something they teach in dental school, though they should."

"Huh," I say. I'm fond of my dentist, and we always greet each other with personal comments and how are yous and such, but she pretty much gets down to work after that.

"Really," he says. "There's a lot that can be learned about dealing with patients. Breaking up the rinse-and-spit parts of the visit with some sincere hominess and good wishes."

Eew. I don't like the word spit at dinner (and hence do not watch baseball games on TV while eating, just a thing with me).

"Well I think that's wonderful," Aunt Lucille says. "And it builds a relationship of trust between young people and their dentists."

"It's imperative," Jeremy says.

By now we have our appetizers—one of those giant all-inclusive meat and cheese antipasti with strange olives and a large section of octopus I don't remember anyone ordering. I read not long ago that octopi are brilliant and very sensitive, and that we shouldn't be eating them. After Aunt Lucille and

I put some of the more salad-y parts on our plates, Jeremy digs into the poor octopus. And salami, which probably wasn't all that sensitive in its original form. I'm not a vegetarian, completely, but I'm thinking about it. I'm thinking way too much about the octopus.

"Did you hear that octopi are actually very smart?" I ask, as Jeremy has a little bit of octopus hanging from his mouth. Aunt Lucille looks at me, a little alarmed. I couldn't help myself, I guess. I give her a look that says, *No, I don't date much.*

"Oh my god," Jeremy says, swallowing quickly—and octopus is not easy to swallow quickly, as you may know. "I forgot to ask if you're a vegetarian."

"No, no. I'm not. I'm leaning that way, but I just was so affected by the octopus story."

"It's something to think about," Aunt Lucille says gently.

Jeremy nonchalantly pushes his octopus to the side of his plate. He holds his fork delicately, as if it were an artistic tool. He has nice hands. And it's not like I haven't eaten octopus myself. Wow, I am bad at this.

"I've had lots of fried octopus in my time," I say. "So, no worries."

I never say *no worries*. I don't mind people who do. I've just never felt I could pull it off.

Everyone's staring at the octopus.

We are saved by large plates of pasta, which despite looking like each could feed a family of four, are placed in front of each of us. I've got the Fettuccine Alfredo, an old favorite. I've never been so glad to see fettuccine in my life.

Jeremy silently gestures for the waitress to take away the octopus.

The night is ours again, what's left of it.

Mental note to now add octopus to the things that can't be discussed on a date, like religion and politics.

"One of my teen patients has an eating disorder," Jeremy says, adding to the list of things that shouldn't be discussed on first dates. "As women, maybe you can help me help her."

I am shoving a large forkful of the sauciest, most buttery fettuccine I've ever seen into my mouth as he says this. While I realize it's practically running down my chin, I decide to be proud that I'm a woman happy to shove carbs into my mouth almost anytime.

"Well," Aunt Lucille says over her delicate linguine with clams and lemon sauce. "Isn't that a shame."

"Terrible," I say, after gulping sufficiently. This stuff is excellent. I may eat all four portions. And now I have a good reason to! Dating. Always a surprise or two.

"Well, what do I tell her? How can I help?"

Aunt Lucille and I look at one another. Maybe I should bring up politics.

"You've mentioned this to her parents?" I ask.

"They're so totally in denial," Jeremy says as if he were fourteen, but it comes out sounding kind of cute, actually. A dentist who uses valleyspeak. I'll bet he's popular with his teens.

"You probably have to be very careful," Aunt Lucille says.

"But firm," I say, reaching for the garlic bread, which is incredibly aromatic. I want to lick the butter and garlic off, but I'm not that bad of a dater. "Make it clear to them what's at stake and recommend therapy right away." I think I read this in *Health* magazine or somewhere. I'm not an expert, thank goodness. Susan and I always eat what we want and walk it off later. Aunt Lucille is one of those tall women who can eat anything at all and are perfectly proportioned. Statuesque.

"Do you have any children's books on that issue?" Jeremy asks me.

I think of the Bobby series. Poor Bobby with his broken arm and divorced parents and such. Could Bobby become bulimic? It is a terrible idea that makes me snort, which I cover by pretending to cough, then drinking a good amount of Merlot, which tastes a little thicker than I usually like. But then, I know nothing about wine and have a mouth coated in butter.

"I think it's way beyond my expertise," I say.

"But I'll bet you could find a good teen book about it," Aunt Lucille says to Jeremy. "To give your patient in private. That's a very thoughtful idea."

Jeremy nods. It is a nice idea. It is nice that he's concerned. It is clear he's really bad at small talk, but isn't that endearing in its own way?

"Do you like sports?" he asks. Does he have a list of topics he's returning to?

"Sure," I say. "I like watching tennis and swimming. And actual swimming. But Aunt Lucille is The Swimmer."

"I am," she says proudly. Aunt Lucille takes over at this point, recognizing a sinking ship when she sees one, regaling us with stories of swim medals she's won, stories about rivals and lifeguarding days. I love my aunt.

Jeremy and I eat and make interesting *Wow* sounds (which are heartfelt, as Aunt Lucille has some stories worth hearing). He glances at me and kind of shrugs, guiltily, making it clear he realizes he's no conversationalist, either.

I'll admit I don't mind looking at him while Aunt Lucille talks (and I suspect she won't mind, either). I think Jeremy seems like a nice guy, one who orders regular coffee instead of a cappuccino, which I really like about him. I can actually sit back and enjoy, as my aunt lets us in on her role in a 1960s Olympic swimming race, at the most tense moments taking a delicate sip from her herbal tea.

* * *

After dinner, Aunt Lucille calls a friend from her building to pick her up, and once we've installed her carefully in her friend Margo's shockingly clean ivory Toyota, Jeremy suggests we walk along the promenade. Since we had dinner at 6 p.m., it's still shockingly early to call it a night, I guess. Though I'm often in bed by 8, I'm not sure this is something to reveal on a first date, or even a second.

"Well, although we've left the restaurant," Jeremy begins, "I guess the big decision of the night is still to come."

I have no idea what he's talking about and don't even think he's making some kind of comment about kissing or sex. Though he might be.

"Oh," I say.

"Tiramisu or gelato?"

"The eternal question, I hear." I'm not fond of tiramisu, though I've never said no to a chocolate gelato. Even the worst date anxiety wouldn't make me say no to gelato and might even propel me into a double scoop.

"There's a nice gelato place up ahead."

"I am always up for gelato," I say, despite the four portions I've just eaten. This guy really likes it when you eat a lot.

"Gelato's easy on the teeth," he says. "Let's walk a bit?"

So, we do. We stroll with the other people out on this incredibly nice night. People all across the world want to live in California, in Santa Monica in particular. I envision myself on a kind of digital map, the words You Are Here circling above me, following me around. I'm not sure how much Merlot I drank.

Then it dawns on me: Is there even still a bookstore around here? Have they all closed? If so, this is an entirely new era of dating. Where are the independents? The art books? Home and garden sections? It dawns on me how out of date I am, and I can feel my body slow down in its steps, as if I'm aging ten times faster than normal. Perhaps dating is bad for your longevity. Feels like it.

But then I see it and a kind of eureka moment comes over me. This is the place. This is the new substitute for a bookstore, where you can ogle at what's for sale and run your fingers over it.

It's the Apple Store. You are here, Amy.

"Shall we?" he says.

I have a Samsung phone and a Sony laptop. I keep this to myself.

"New gadgetry," I say.

"The latest must-haves." I can tell he's a Mac person by the excitement in his eyes. Maybe he wants to keep up with the teen patients, be able to understand everything they say about their apps and profile pages and such. I nearly stop in my tracks, a little wary, and wonder: Could he be on Facebook?

Ben's probably on Facebook. Geez, Chester's probably on Facebook. Aunt Lucille is probably on Facebook. She probably has more than one page.

The store is crowded, with people of all ages. Like a zoo, but with more of a buzz going on. Grey-haireds look at phones. Millennials roam around excitedly and have to be reminded not to run several times. People my age (and Jeremy's) carefully examine MacBooks, reading the fine print on the screens. You can't see anyone buying anything, but you know they are. I like the blue shirts and could see us dressing like this in the office. We could use some cute shirts that say Kids Press, not that anyone would come up to us to ask a question or anything. Maybe it'd be fun to have on the days we visit the schoolkids. Maybe they'd like some, too. Everybody's wearing T-shirts with a logo, or two layered on top of each other totally unnecessarily.

"I should have worn a T-shirt," I say.

"You look wonderful. Maybe just a little dusty," he says, swiping a little at my sleeve.

"No, it's dusty pink."

"Oh, that's what I meant," he says, making some sort of bad joke or worse—a pun.

Now he just looks embarrassed. I've never been dusted on a date before. But it's certainly not the worst thing that's ever happened.

We examine iPads, which I admit I think are cute. I've borrowed Chris', but for some reason just can't get it to do what I think it should do. Like we speak a different language, and it's not about to speak mine.

"They're the best," Jeremy says. "Just so practical. I carry mine everywhere, except tonight."

"How come not tonight?"

"Oh, you never know what someone else might think about you."

"So, if you'd walked in and I'd been doing something on my iPad, what would you have thought?"

"I'd have probably thought that you use your time very

wisely," he says.

"Really?"

"Sure. Why, what if I'd been typing away on mine when you came in?"

"Well, I'd have thought it would be rude to Aunt Lucille sitting beside you."

"And if she'd been typing away on hers, too?"

Well, it would have made the date even weirder, I think but don't say. "I'd wonder why you weren't talking together."

"Yeah, it's a bad example. It's never boring with Lucille around."

Odd quiet moment.

"True," I say.

"So, the iPad probably isn't the best accessory for dating," Jeremy says. I kind of laugh when he says accessory for dating. It sounds very *Teen* magazine. Or maybe *GQ* But it's kind of sweet.

"I don't date all that often," he says.

"Yeah, me either."

"But look at this great screen!" Jeremy says, arms flying. Ah, he's into technology. This is not a bad thing. Hooper didn't have an iPad. He had a secretary. Not that he brought her along on date nights. Just that she planned them, I think.

Bad memories. I look at the colorful screen. It is pretty. The littler iPad kind of reminds me of My Bug. There's no denying the appeal, or what technological direction we're all headed in. The artist in me wants to make sure we make this technology look the best we can. I'm not as excited about it as Jeremy, but I don't feel appalled by the devices, the way I once did. I'm readier than ever to welcome them into my life, once they have a good talking to and we make it clear who's in charge. I'd never felt in control of them much in the past.

My wandering mind slowly comes back to the present, standing in the Apple Store in Santa Monica, as I feel someone looking my way. I'm stunned, then I'm smiling, then (I can feel), I'm turning a shade of (dusty) pink.

"Um," I say.

"Amy," Ben greets me from just a few iPads away. "Come here often?"

"Wow, like is this the hot pickup spot?" I ask, then feel really weird about it because why would I ask such a thing? Oh yeah, wine.

"Now that the bookstore is gone," Ben says.

"I know," I say. Jeremy is still staring at his screen, kind of caressing it with his index finger. He looks up.

"Jeremy, Ben," I say. I have always hated introducing people.

"Hi," Jeremy says, "I'm a dentist." They shake hands. Ben seems to take Jeremy's news just fine but offers up nothing about himself.

"Nice to see you guys." Ben says, "Girl in the '67 Beetle." He looks like he's trying not to smile too hard. I don't know why. Jeremy and I aren't nearly the oldest people here, at least. And Jeremy clearly knows his way around an iPad, even if he's no better at introductions than I am. Proud to be a dentist? Well, why ever not. I feel myself adjusting whose side I'm on, not that sides need to be drawn in an Apple Store.

"Ben fixes my VW Beetle," I say to Jeremy. "Actually, it was Aunt Lucille's Beetle," I say, as if this just shows you what a small world it really is.

"Car guy," Ben points at himself.

Car guy, teeth guy. Goldilocks girl. Actually, car guy sounds the best of all of us.

"I didn't know you were a Mac person," Ben says, no judgment in his tone.

"A girl can change," I say. "A girl in a '67 Beetle." I'm starting to like the moniker. It's fun. Like I'm a girl in a romance novel. A woman in a romance novel. With a cool car and too many guys staring at her at the moment.

Can you have too many guys staring at you at the moment, I hear Susan's voice say. I feel dizzy.

"Bye, Girl in the '67 Beetle," Ben says. "Nice hair," he adds, softly. It's a little more gold than last time he saw me, like maybe I've been hanging out at the beach. Or, let's face it, at the hair salon. I've got a little kickier haircut, too, although it's still near my shoulders. The short haircut I got post-Hooper that I liked so much? Well, one day you wake up with the short hair you love and look like an unhappy donkey, and then you have to wait months and months to get to the next stage where you look okay again, especially to yourself. Then, you're The Girl in the '67 Beetle. I give my hair a little shake. What the heck.

Ben nods to Jeremy, who waves, then starts an app on another iMachine as if nothing even happened. Funny, I feel like the evening just ended. I don't even care about the gelato anymore, and that's saying something.

But Jeremy reads my mind. Maybe we do have a connection going. "I promised you gelato, didn't I?"

Or maybe we're all just basically thinking about gelato most of the time. This seems the best explanation.

"How about next time?" I ask, then realize I've suggested something maybe I don't want to suggest. I don't know. Maybe it's just a thing we all say.

"Absolutely!" he responds, as if he doesn't hear maybe next

time all that often. We leave the Apple Store as four teens on skates enter but set off some alarms. I'm not sure how this can happen, but I don't really care that much. It makes Jeremy laugh. He has a good laugh, and a nice smile (and really good teeth, by the way, but then he would). He looks younger when he laughs, like maybe someone carefree is trapped inside.

Jeremy walks me to my car and tells me a story about Jessica, a young patient he's known since she was five, who is now starring in her junior high musical. Despite braces. He is all encouragement and excitement. He's seen the show twice. He's a dutiful dentist, I think. Kind and nice. He likes his iPad and loves my Aunt Lucille. He probably drives a Toyota Camry. Maybe a Lexus. I hope not a Lexus.

I'm such a reverse car snob.

"This is me," I say to Jeremy, or maybe to the Beetle, who already knows me of course. I'm glad to see it again.

Jeremy stands back and admires my car. "Well, that is a beauty."

"Thank you for tonight," I say. "I think it was awfully sweet of you to bring Aunt Lucille. Really thoughtful."

Jeremy smiles. (No dimples. In case you're keeping score.) He leans in and kisses me, and let me tell you, this goes on a bit and surprises me, the Beetle, and a few people walking past, I think. It's gentle enough but commanding, inspiring. Jeremy can really kiss. You'd have to wonder why a single guy who can kiss like this is still single. I mean, wouldn't you?

I picture us: It probably looks like a kiss in the movies. That postdate garage good-night kiss the whole first part of the movie's been leading up to. So, I'm both inside and outside the kiss.

Way too much thinking, Amy.

Is it a good kiss? Is it a better kiss than, say, Ben's?

Why am I being so analytical, anyway? So scientific? Why am I so doubtful?

Somebody walking by gives a low whistle, which embarrasses me to pieces. Clearly, he or she thinks it's a good kiss.

"Goodnight," Jeremy says, once he lets go, which feels like about an hour later, or at least, the people I noticed out of the corner of my eye are gone. It's not like I'm timing it (though an onlooker might be). He tastes like chocolate gelato, though this can't be. So now, I'm really confused. Is it too late to blame the Merlot?

13

Let the Games Begin

I t occurs to me that I may need help sorting through my newfound quandaries. Help looking for a new place to live in my super expensive neighborhood for one single girl and one single cat (no pets is not an option). Help figuring out what's going on with my job. Why am I having so much trouble plotting Goldilocks' future? Will I remain the co-artistic director if we merge with the bug people? And then there's my after-work life: What's up with my sudden rise in demand among males? Is one of them too old? Too young? Just right? Is there such a thing as just right, or is it time to transform this fairy tale all together?

Since I think it would take way too long to explain this situation to a therapist, I gather my best friend Susan and our pal Miralise Silva-Abramowitz before work at the café. It's time for me to kiss (though I've already done this part) and tell.

"Three guys," Susan says. "This gets better and better."

"What about my impending homelessness and joblessness

problems?" I ask them.

"Geez, not before coffee," Miralise says.

"Not before dinner and drinks," Susan says.

"Speaking of dinner and drinks, and three guys to kiss ..." starts Miralise.

"I didn't mean to kiss Ben, exact—" I say. I can barely keep the "exactly" in.

"Ben?" Miralise questions.

"The young mechanic," Susan reminds her. "Keep up."

"Please," Miralise says. "I have three students named Benjamin. I keep seeing six-year-olds."

"No, he's in his twenties," I say.

"I like that about him," Susan says, running her spoon through her latte suggestively, if you can do that.

"Okay, let's start with last night's guy," Miralise suggests. "You're becoming so *Cosmo.* Different guy every night."

"It was a date with a guy recommended by my aunt, and it was not the whole night, thank you very much," I say. "Is *Cosmo* even still around?"

They both shrug. "I think we aged out of Cosmo once we hit sixteen," Susan says.

"I never aged into Cosmo," I say.

"No one really does," Miralise adds. "Probably why we don't even know if it's around anymore."

"So, the den-tist," Susan says, enunciating precisely.

"You guys are such snobs," Miralise says. "Dentist is good. Dentist means vacation time and, well, dental coverage, like for life."

"Dentists poke people with sharp painful instruments," I say.

"Not intentionally," Miralise says. "So, dinner."

"With Jeremy and my aunt," I say. "This following coffee with Jeremy and my aunt not so long ago."

"That's sweet. When's the last time I met a guy who would bring my aunt along on a date?" Miralise says.

We stare at her, wondering when, too.

"Oh. Never," she says. "So, he's thoughtful," Miralise says. "What do you want, obnoxious and uncaring."

"She married that one," Susan reminds us all unnecessarily.

"Just because it's what you're used to ..." Miralise says.

"True," I say, finishing her elliptical thought in my mind.

"Maybe you don't recognize nice as the good thing it is," she says. "Maybe you're hung up on looking for the wrong thing."

Looking for the right thing/person/chair/planet. I'm reminded of Goldilocks. Or Dr. Goldi Locks. In search of something just right. Someone?

"Don't go looking for another Hooper," Miralise says.

"Is that why you're being so fussy?" Susan asks, though I don't think I've been fussy since I've kissed all three of these guys and am perfectly happy to do so again.

"They're not Hoopers," I say.

"You missed all the signs with Hooper," Susan says. "But then, didn't we all."

"Yes," I admit.

"But you were having a rough time then, what with your parents dying and all," Susan says. It's true, my parents died in a really rotten plane accident that left me terrified of flying and overall extremely mousy, timid. Like half myself, maybe less.

"Oh, sad," Miralise says. "Sorry. Sounds like the ex took advantage."

"We did all think he was fine," Susan says. "Robert will

never forgive himself."

"Your husband-lawyer isn't a jerk," Miralise says.

"Not that I didn't ask Robert a few questions about him," Susan says. "He didn't know, you know."

"What do you mean?" I ask.

"Robert didn't know Hooper lied to you about having a vasectomy," Susan tells me. "Robert feels awful."

"Oy, I missed quite a conversation! What?" Miralise asks.

"Hooper had a vasectomy but didn't tell me, and I tried stupidly to get pregnant and felt awful about myself when I didn't," I say.

"Wow, really big plot of a romance book," Miralise says. "I hope you've checked these guys out plenty. Make sure they're for real, at least as much as you can."

"Do you mean have I checked to see if one of these guys is a jerk, like under the hood?" I think of Ben raising the hood on the Beetle—and yes, it's in the back. No jerk there as far as the eye can see, not that I've exactly searched his whole body. Yet.

"I don't want to be spending my time and energy looking for anyone," I say. "I don't want it to be an active thing taking up part of my mind I could be devoting to something else. 'Man hunting.' It sounds so antiquated. Kind of noir."

"Man hunting in stiletto heels," Susan says.

"So not me," I say.

"So, what would you rather be doing, knitting?" Miralise asks.

"Knitting? Isn't that sexist or at least overly gender specific?" I picture an old me knitting. I've knitted, I just leave a lot of holes and then give the sweater or whatever it was supposed to be to Lulu. She deserves better. She deserves organic cashmere in shades of cranberry. I should go home and pet Lulu.

"Can't I spend my time focusing on something else more manly?" I ask.

"Like the Beetle's mechanic," Miralise adds.

"Well, you don't want to settle for whatever comes along," Susan says.

"Wait," Miralise says. "You've already got three to choose from. They seem to be appearing in front of you pretty easily, if you ask me."

"Three that we know of," Susan adds.

"This is not helpful," I tell them.

"Let's come at this a little more scientifically," Miralise says.

"Break it down into theorems. Guy number one, go."

I shake my head as if to clear it. "Okay, I'll play," I say, giving in a little. "Chester, I like. He's fun. He's adorable. He's inventive. He's a little exhausting," I say.

"Sexually?" Susan wants to know.

"I'm not answering that," I say.

"Older," Susan says.

"Older's ok if he's still, you know, vital, sexy, interesting," Miralise says.

"He's always energetic," I say.

"You say that like it's a bad thing," Miralise says.

"I'm still worried about the older part," Susan says. "Let me be the voice of reason."

"I am fond of Chester."

"Urg, fond," Susan says, sticking out her tongue.

"Let's talk about the medium age one," Miralise says. "And you'll notice I did not say middle age. I'm not going there. Have you ever heard middle age used as a compliment?"

We shake our heads.

"The middle one," Miralise says. "Jeremy the dentist?"

"Jeremy the dentist," I say. "Why is that how I think of him? Kind, nice, decent, respectful. Referred to me by my aunt. Not a bad, bad person like someone I might have married who would never in a million years invite my aunt to dinner or even to our own home without my begging him to. That said, Jeremy's little dull. A good kisser, technically speaking."

"Now we're getting somewhere," Susan says.

"Wait," Miralise says. "Technically speaking?"

"Well," I say. "I could tell it was technically a very nice kiss."

"Eew," Miralise says. "You're not using strong, supportive adjectives here."

"Yeah, I don't think I'm supposed to be giving him technical scores as he's kissing me," I tell them.

"But says who, really?" Susan adds. "I mean, it's a first kiss, right?" We nod. "All that tension and anxiety, so much pressure from all those movies. So, if the technique is already in place, maybe there's a chance it will only get better from here."

"Better than a guy who can't kiss at all," Miralise says. "Trust me."

Miralise has been marching along with a string of (monogamous) relationships. Her current sort-of boyfriend is named Dwayne Lipschultz. He's a personal trainer and (obviously) never changed his name, which Miralise thinks is brave. He's a super muscle-y type, which I find just a little repulsive, but it doesn't seem to bother Miralise one bit.

"It was a good kiss," I admit.

"Come on," Susan says. "Let's get to the young guy."

"Oh as if I forgot," Miralise says. "Did you kiss the young guy?"

"Ben." I say. "His name is Ben."

"She said he's really cute," Susan tells Miralise.

"What is this junior high?" I say. "But yeah, he's cute. And yes, the kiss was nice. Very nice."

"Very nice," Miralise says, nodding. "Maybe we should rate them, scale of 10, like it's the Olympics."

"It's more like Olympic trials, the way you're doing it," Susan says, not harshly but with admiration.

"Let the games begin," Miralise says.

"Neither one of you is any help at all," I say.

"I think we are. We're cheering you on. We're your support system," Susan says.

"We know you can go the distance."

Then Susan says it. "Go for the gold, Goldilocks."

That's Dr. Goldi Locks, although I think I'm mixing metaphors, and before lunch, too.

* * *

After working for a few hours in which I've managed to take the Goldilocks manuscript and remove all mentions of chairs, beds, and porridge—okay, I tried granola instead, but it's gone, too—and pretty much start fresh, all of my office mates assemble for a field trip. Now might be a good time for those matching office T-shirts, but at least we know each other very well and rarely leave anyone behind. All right, our young artists Jefferson and Gabriella—but just the one time.

As usual, Nelson has rented us a little bus. It's not exactly a van, as it's too round for that, and not a tram or limo or anything like that. Paint it yellow, and it's a little school bus. As it stands, it's painted in primary blue and red squares (not too obnoxious, right?), and not totally unlike the bus (albeit greatly shrunk down to size) from *The Partridge Family*, if you happen to be a fan of reruns and stations like TV Land. I am and don't care who knows it. Not that anyone ever talks about this kind of thing, outside our office at least.

We assemble. Me, Chris, Robbi and Bobbie (sales and marketing, or wait, marketing and sales), the young artists, Kelly with a notepad, Hannah who still hasn't left, and Nelson. So yeah, it's a fair-size busload.

"Seat belts, everyone," Nelson says, and Kelly giggles.

"We are not singing songs," Hannah says, then buries her head in her tablet.

"What else can we sing if not songs?" Nelson asks.

"Buddhist chanting." Chris, ever helpful.

"Silence is golden," Hannah says.

Jefferson starts humming "The Wheels on the Bus," until we all are, and Hannah places large headphones over her ears. And yes, they do look like the expensive noise-cancellation kind. But I like humming, and if those headphones are as expensive as I think, I suspect we could sing and she wouldn't hear a thing.

I want to say that our building at Kids Press is homey and sweet, small but (as they say in real estate) cozy. Sincerely. We know each other in ways that people in large fancy buildings couldn't possibly, and I'm talking about good ways. A good closeness that embraces sharing, collaborating, chatting freely, and a sense of collective purpose. Our office is all things good. The plumbing's not great, but hey. We work in the center of sunshine and sea air. We know better than to complain about details.

But upon reaching My Bug Unlimited, it's clear that their

office is so much better. Not just bigger (it's that, too), but way better.

"Oooh," Chris says, admiring the clean lines, the vast expanse of space. The office spans the entire floor of a modern, shiny, darkened glass building in Marina Del Rey. The building screams "I'm cool and was designed by someone famous," as you can tell by the pronounced, almost-pyramid-like structure on the right side. I bet it houses a juice shop. Ocean views and seagulls overhead. Boats at sea. A small park area down the street perfect for outdoor lunch. I smell excellent roasted coffee not too far in the distance. It seems too good to be true.

The Marina has just always seemed better than everywhere else. It's like it knows it, too.

Except that compared to our Santa Monica office's home, it's a little soulless. Inside are all-white walls, vast expansive spaces. Not a plant in sight—healthy or dying, or even plastic. On closer look, the guys' desks are piled high with papers, odd materials, plastic, and general stuff. It's sticking out, so I don't know what you call it, but it's too straightly piled up to be called a mess. It's beautiful in here, but there's no here here, as Gertrude Stein might have suggested, if she could tear herself away from the view.

A room with a view is a terrible thing to waste in Los Angeles. Jefferson and Gabriella have run up to the windows as if they've been locked up in a cell for years, when really, we have a perfectly nice spot in Santa Monica within walking distance of three coffee shops, two bagel places (one gluten-free), and a real-ish French patisserie with pink poodles painted on the walls (hence the −ish). But the windows hold some kind of allure.

We're escorted into a conference room, where Hannah

immediately begins placing broken Bugs from our office on the fir wood and marble table (and I wouldn't have thought fir and marble would go so well together—who knew?). Suddenly there's a lot more MyBugs than I thought we had. How did we get a hundred so quickly?

"I thought we only had ten?" I say.

"Well, I couldn't stop at just ten," Nelson says. "I needed more. I wanted more."

"And now they're all busted," Hannah says, looking at them as if they were, well, dead bugs.

The MyBug guys crowd around the table, same nerdy guys as last time, broken glasses, stretched-out T-shirts, everything you'd expect. More than one looks as if he's had the flu recently. I keep my distance.

They begin disassembling bugs. Plastic pieces fly in the air.

"I didn't realize they were dangerous," Kelly says, ducking while writing something down.

Some of them make those chirping sounds (the MyBugs, not the boys); some make warbling sounds. None of it sounds just right.

"It's a minimal production error," says the tall one, Steve.

"Nothing wrong with the initial programming," responds Paul, robot-like and superfast.

"We don't want to be associated with toys that act like dead chirping bugs," Hannah says.

"Would a dead bug really chirp?" Nelson asks us rhetorically. "People, let's relax. I like these contraptions, games, whatever you want to call them."

"Dead chirping bugs," Hannah repeats.

"We can fix the problems," says another of the guys.

"It's Beta," Paul says. The other guys nod. This explains it all, apparently.

"So," I ask. "You really want to program books on these."

"Yes," they all say as one. At least they agree. Maybe that's how they've gotten together enough backers to have these really nice offices.

"It's the future," Nelson tells me.

"So's air pollution and a lack of water resources," says Chris.

"Somebody's been watching *Blade Runner* again," Hannah says dismissively.

"I like books," I say. "For the record."

"There's nothing wrong with books," Steve says. "They're great to have—"

"—and to hold," says Paul quickly, as if they're getting married. Oh wait, maybe they are married to each other. These things are fine with me of course. I didn't mean anything and am thankful I didn't say it out loud. No rings, I notice, though.

"We can produce some books," says the one who likes Kelly, the really neat one, and by neat I mean unwrinkled and clean, with straightened and trendy eyeglasses, not that he's exactly cool. He stands a little too straight to be cool, but cool is a relative term. He's at Kelly's side again. She looks like she's pretending she doesn't notice he's right there. But I can tell. I glance over to Chris; he can tell, too. We work together closely—we can read each other's minds. It's how it goes when you drink from the same primary colored water cooler.

"I'm still not sure about the sale," Nelson says, and I feel a hopefulness overcome me. Do I not want to merge because I'm afraid of new things (like MyBugs, not that they're really scary)? Am I stuck in a rut? Am I not reaching out to discover the possibilities of my own life?

"Here we go, guys," says the one called Joel, whom I

remember as sweet, something of a counselor to the others. "These babies just hatched." He empties a box of MyBugs all over the table, and they roll and slide and, it strikes me, hop.

"That one's moving," Kelly says critically, backing up a little.

"Oh my god," Nelson says. "You've made them mobile! I love this!"

"Only the pricier ones," Steve says. "It's not a particularly educational feature—"

"—it's for showing off to your friends!" Paul says beyond enthusiastically. Oh that's right, he and Steve finish one another's sentences, I remember. He starts pushing buttons on some of them, causing them to move forward or spin, or both.

"The moving ones are glowing!" Chris says, getting into it. He and Nelson start playing with them together. Jefferson and Gabriella have taken a few to the corner of the table—though it doesn't really have corners, as it's somewhat rounded but not quite oval, and I don't know what the shape is called. Geometry was a problem for me, as I may have mentioned. They're murmuring about the MyBugs and have stopped paying any attention to the others. Nelson pokes me.

"See, technology-obsessed youths," he points at Gabby and Jeff.

"They're in their twenties," I say.

"Party pooper," Nelson says. I've been called this before. It's not my favorite thing.

Everyone starts to play with the MyBugs, although Hannah just watches, every now and then goading one with a pencil. They're tougher to knock over then you'd think, which seems to amuse Hannah. After stabbing at one five times without making it trip over itself, she nods.

"Good," she says to herself.

I look to Kelly, who seems to be taking in the vast emptiness of space around the office that could be fixed up with a few knickknacks and human beings who enjoy working together on real, material, informational, lovingly created books. Though I may be projecting.

"But a walking book?" I ask. "I mean, that's really the question, right?" Nelson looks up.

"A walking, talking, buglike book?" Chris says.

"That lets you decide the ending?" says Steve.

"A walking, talking book that lets you decide the ending," Paul repeats quickly. "I don't see a question mark there at all."

"But do you?" says the nice Joel to me, then looks to Nelson. "That's the real question." The boys look to us with hope. Paul hugs his Bug. They want this and are young and well-funded, but they still need the right answer, a pat on the head, approval from the room. Like anyone.

Nelson only sighs. We watch as two of the moving, hopping Bugs begins to chirp, then fall over, warbling incoherently. And not in a good way.

"Oops," Paul says. "Problem!"

There will be no singing on the bus ride back.

14

Meditation à la Mode

At least there's dinner with my favorite six-year-old to look forward to, and yes, I have quite a few six-year-olds to choose from. Libby and I play Twister (the innocent, old-fashioned way) because Susan's yoga teacher says it's better for you than Hatha yoga, which doesn't have one of those fun little spinners anyway. I'm sorry, but Milton Bradley has always had it way over yoga in every way, including that the Twister mat is more fun and colorful. They make slipping part of the game, something yoga has never really learned to do. But should.

Susan's home near the Venice canals is everything the Chroma museum lacked. It's warm. Here are the Pottery Barn red slipcovered sofas that are both homey and practical (and machine washable on just about any setting you'd like to use). Light maple wooden floors run through the whole house with an assortment of colorful cotton rugs that are also washable and in no way fine or antique. Everything is soft. Even the white on the walls isn't bright but a paint color called Warm

Light. I didn't believe this at first, but Susan showed me the label as, after all, I helped paint. We go way back.

A family lives here. Libby's drawings are taped to walls. Nothing snobby about it, though of course it's a tough neighborhood to crack (meaning really expensive now), and the house, when Susan and Robert bought it, seemed to have an earlier life as a shack. As a co-art director I'm comfortable saying that paint goes a long, long way.

I hand Libby a MyBug, even though I know it's dysfunctional.

"That's a boy's toy," she says.

"Why?" I ask. "Because it's electronic? Because it's blue?"

"No, those are just stereotypes," Libby says. I've told you she's a smart first-grader. I'm pretty sure I didn't learn about gender stereotypes till Women's Literature in college. Third year.

"What if I gave you this one?" I hand her a magenta one.

"Better," she says. "And not just because it's pink. But mostly," she says. "Not all stereotypes are without merit."

"What if it were purple?" I ask.

"Purple is my favorite," Libby says. "But you know that."

"Yeah, I only had the pink handy."

"Does it do anything? Boy toys often do something stupid like turn into something you'd never want to play with. Or something that you know will break, or your mom will step on. Either way, you're bound to get into trouble for it."

"Same goes for boys in general!" Susan screams from the other room.

"I hear you," Libby says.

"Not all boys," Robert, Libby's dad says. "I'm a boy."

"You've outgrown your trouble-making days," Susan says. Libby points at her dad, who is holding an iPad mini. A blue one.

"You love the mini," he says to her.

"But it isn't pink," she whispers to me. I make a mental note. I like pink, too. Always have.

"Right now," I explain to Libby, "it just does games and stuff, but they're thinking of putting books on it."

"Like the mini," Libby says.

"Yes, but books you can change around, so you could make your own ending, or change a character's wardrobe or behavior." I realize I don't know what they want to change about the story, exactly, and though at first I'm annoyed by this, I start to wonder.

I ask Libby: "Do you think that's a good thing? Changing the story or characters."

"Sure," Libby says, no question in her mind. "How many times have you wanted to tell a character not to trust another character, or to comb her hair before someone sees her, or to avoid any number of boys she's about to encounter." She looks to her dad. "Not all boys, just the ones you can tell she should go around."

"Fair enough," Robert says.

"You wouldn't miss holding a physical book?" I ask her.

"I still have books," Libby says. "I'm not afraid books are going away. My friends and I don't buy into that."

"You've discussed this?"

"In current events," says the first-grader. I guess this subject followed their discussion of gender roles. Or maybe preceded it. "But this doesn't work."

"It goes on the fritz," I say, taking the toy and pounding it on the ground. It comes back to life.

"Oh, it is like the iPad mini," Robert says. Libby just nods.

"Technology," she says with some dismay.

"Do you know about the Goldilocks planets?" I ask Libby.

"No, I don't think so."

Thank goodness, I think but don't say. I still have something to teach.

"It's this idea that scientists are searching for a planet, or more than one, that's most like the Earth. As in not too cold, not too hot, that kind of thing."

"Why do we need another Earth?" she asks. "What's wrong with Pluto?"

"What is wrong with Pluto, anyway?" Susan asks. "Perfectly nice planet just minding its own business."

"It's not a planet," Robert says.

"It's a planet again," Libby says.

"Really?" her dad asks. "Did I miss something?"

"Too much time with your electronics," Susan says.

"It's a sort-of planet," Libby says. "I read it in *Time for Kids.*"

"The magazine said it's a sort-of planet?" he asks.

"Yes," Libby says. No one's going to disagree with her. Besides, I don't object to this terminology at all. Sort of a planet. Thank goodness there are still printed magazines for kids is all I'm thinking.

"Anyhow," I continue, "scientists think it might be good to find another Earth-like planet to grow food on or maybe move humans to, I guess." I don't really know why they're searching for another planet, but this must be close.

"Like *Wall-E,*" she says.

"Not everything is like a Disney movie," Susan reminds her daughter gently. "Most things, in fact, aren't at all like a Disney movie."

"But it's a good movie," Libby says.

We all agree. It's a conundrum.

"So, I'm thinking about using this Goldilocks Planet idea to rewrite the Goldilocks fairy tale," I tell Libby, and anyone who'll listen, really. "Goldilocks could be a scientist, looking to save the world, or at least find a nice planet out there."

"A purple one," Libby says, because she is still six.

"It should definitely have purple." I agree.

"It would have to have all the colors of Earth, wouldn't it?" Robert asks.

"Why stop there?" Libby says. "It could have colors and textures and all sorts of things," Libby says. "Purple comes in many shades," she reminds me.

"True."

"So, if it's on this thing..." she holds up the Bug.

"The MyBug."

"Okay, though that's a little babyish of a name for me."

"Sounds like iBug!" Robert says positively. Libby makes an *sssss* noise that's definitely skeptical.

"If it's on the MyBug, if you have to call it that," she says, "you could pretty much make a planet that looks like anything you want as long as it's like the Earth enough in other ways."

"*Imagine there's no countries,*" Robert starts to sing.

"No singing, Dad," Libby says very seriously.

"*It isn't hard to do...*"

"The countries could be purple!" Libby says. She tries again to make her MyBug work, determined, with an expression that says anything's possible, an expression like Goldilocks herself might have, were she, say, a scientist looking for just the right planet, in a nice shade of plum.

* * *

175

I've done a little meditating in my life. I've learned how to breathe in properly and breathe out slowly, counting silently, that kind of thing. I've never gone in for a mantra, mostly because I can never think of one, and I don't like the idea of paying someone to assign me one. It seems like something that should just come to you naturally, meaningfully, or I could have the completely wrong idea about this. Regardless, when Chester calls to ask me to go meditating with him, I'm only as surprised as the next girl. I've never thought of it as a date thing, but then, it's Chester, so all bets are off. Maybe people go meditating together all the time. Maybe people use it as a pick-up spot, although it's probably kind of a quiet one. Not that that sounds so bad.

Do I want another date with Chester? I don't know. The phone isn't ringing off the hook, no matter how many guys Susan says are interested in me. Chester is such a curiosity, I somehow just want to give it a try. We should all meditate—isn't that what all the websites say? Can they all be wrong? The answer is yes, of course they can, but still, don't you have to wonder?

So, off we go on a beautiful Saturday morning. Chester has registered us for a free session not far away, where we're to be led by an expert in the field, who has a PhD and MD, which is pretty excessive and probably says more about him than I need to know. I've been to a few meditation classes. I've tried walking meditation (this doesn't work for me—I trip too much), the counting thing, picturing a relaxing forest with birds chirping but no insects biting, etc. I don't hate any of them—I just can't stick with it. I feel embarrassed meditating, even just by myself. I could probably meditate about this and it would go away. I may need expert help, but I can't picture myself with a swami, if that's what they're still called, though I doubt it. I'm not hip on the meditating lingo. Maybe I should have Bobby from the picture books try meditation. This can really be research for me—rather than just an old-fashioned date. God forbid, right?

"He's well-known, and not just in SoCal. He's from Berkeley," Chester says admiringly. I feel a little comforted, too. Shouldn't all meditation leaders come from Berkeley (by way of India, of course)?

"I have trouble getting myself to meditate," I admit to Chester, who has picked me up in his rounded Volvo.

We drive to an old building in Santa Monica that could have been a small school, or maybe a large lighting supply company: It's hard to tell. It's nondescript and boxy, like a community center that needs a remodel and will no doubt become a huge dark-windowed building in a few years. Let's face it, practically anything could be going on inside, although I don't know why the look of an innocent square building makes me think this. We find a space not too far away (but isn't that suspicious? It's Santa Monica—why is it so easy to park here), directly behind two identical dark blue Priuses. Or is it Pri-i? A small sign reads Inspire Within Meditation, and although I'm not sure how that works grammatically, some lovely pink-flowering bushes bloom by the door with a scent of something jasmin-y.

"This is so exciting," Chester says. "I've been trying to find time to see this guy for years. It's like we're never in the same place at the same time."

"Kind of metaphysical," I say.

"Exactly. Maybe this is our moment!" Chester is kind of new-agey this way but seems to mean well. "I think he may have a lot to offer us."

"I want to know how to stay awake when meditating," I say. And *why to stay awake,* I don't say.

"Focus is everything," Chester says. "And we're not supposed to be good at it, at least at first. Failure is almost a requirement, but then you get to surpass it. Failure indicates we're human."

"How often do you meditate?"

"Oh, twice a day if I can," Chester says, "unless I'm entertaining," he says a little suggestively but sweetly. "For about thirty minutes, morning and night."

"That sounds like a good amount," I say.

"It's a start," Chester says.

"I'd rather listen to music, though," I say. Or watch TV or pet the cat. I should pet the cat more. Maybe there's a kind of pet the cat meditation, if you breathe properly but don't inhale too much fur—Lulu has such long hair. Maybe you and your cat can do tandem breathing. But that sounds a lot like sleeping, which Lulu and I already do together very well. And if I just sat there breathing, not petting her, wouldn't she feel bad? Wouldn't I be deepening her unhappiness by not petting the cat in my spare time, twice a day? That sounds more utilitarian, but maybe utilitarianism doesn't apply to yoga. Maybe yoga just is. I suspect house cats rarely think about such philosophical theories, anyhow. This lack of concern hasn't hurt Lulu any, although she could stand to lose a couple pounds.

Hmm, cat aerobics.

My mind is wandering, and I haven't even started trying to meditate. Plus there's something else I need to talk to Chester about. I know this.

"To calm the mind, you need to empty it," Chester says,

and I see a little trash can icon like on the computer. With a ding-ding sound. I'm not good at this.

"But the term empty-minded is pejorative."

"Clear minded, not empty exactly—open," Chester says lightly. Sounds a little dirty, but I know he doesn't mean this. Still, I remember some professor in college talking about keeping an open mind, and I know he meant it in a dirty way, judging by his syllabus.

Inside, the place looks like a 1960s small meeting room turned into a yoga studio, but at least it isn't heated like one. Padded chairs are lined up, ready for a speaker. Most of the people sitting down are older than me and already seem to be silent, practicing maybe. Okay, a couple of older men are asleep, but since the program hasn't started, I don't think there's anything wrong with it. No one's trying to wake them. Maybe it's the kind of place where judging others is frowned upon. I hope so.

"Aren't we supposed to sit on the floor?" I ask Chester.

"Ideally, there's no supposed to," he says. "Though we all love our rules so much. But I'm sure no one would mind if you took off your shoes."

"No, no," I say. My shoes are always sort of shapeless comfortable flexi things. I can barely feel them on my feet as it is. I like it this way. I have no interest in being aware of the shoes on my feet at any/all hours of the day. Though Libby has claimed red sparkly shoes are nice, and I do see the attraction.

The guy comes in. He's older than us (than Chester, too), with all-white hair that's almost coiffed, but naturally. *Naturally curly hair,* it comes to me, like the girl in the Peanuts cartoon who puffs up her hair. If he's a meditator, I don't imagine he spends much time fixing his hair, but then I may not understand the role of meditation in one's life (and have never had curly hair). He's dressed in nice dark pants and a light blue button-down shirt, wears sports shoes that aren't beat up, unlike the ones in my closet, say.

"I'm Dr. Randall McKee," he says, "and I've been a physician and meditator for forty-five years."

No one says, "Hi, Dr. McKee," but I do think it, and there is a pause. I guess we're all a little shy, or it just isn't that kind of meeting.

"I'd like to take you through a little meditation to bring you all to this place that's hosting us today. You may feel like you're here physically, but let's make sure we bring our minds to center here as well. In totality."

He gets us started, everyone comfortable, closing eyes, deep breaths. We go down a garden path, over a wooden bridge, up and around by large shady trees, lots of directions, flora and fauna. I can't remember how many times I've gone down some steps and then back up another path. I get a little lost even in my mind, though you'd think I'd know it pretty well by now. There are butterflies. Deer by a creek. That tiny hum of dragonflies nearby. The smell of a fresh honeysuckle. I try to focus on this place, but of course my mind wanders (not my first rodeo, er, meditation). I admire a trail of busy ants on a tree. Why are there ants in my dreamy meditation? Still, I suppose it's good to be detailed. I name one ant Stanley. He's not the leader, just an ant in the middle. We all stay at our happy places where there are bluebirds and evergreens. Fresh flowing water by the fall. Are we even in California anymore?

He brings us back to the room, and we open our eyes, happy, although I do have to think, *Why didn't Chester and I just go someplace like that instead of here?*

The room doesn't smell that forest-y fresh way, just basically more like reality. Can I go back? Is that the goal?

"Meditation is the key to happiness," he says. I can almost feel the little birds chirping in agreement. I have a vivid imagination. You'd think I'd meditate more often. Which makes me wonder: Does daydreaming count?

"It will help you be present, understand how to appreciate every day, and help you to deal with the most important thing in life—"

He looks at all of us. I smile. I'm the kind of audience member who smiles at the lecturer in agreement. I always figure, if I were giving the presentation, I'd want people to smile. Plus, I'm pretty happy about that waterfall.

"And what's most important for you to understand, to really come to peace with, is that you're all going to die."

Several people gasp. I might be one of them.

"Huh," Chester says quietly.

The suddenly scary-looking doctor looks at Chester. "That's right, you know it," he tells Chester. Chester nods unhappily.

"Well," Chester says.

"Comments later," doctor tells us. "Accept that you're going to die. That's what it's all about. Picture someone you love, your child, your parent, someone you've always loved deeply."

I see Aunt Lucile. She's diving off a high board, in a lion-print bathing suit that's very chic. She dives in and does that stroke where you go across the pool on your side, like a bathing beauty from long ago. She is healthy and strong, and I couldn't admire anyone more.

"Do you have them in your mind? Think about how much you love them—"

He pauses and I think of Aunt Lucile. I wonder if she'd like to take the trail to the waterfall. She loves water.

"Now that you can picture them, realize ...that they are going to die!"

"Oh my God," someone says. A few someones.

In my mind, Aunt Lucile gives the meditation guy a look that could kill.

"I thought we were going to talk about meditation for health," Chester says loudly.

A woman at the back says, "Am I in the wrong place?"

"It's all about death," doctor tells us. "All of it! You have to accept! Free yourself!"

A few people in the back sneak out. We are in the second row, so yes, front and center.

Chester turns to me: "I thought we'd just count our breaths." He turns to the doctor. "We just want the part about counting our breath."

"No counting!" the doctor says.

An older woman in the back starts crying.

A younger woman in the front starts crying.

A woman on the side drags her teenager from the room.

"You are going to die," the doctor repeats.

I see Chester do something with his phone in his pocket.

A fortysomething woman wearing a cape behind us stands to say something about her religion, and the doctor says something about following the wrong God.

Chester's phone rings.

"No phones in here!" The doctor is screaming loudly enough to scare someone to death.

Chester says, "Right," grabs me, and we tear from the room. Several others follow us out. We run down the stairs and out the door.

"I've always found meditating a little scary," I start to say.

"I'm sorry," Chester says, (deadly) serious. "This is not right."

"Quack," a man says, leaving the scene. "Meet ya at the waterfall!"

"I think we need to do a few minutes of calming breath after all," Chester says, leading me to a yard with a track around it. We start walking the track, then he turns to me and smiles.

"Race?" he says impishly. "Go!"

We start running wildly. My shoes aren't meant for running, but they'll do for an impromptu track star moment. Chester is wildly fast. Small but athletic and laughing hysterically.

He gets ahead of me, turns around, and says, "Don't forget to focus on your breathing!"

We make it around the track. People in the park, some from the class, are cheering us on. Chester slows down at the end so we can tie.

"Let's go meditate over pie," I say.

"Really focus on it!"

We go for pie.

* * *

"Worst free class ever," Chester says. We're at the diner on Fourth, sharing a piece of cherry pie large enough for five people called The Cherry Share-y. They serve it with sporks, so you don't have to decide whether to use your spoon or fork. It also comes with whipped cream and ice cream (also for five people). We deserve it.

"I've been to some bad free classes before," Chester continues, "like the vegan one that showed horrible cartoons of what happens to farm animals. Cartoon animals screaming. Cartoon blood everywhere. Not your G-rated Saturday morning special."

"You go a lot?" I ask.

"Sure, some," Chester says. "That was supposed to be a talk about how mediation can be the solution to health problems, how it can bring you peace and happiness."

"And death, apparently," I say.

"No, that was something else. Maybe a cult or something. Who wants to meditate about dying? Defeats the purpose," Chester says.

"The waterfall was nice," I say.

"I love how you see the silver lining," Chester says. Chester said the L word. I almost didn't hear it. But I did. Do I love anything in particular about Chester? Okay, besides the car and the fact that he slowed down so I could win the race?

"Silver linings are my specialty," I say, not bravely or particularly proud of myself.

Chester just smiles. We're quiet a moment.

"I have done long, meaningful meditations on pie," Chester says, licking ice cream off his spork.

"Pie would have made all the difference at that lecture," I say.

"Yes," Chester says, "but no doubt we would have ended up throwing it in that doctor's face. Which is just a waste of good pie."

We meditate on what he has said. And what I haven't.

15

Analyzing Your Data

J eremy calls me on a Tuesday night as I'm trying to wrap up a ball of yarn for Lulu. I'm not much of a crafter, but I do try to pick up soft skeins of yarn when I come across them because I know she'll play with one, if she's in the mood of course, but only if the texture is just so, like your best sweater or that cashmere scarf you haven't bought for yourself yet even though you know the color you want is going to go out of stock and you'll have to wait for it to go on sale a whole 'nother year. I'm pulling the yarn out of the skein before it gets too messed up, and she's grabbing at it, so we become something of a Push Me—Pull You with strings attached. Cheap fun for both of us on a Tuesday night and at least usually, no one gets hurt.

I haven't heard from Jeremy in a couple of weeks. He seems like more of Aunt Lucille's boyfriend at this point than (one of?) mine. Except for that big kiss. Not the way you'd kiss someone's aunt, I suspect and truly hope.

After he says a few hello, how are yous, and drops the phone once, he says: "I've promised your Aunt Lucille that I'd take her to this restaurant she's always wanted to go to, and I thought you might like to come, too." Maybe he is dating Aunt Lucille. The term *triple dating* comes to mind, but I don't think this is what it's supposed to mean.

"Oh," I reply. "That's nice..." I guess.

"It's her birthday," the dentist tells me about *my* aunt.

"It is, soon," I say. I know this. I have a present ready and have ordered the black forest cake she likes from the place in Brentwood. I'm trying to be a better niece. I'm checking rental ads every day. So, what if I don't know about some restaurant she's been wanting to go to for however number of years? This call is making me feel guilty, and Lulu has run off with the entire skein, so now on top of it, I have nothing to do with my hands and am about to start twirling my hair mercilessly, which it does not deserve.

"It's in Topanga," he says. "Inn of the Something Stars. I have it written down—" I hear things dropping, which makes me giggle, not at him, really, but with him. I'm like this when trying to find something I wrote down. Which is why writing on your hand really never goes out of style.

"Inn of the Seventh Ray?"

"I thought it was stars, but that sounds right," Jeremy says. I like that he isn't one of those snobs that knows the exact restaurant name and Michelin ranking or whatever. "So, what do you think? Should we take her? It sounds like it would be nice of us," he says.

I wonder if this is a setup, if I should say no, thanks, I can happily find a way to celebrate my own aunt's birthday. But the truth is that it would be nice of us, especially if that's what she wants, even though my understanding of this restaurant is that it's the kind of place you take your soon-to-be fiancée to hide an engagement ring. But for Aunt Lucille, yes, it would be nice of me. It would be very nearly the least I could do.

"Yes, of course," I tell him. I feel so untrusting. But then I have reason to be, in the man department, that is (different from the men's department, but that one, too). I gained a lot of experience from trusting my ex, a distrustful, lying human being. I have a right to be careful, confused, me. But I trust Aunt Lucille, even if she is often up to matchmaking shenanigans.

It's a date, sort of, again.

* * *

"I've given notice," Susan tells me. We're with Miralise after school at the Latte Lesson, in my work neighborhood. So okay, it's not far from my home, either. I like this about my life. She continues: "I'm leaving the museum."

"Wow, I had no idea. Plus, I'm impressed by your ability to make a decision," I ramble. "Not that you have problems with decision making. Just thinking about myself of course. How do you feel?"

"Stupid, terrified, massive failure, that kind of thing," Susan says, slicing a chocolate croissant into a tiny bite like that will make any difference at all as to how much either one of us eats.

"I'm proud of you, except for the feeling like a failure thing, which you are not."

"The press got to me," she says. "I never expected to have bad reviews in my life. I don't mind working for a place that represents something small and valued. But even I couldn't stand the yellow room. In my heart and mind, I'm afraid I always called it Romper Room. It was gnawing at me."

"You'll find something," says Miralise. "We believe in you. Girl power. Move on up."

"You're a powerhouse of skills and knowledge," I add. I mean this, but then so did Miralise.

"Oh, yeah," Susan agrees halfheartedly, or maybe even less. "Because art history majors who've curated color museums are so highly valued by our economy. Why do we identify ourselves so much by our jobs, anyhow?"

"Something ingrained in us, probably by the evening news. Or Mary Tyler Moore."

"I blame Diane Sawyer," says Susan.

"She's great to blame," I say. "Wait, let's blame a man."

"Right. Let's blame all men," Susan says.

"It just doesn't feel the same as blaming a woman by name, especially such a blonde one."

"That's how ingrained it all is," Susan says. "And probably why we're so comfortable blaming ourselves, even without the perfectly coiffed head of hair."

"Oh yeah," I say. "That."

Susan waves her hand in the air in an attempt to wash away the worry. "Enough about me. Clearly at least one of you has some unsolvable problem."

"The Goldilocks Problem," I say.

"Oh, you mean the Goldilocks Planet," says Miralise, first-grade teacher that she is.

"Oy with the Goldilocks Planet!" I say.

"Libby was talking about that the other day," Susan says. "Interesting."

"Okay it's official, every person I know has now heard about this," I say.

"I gave the kids a lesson," Miralise says. "NASA's got all

sorts of materials. Pretty. Oh, listen, you'll like this," she says to me.

"It started with three planets," Miralise begins. "So, you've got the Earth, Venus, and Mars. Mars is too hot, Venus is too cold, but the Earth was just right. Then they extrapolated to other planets and stars. Kind of like making a list of the three and listing the pros and cons."

She stares at me.

"And," I ask.

"So, say you have a choice of three, Goldilocks," she continues. "Three bears, three bowls, three eligible men."

"Three is a good number," Susan says, nodding.

"Right," says Miralise. "So, you can ask yourself the important questions: Which planet, so to speak, is hotter? Which is colder? Which feels just right?"

"Oh, I get this," Susan adds, "You get to test them out. Actual touch required, for scientific discovery's sake."

"What is each surface like?" Miralise asks.

"Yeah," I say. "I see where you're going with this."

"It's all trial and error, testing your hypothesis," Miralise says.

"Proving your chosen theory," Susan says.

"Or suddenly coming across evidence that utterly upends your thinking," Miralise says.

"So to speak," they both add.

"So," Susan says, changing the subject but not really, "got another date with the dentist?"

"Gathering your data," Miralise says. "Nothing wrong with that."

"I guess," I say. "Is it dating if your aunt keeps coming along?"

"Depends how many times she gets up to use the bathroom," Susan says. "More than once? Date. Not at all? Not date. Or at least, not a good date. Your Aunt Lucille's seen enough chick flicks to understand how this works."

"Aunt Lucille knows her way around a setup," I say. "She is Dear Aunt Lucille, advice-monger to the West Coast, or at least our little part of it. I may be her biggest failure," I say.

"You wish," Susan teases.

"What if Aunt Lucille is the best part of the date?" I ask.

"Then maybe you need to start seeing the dentist on a professional-only basis. Or get another cat. Or both."

"No making fun of women and cats," I say. "Lulu is my rock. And she almost never tries to divorce me."

"Lulu provides a reliably good time, it's true," Susan agrees.

"And never cares if I wear makeup or not," I say.

"Excellent feature in a companion animal," Miralise says.

"Actually, she likes to lick off my blush."

"Which might not be good for either of you."

"Yet another vote for the clean face look," Susan says.

"Which might not be what your aunt has in mind for her birthday dinner," says Miralise.

"Oh, I don't know, anymore," I say. "Sometimes a birthday dinner is just a birthday dinner."

"Hah, a birthday dinner is always something more than a birthday dinner. Often, it's a total disaster," Susan says.

I'm hoping Susan's wrong this time, but yes, I've had my share of off-putting birthday dinners. Special occasions always spell danger, somehow, if you mix up the letters just right plus add a little alcohol. We all know this.

"I'm tired of so much of everything being about men," I say.

"All women are, or at least should be," Susan says.

"I don't want to think about it so much," I say. "I want to finish illustrating my book—or at least get a better start. I don't want a second cat, but if I do, I don't want it to mean anything significant about me other than I don't mind the changing-kitty-litter part of life and rarely wear black pants. Why does everything have to be so symbolic? Who decided this? I mean, can't I just have a lightly romantic birthday dinner with my aunt and her dentist? Does the world have to have such high expectations just because the restaurant has a lot of sparkly twinkling lights in a romantic canyon setting?"

"I don't know who made up the rules, but it does feel like we always get the short end, not to mention a seat by the kitchen," Susan says. "I suggest you slip your credit card to the maître d' before the meal. You pay, you play by your own rules."

"I like it," I say.

"There's no such thing as a free meal with sparkly twinkling lights. Ever. We haven't come that far, baby," Miralise adds.

"The romantic restaurant. We've all seen that scene in the movies, haven't we? Does it ever end with anything but hurt feelings or worse, an actual pie in the face?" I ask. Though I know the answer.

III

Part Three

16

You Get a Furby, and You Get a Furby...

I'm driving to work when my rear-view mirror falls off and somehow lands inside my purse. I'd like to say this hasn't happened before, but then I'm driving a car that's much older than I am. (Ooh, I'm involved with an older car.) I suspect I won't fare so well when I'm the Beetle's age—and wonder who'll be around to pick up the pieces. Which is a bad metaphor to start the day with, I recognize. I hate when bad things happen to the car. I go straight to panic mode.

So, I head to the mechanics' shop. Just an innocent trip to the garage. It's not like I'm looking for anyone. And now I can't even check my hair in the mirror as I pull into the garage.

There's a guy behind the desk, which is old and chipped like any good front desk that's been around even longer than my car has. His name, I know from experience (and his name tag) is Inky. He's a guy around my age who wears those fashionable thick black glasses (with thick lenses) and has inky black hair, and he doesn't talk a lot.

"Hi," I say, handing him my mirror. They know me here,

even Inky.

"Ah," he says.

"Again," I say.

"Happens." He writes something up.

I'm casually looking around. Nothing more than that.

"Is Ben here?" I ask not very casually.

"Somewhere," Inky says. He hands me a receipt that in big black letters that says No Charge VW Downed Mirror.

I like it here.

I walk around a little. I leave the front room and go to the waiting room, which also doubles as a really low-key coffee room with an antique-looking snack machine that sells M&Ms. It's all M&Ms—rows and rows of different colors and types. It's somebody's idea of a joke, but it's also just what I always want. There's also an ancient cigarette machine that still works but is rigged so that when you push the button (no change even needed), you get a Hershey's Kiss. So there really is a God, and he likes mechanic shops, too.

When people ask me if Santa Monica is as good as it sounds, I tell them it is. And I think of this place before the beach, even. Maybe it's just me, but I doubt it, as the little coffee room is filled with people waiting for cars and eating candy with their coffee. I've gone to my happy place.

I get close enough to the room to admire the old Naugahyde chairs and Formica tables, and the smell of coffee and creamer (it's stir your own here), when I notice a few guys over at a table by the window. I take three giant steps back behind the door and listen. I'm hiding in a mechanics' garage just outside the snack room listening to Chester talk with Jeremy the dentist, as Ben (their mechanic too?) leans near them against the M&M machine. I didn't see what kind of M&Ms he has, but I hear him crunching. So, yeah—peanut.

I try to get the *What Are the Chances of This* thoughts out of my head so I can eavesdrop more freely. Two moms are at another table speaking low (but I can still hear it's about yoga so I'm not about to listen, even though their tone does seem to be kind of a complaining one, which I respect). The guys are all crunching. Maybe guys don't know how to talk in a group. It's not as if they have all that much in common. I position myself: I can just barely see them. I pretend I'm just standing around waiting, which is actually a skill of mine, as I'm often standing around waiting. Maybe it's more talent than skill.

"I just don't know if I could handle it," Jeremy the dentist says. "All the insecurity, all that never knowing if you're going to be left entirely alone."

"Stranded," Chester says with a nod. Oh look, he has a bag of the pastel M&Ms.

"I like knowing for sure what's working when," Jeremy says.

"I don't know," Ben says, clearly disagreeing, then leans his head back to dump some M&Ms right from the bag into his mouth, which I do consider a skill.

He chews. The older (and oldest) lean in.

"I find it exciting, just never quite being positive what'll happen next, when things'll get started," Ben continues.

They're not talking about me. C'mon, I know that, right?

"I like things to run the way they're supposed to," Jeremy says. "I like to have my expectations fulfilled, no bumps on the road, nothing faulty at all."

Now it really doesn't sound like me. Bumps on the road. Or does it?

"But it's exciting," Chester says, getting a little impassioned. "It's nostalgic; it's will we or won't we? It's what life is about."

"You take your chances," Ben says solidly. "You plan options, keep your mind open."

"Uh-uh, just don't think so," Jeremy says.

I can't say my heart is broken at his dismissal of, well, whatever it is.

"But the challenge!" Chester says. I do appreciate his zeal, misplaced though it might be. "The Will She or Won't She?"

"Yes," Ben agrees. "You have to go for the ride, just feel it out." Kinda suggestive, seems to me.

"Well, of course," Chester agrees.

"No. No, no, no," Jeremy the dentist says. "No. I'm not about to trade my brand-new Toyota for any old classic car— I don't care what the charms are."

Oh, they're not talking about me. Of course not. They're talking cars. But just cars? Cars as transportation? Cars as art? Cars as...metaphor?

"A classic, though?" Chester says. "A classic has its place. A classic can't be denied."

"Uh-uh," says Jeremy. Jeremy, I have to say, seems to be getting out of the race.

"Driving a classic with style, spending whatever it takes, really caring about a thing of beauty..." Ben trails off.

"Yup," Chester agrees.

"Well," Ben continues: "The girl who drives a classic is always right."

"Girl?" Jeremy says.

"Sorry, um, guy," Ben says. "The guy who drives a classic is always right. A girl in a classic? Just right."

I'm not sure even they know what they're talking about, though it's clear where their allegiances lie.

I sneak off, with lots to think about and no M&Ms whatsoever.

* * *

I mope my way into the office not because I have anything to be particularly sad about but because a lot of little things are starting to pile up. I need to get going and find somewhere to live so Aunt Lucile can have her place back. I need to finish Goldilocks, or finish her off, or whatever. Plus, I seem to be dating two or three guys, which probably isn't considered a problem in *Cosmopolitan/Elle/Glamour* magazine. But for me—it's a little outside the norm. It's a continent away from the norm. What am I doing? Who am I doing it with? Yuck. I'm not really sleeping with Chester anymore. It was really just the two times, and they seemed more like exercise or a successful sporting outing than moments of significant intimacy or soul connecting or whatever the open-shirted-man-on-cover romance novels say.

Walking into Kids Press, I see what looks like a garage sale, or maybe a flea market. Basically, there's stuff everywhere.

"What's going on?" I ask no one in particular

"I'm setting a date for leaving," Hannah says, moving things around the table. The whole crew is here, admiring a motley collection of stuff I haven't been able to identify at first glance.

"You're leaving a sinking ship?" I ask.

"It'll never sink with all this junk around. Grab a piece and float."

"What is all this?"

Chris answers, holding a little stuffed monkey. "Hannah unearthed it in a back storeroom." He makes the monkey play the cymbals just like every old nightmarish monkey must have done in a premodern time, or at least before I was born.

"Ha!" Chris yells when it does what it's supposed to do, as if he's never seen a monkey cartoon in his life.

"Nelson's collection," Kelly says, twisting a hidden knob and making a donkey walk across the table. "This is an official donkey from the 1960 election!"

"It's junk, and it's going," says Hannah.

"Like you?" Chris says.

"I'm not as an antique as you think," says Hannah. "But timeless."

"You're fortysomething," I say. I'm only a couple years younger and not willing to let myself be called an antique either, or even a reproduction.

"Publishing ages us," Hannah says.

"Cruel, cruel publishing," Chris says sweeping back his lightened blonde hair and picking up a Furby in what looks like its original packaging. He waves it around.

"Those scare the crap out of me," Hannah says with no emotion whatsoever. I've never understood Furbys. Hannah actually takes a step back.

"Like a witch doctor's toy or something," she says. Chris puts it down quickly.

Gabriella and Jefferson play with old-time marionettes they've unwrapped from heavy plastic.

"Macs are better!" Jefferson makes his guy marionette say.

"Brainwashed!" Gabriella's girl marionette says. They look a little Charlie McCarthy–ish in that hideous unhuman way.

"Mac!" Jefferson says, swiping at the other doll

"PC!" Gabby replies, picking up a pet rock and throwing it at Jefferson's doll.

Nelson comes in. "My toys!" He tries to hug each one,

mumbling "Hello, old friend; hello, bad doll; hello, creature from the black lagoon...."

"Hello trash," says Hannah. "I want this place truly cleaned up before the merger."

"We're merging?" Nelson asks.

"Aren't you the one to decide?" asks Chris.

Hannah nods her head. "Yes, he's deciding. I'm putting things in order; he's deciding. That pretty much sums up my job as editor in chief here for the last how many years."

"How did you gather all of this, Nelson," Chris asks.

"Not to mention why," Hannah says with a glare.

"I'm a toy person," Nelson says. "How could you not have noticed?" He waves toward his small glass-enclosed office and yes, there are airplanes hanging from the ceiling and creatures lining the bookshelves. He points over at Jefferson and Gabriella's little toys near their desks, a collection of windups and dragons and trolls. He swerves and sways his arms all across the office. It's Kids Press, so yeah, there are toys just about everywhere.

"I've got hundreds more at home," he says.

"Really, hundreds?" Hannah asks doubtfully.

"Okay," he admits quietly, "maybe thousands."

Jefferson and Gabriella have been inching closer and closer to Nelson. But then face it, we all work on kid stuff. We're all pretty interested, except maybe Hannah, who I suspect figures she may have to clean it all up or categorize it or something before she goes. Though I notice she didn't mention an end date.

"Wow," Jefferson says. He picks up a Godzilla that really looks like Godzilla. Let's put it this way: It's not at all cute.

"Ooh," Gabriella says. The two turn it this way and that.

Hannah makes a loud sigh and moves away. The rest us of move in to unpack the stash.

"Everybody collects something," Nelson says somewhat apologetically.

"Garage sale," Hannah says succinctly, grabbing an old *Where the Wild Things Are.*

"Don't touch that, it's valuable!" Nelson says.

"Eight-ninety-five at Target," Hannah says. But Nelson has whisked it away.

"You can't sell this stuff!" says young Jefferson.

"I can try," Hannah says. "But maybe you're right. Let's bag it up and take it to Goodwill."

"No way," Gabriella says, holding what looks like a fuzzy pink unicorn close to her chest. "This stuff is worth gold."

"It's original," Jefferson says.

"EBay here we come," Hannah says.

"These are priceless!" Nelson echoes, grabbing a hot-pink Barbie car that looks fresh from the packaging.

"Garbage bags, please," Hannah instructs Kelly.

"No!" Nelson says. "No," he says more gently, grabbing a small doll with weird, gigantic, sort of psychedelic eyes, which is still in an unsealed box (it looks unsealed from here, at least). "I have to say no."

"The boys are coming," Kelly says.

"Boys?" I ask. "Kids? School kids?"

"No, the Bug boys," Kelly says.

"We've got to clean up!" Hannah instructs

"To impress the Bug boys?" Chris asks. "They barely change their shirts." I agree. Those guys seem young enough to still have piles of laundry in their rooms, if not their office.

"They're he-re," Chris says, *Poltergeist* like.

And in they come, all wearing green shirts, which I doubt they even planned.

"At least the shirts aren't red," Chris whispers to me.

They come in saying variations of hi, hello, whoa, hey, yep, and uh. The neat programming guy looks at Kelly then his eyes flash to the table strewn with stuff. The toys of our childhoods, or our parents' and grandparents' childhoods. Toys that someone young once whispered secrets to, toys that have been held and caressed and tucked under pillows—albeit maybe not the dolls still in boxes, but who can say for sure? I slept with a kitty stuffed animal for many years that developed its own kind of stuffed animal mange after a while. And I still slept with it. We are creatures of habit, and we love our toys to pieces, literally.

"Oh. My. God," says the tallish Steve. The Paul guy runs for a Furby in a box (there are several out of the box, too, but the boxed one, I have to say, is the creepiest).

"Tell her," Nelson says, pointing at Hannah, who fiercely rips the tab off a huge box of heavy-duty black trash bags.

"Do you know what you have here?" Steve says staring at the toys.

"A mess," Hannah says.

He walks over to her and takes the box of trash bags away, then hands it to the quiet guy Joel, who walks over to the window and throws it out. I hope no one was underneath. They don't call them Hefty bags for nothing.

Steve turns to Nelson. "Seriously..."

Nelson replies, "I don't have an inventory or anything."

"Is there more? Is there more?" Paul says excitedly, grabbing boxed Star Wars figures. The guys are really, although I find the term not quite descriptive enough at times, freaking out. He keeps saying, Ah, Ah, Ah! I can practically hear his heart beating from across the room.

"There's more at home," Nelson says. "Including a big Godzilla."

"How big?" one of them whispers.

"Big. Large." Nelson says. "Big and large."

"Priceless," says Paul quickly like the commercial.

"Oh, my," Steve says. He walks over to Nelson and puts an arm around him. "Have I mentioned," Steve says, nearly crying, "that we've just been given another two million dollars in funding?"

He and Nelson walk off into the sunset together, each picking up, then cradling, a cabbage patch doll. It's a moment all right.

17

I Get No Kick From Champagne

The previously mentioned birthday lunch has become a birthday dinner, and still I wasn't too suspicious. Aunt Lucile said she much preferred early dinner to lunch, that it made the day feel more complete, as where can a day really take you after a big lunch but downward, or worse, leave you hungry at 9 p.m.?

I see her point. We're neither of us usually big eaters, so we like to enjoy what we do eat.

But I suspect there's a difference between lunch at Inn of the Seventh Ray and dinner at the Inn of the Seventh Ray (even an early one, say, with your aunt and her handsome, well-kissing dentist). The twinkle lights alone, turned on against a just darkening sky—well, maybe you don't always want to find yourself in a twinkle-lit restaurant at a certain hour. Again, with your aunt and her dentist.

I meet them there in Topanga Canyon, since driving with people makes me feel funny—what do you say on the drive? Do you use your best conversation or save it, and how much weather talk is appropriate? Do you go into inches of rain per season or stick with levels of sunburn, and leave air pollution levels out entirely? Plus, radio or no radio? NPR? Baseball? (In season). It's possible I drive alone too much, but maybe I just like it that way.

Jeremy offered to pick up Aunt Lucille "like a birthday date," he said. So really, he already used the word date, albeit not in reference to me. I said I'd meet them as I had to stop off at the office (I often forget things at the office, so this is always a possibility, as opposed to an out-and-out, know-in-advance lie). I know it's not eco-conscious, but did I mention how much I love my Beetle? I find it calming to drive in the Beetle, whether it's an impending date or not. And I'm worth it. (I have to force myself to believe this, but I think it's one of the greatest ad lines ever, so I give it a whirl now and then.)

But oh, those twinkle lights. Let me set the scene. The Inn at the Seventh Ray, though it sounds new-agey if not completely hokey—and I'm not saying it isn't—is a romantic spot chosen by many for their wedding or proposal, or engagement celebration, or a meaningful moment that might lead to any of those three. It's probably not the place to tell your soulmate you're filing for divorce. (Hooper told me at a little crepe place in Venice Beach, which is only one reason why I can't see the point of crepes.) It's romantic here with a capital R. A capital, lace-trimmed, flowery, hand-scripted R made of twinkle lights. Like R but frillier.

I'm here first, just before 6:30, dusk approaching on a still warm night. I want to be first because it's someone's birthday, my aunt's in particular, and I still feel a little guilty for not riding with them. Not that Aunt Lucile would mind because Aunt Lucile has the gift of gab—and I mean it as a compliment. The gift of being comfortable making conversation with everyone, and it is a gift. I wait for them by the parking and see them arrive in Jeremy's perfectly acceptable Toyota Avalon, white and newish. A stylish but still stuffy kind of car that makes sense for a dentist, I think, car snob that I am. Actually, I think those cars are pretty expensive. At least it's not a Lexus, I tell myself, which seems like a conceited, overly expensive car to me (in all styles—I think it's the annoying Lexus logo). I'm an old car snob. I want to see people spend their money on a groovy ride, not a metal emblem. So, an Avalon is pretty middle-of-the-road to me, a Japanese car with Swiss-like neutrality, if you will.

Not too hot, not too cold, I hear my Goldilocks character say. *But still, not quite right.*

Dealership license plate holder—nothing personal or individualistic, I don't fail to notice. I am mean when it comes to cars. I wonder if I'm mean about everything. I wonder if I'm approaching the age where it doesn't matter, where no one cares what I'm like and everyone has just about had enough of me. A woman over a certain age. Is 34 that age? I'd hoped for more time, I think. But then I see Aunt Lucille, who is nothing if not a cool older lady. And I don't think I've ever heard her be mean.

Jeremy escorts Aunt Lucile from the car, and I hug her. Aunt Lucile loves lavender scent, which is one of the few fragrances that doesn't make me sneeze. Plus it rubs off a little on me, which always makes me think I feel more relaxed, whether I do or not. I take all those health magazines to heart. Even just imagining I smell lavender makes me smile. Sometimes, all I need is just the word. *Lavender.* Maybe it's just me.

It's ridiculously pretty here, the kind of place that is dream come true, picture-perfect. Splashes of purple. (I do so like a thick purple napkin—who can explain it?) Shining crystal glasses or maybe just glass glasses, as I've never known how to figure out which is which, or why it matters.

Though I suspect it does in some way I will never be wealthy enough to understand; a way, for instance, that would never matter to my cat Lulu, so how important can it be? Sometimes, I do judge things on a Lulu scale, especially on a bad day, like: Would it matter to Lulu that my hair is parting funny so it looks like I have a balding spot when I really don't or at least don't think I do? She might give it a 2 on a scale of 10 of caring, maybe lower. Would it matter to Lulu that I tromped through mud at the gas station and have to wash my pants, when I'd hoped to get two or three more wearings out of them? Maybe Lulu would give it a 4, as actually, she likes warm laundry fresh from the machine. And who doesn't.

Yes, I'm digressing. I'm nervous, I'm on a threeway or whatever. I do not need the champagne that is appearing in the pretty glasses set off by the dimming sunlight and twinkling lights, which are everywhere. I almost got one caught in my hair. But let's face it, Lulu would like this, too.

Aunt Lucile, perhaps sensing my nervousness in a little bit of an awkward situation, is regaling us with another story and has been since we came in. Not in a way that bothers anybody. More in the lifesaving way that might motivate you to send a thank-you note later, or flowers, or a hand-painted vase trimmed in gold. That kind of talking. So, you can take in your surroundings along with the face of the dentist, his whole demeanor, actually, which can I just say seems a little one step up from previous not-exactly dates? Or is it just the twinkle lights?

Maybe Jeremy got a haircut, or a hairstyle, or a makeover from *GQ* or one of those shops in Beverly Hills where they assign you a team to attack every feature of yourself you've never liked that makes you feel there's hope, and allows you to believe that they've has seen worse. Jeremy is a new man, a little less average Joe dentist, a little more, what is it? A little more Kevin Costner. Younger Kevin Costner like *Dances With Wolves,* which, although lengthy and a little violent, is really worth lingering over on a couch with your cat. Jeremy seems a little lighter, a little more tossing back his head a la Costner with a funny little smile. Where the heck did that come from?I'd wonder if he just responds more to Aunt Lucille, but this isn't our first group date. Something has been professionally adjusted, and not in a bad way.

Casual sport coat, good blue shirt (heavy fabric, nothing weird or polyester), something or other different about the hair near his ears. Something more relaxed. Man these twinkle lights. I kinda hope they're working on how I look, too.

But why would I care? Aunt Lucille has seen me with the H1N1 flu, definitely at my worst. But Jeremy Costner hasn't.

Hmm. This champagne.

"Right Amy?" Aunt Lucille asks me. "Are you with us?"

"This place is so beautiful," I say. "Doesn't it make you feel a little better about, well, everything?" I ask.

Jeremy smiles. "I've always had a feeling about this place."

"It's magical," Aunt Lucile says, raising a champagne flute. "Thank you both for bringing me. It looks like a great place for a wedding," says my aunt innocently, if you don't know better.

"I've heard it is," says Dr. Jeremy Costner, DDS, with a little masculine hair toss that's not a bad habit at all. Goes with the little side shrug he's doing. The DDS is getting cuter. I cannot believe this.

"Let's not talk about anything serious," Aunt Lucile says.

"Why's that?" I ask

"Why waste this? I know the world is practically falling to pieces in most places, but not here and not this minute," Aunt Lucile says, raising her glass.

"Here, there are twinkle lights," I say, smiling, enjoying the scent of what must be hundreds if not thousands of blossoms in the distance that might bother me any other day in any other place lacking in twinkle lights (and champagne—I'm on my second very tall glass, that I know of).

"Here, there are beautiful landscapes—and beautiful women," says my new dentist, clinking glasses. "And I do have some friends who got married here recently. The photos were gorgeous."

"You didn't go?" Aunt Lucile asks.

"I meant to, but then," he says, with an amusing little head toss that's really not too much at all for a guy, "emergency crown situation."

"Ouch," Aunt Lucille says.

"Sorry, no dentistry talk today," Kevin says. I mean Rusty, er, um, I'm not sure of his name. But his hair looks a little redder suddenly. I hadn't noticed that. Twinkle lights can't give a dentist a little glow, can they? I have got to get some for the apartment. (Lulu would say 6 on a scale of 10. Hmm, I'd forgotten about her.) Could twinkle lights possibly be the answer for many of the problems we face today?

I probably always feel this way after champagne but forget before drinking the next time, as I'm always a little dulled by headaches I know will follow. I wonder if the headaches' effects compound over the years and mean something like I've lost brain cells or the ability to focus at dinner with a man (yes, plus my aunt). Say.

"What are your plans," Aunt Lucille asks me. My mind is in the champagne, but my body seems to have remained at the table.

"For?" I ask lightly as if I've been listening (bad niece) but am just in need of a little clarification.

"The autumn," she says. "I always feel like my birthday is the start of the season," Aunt Lucille says. Well, it is September 1, so this is somewhat reasonable.

"Everything," I say with a profound sense of freedom, determination, liberty and justice for all. "I want to finish the Goldilocks book I'm writing and drawing. I will finish it. I will resolve all the living arrangement problems; I will get Lulu a professional grooming. I will get my car detailed even though I have never known what this really means and why I can't do it myself. I will help my boss decide what to do about our company and, quite possibly, go in search of a new job."

And then I start to tear up. My eyes are full, and words start spilling out of my mouth.

"Job?" I say. "There are no jobs out there. I don't know why it's taken me so long on this book. I don't know why I can't get it together."

Aunt Lucille reaches over and moves my champagne glass in her direction, though it's not as if in this condition I'd care at all about looking impolite and reaching across the table for it, or even getting up and getting it from another table, not that this is likely. Even weirder, younger circa 1990s Kevin Costner covers my hand with his own, and it is warm. It's a little cold out here even though I have a sweater because my Aunt Lucille always told me to take a sweater—and since she's here, you better believe I have one, albeit half falling off my shoulders. One shoulder.

But oh yeah, the hand. He gives me a Kevin Costner smile. *Field of Dreams* nice, not *Bull Durham* smirky. A little more seasoned, sincere, maybe even cornball. Not smoldering, just relaxed, involved, entranced if not utter magical realism. Though what about this dinner isn't draped in magical realism?

I am silenced. In a good way. And realize I need to eat.

The menu looks plainer than I'd expect from such a fancy place—no nonsense, although with foods in italic, which I find hard to read. I actually misread the Soup & Salads + organic chicken as Soup & Salad + orgasmic chicken. I know it's really time to eat, and of course, I'm ordering it. With the Hand-Cut Linguine, which sounds fun. I'd like to stand at a long table and cut linguine, not that I think it would matter that much to the eater, nor to the linguine, of course. I hear lots of foodie jargon coming from our mouths: pan-seared, free-range, sunchokes, salmorigilio-rubbed cauliflower (sounds a lot like salmonella, but I don't say anything). Words I don't know: shishito, not to mention tendrils—what is a pea tendril and is it a good thing? Let's not even go into mustard frill, which may be a garnish or perhaps a typo. Words I don't like for some reason (reduction, confit, glace) because I think I'd sound absurd saying them. I suddenly realize how much I want something with croutons on it. When's the last time you had really good croutons? Can't you just feel the crunch?

Before I can think, something appears before me that the waiter calls Roasted Mushroom Toast, kind of creamy, and not utterly appealing. I push it aside and attack my salad with orgasmic chicken, which I think will help me get myself out of this mess I've sipped my way into. Kevin Costner bravely takes over the creamy toast thing, which while its not a manly dish in any way, I admire him for. Brave. *Braveheart.* No, that's that other guy who's icky.

"May I have some more water?" I ask, hoping there's a waiter behind me. The waiter (still assuming it's the waiter) lights three candles on our table. I can't explain why there are three. Unless I'm seeing triple.

Dinner proceeds more smoothly. Talk of new pandas born at a zoo; Aunt Lucille wants to go to a place somewhere in Asia where you can hold a baby panda. Though you have to wear surgical gloves and a doctor's scrubs, supposedly, there's nothing like it. Lots of panda talk for some reason.

"I dream of going," Aunt Lucille says. And the dentist is really into it, too.

"I want to hold a panda!" he nearly screams. (I'm not the only one into the champagne.) "It's just this huge desire I have," he tells her, and they look at me.

"I'd hold a panda," I say, chicken hanging out of my mouth. I'm eating fast, and it's working.

"So cuddly," Aunt Lucille says. Kevin just kind of makes this adorable huggly movement with his shoulder that screams, "I want a panda! I want a panda."

"I love the ones at the San Diego Zoo," the dentist says. "If you go really early, there's no crowds, and the pandas are more frolic-y." The dentist said frolic-y, and I can feel my face getting red. I'm not sure if it's a causation or correlation. But I can picture the pandas, too.

"Oh, I love that zoo," Aunt Lucille says. "Though I don't necessarily love the idea of a zoo, such an unnatural condition. Amy loves the red pandas," she says.

"Do you, Amy?" Kevin asks me.

It takes me a minute to grasp the notion of a red panda, which doesn't look like a regular black and white panda, but is more of a cute, little, raccoon/monkey/like panda-ish creature.

"That's right! Red pandas," I say. "There's something about them..." I can't find the words. Nothing at all like frolick-y comes to mind. I take a piece of crostini off the cheese plate. (I don't go for cheese by itself, but the bread looks fine, and I finish at least three-quarters of a loaf.)

"Maybe we should go together," Kevin says.

"Huh," I say, crunching happily. Hand-cut linguine appears before me, looking not unlike non-hand-cut linguine. The tomatoes seem overdone, but I'm not the kind of girl who'd say anything about it.

Kevin has gnocchi. (Do you say the G? I don't mean are you supposed to, just do you? Because Libby does, and it sounds right when she says it that way. Plus adorable.) I get caught up thinking about gnocchi as one of the dentist's rolls onto the floor, and again, I'm not about to say anything. His tomatoes look overdone, too. At least no one ordered the tartare, the thought of which I just can't handle. Aunt Lucille has the scallops with veggies. I remember there are supposed to be tendrils in there, but I can't particularly identify which ingredient that might be. I don't see anything green on her plate at all. Focus on your linguine, Amy. Don't slurp. I ask the waiter for more crostini or just bread. I know when I need to sop up some alcohol from my system.

Though the lights in here are lovely.

"Aren't they?" Aunt Lucille says. So yeah, I said that out loud. "I love it here," she says. I'm pretty sure she's the one who said this, but Kevin is smiling at me and—wait for it—there's a dimple. Oh my God, just where you want it to be. I reach out for it but somehow manage to get my hand to land on sourdough bread instead. Thank you, god of dating. I don't even care if it's gluten free. I'd even have thankfully landed on the Brie then take my chances and see what follows actually touching the dimple. You never know what might happen when you reach for someone's dimple.

And as if we weren't full enough, let me just add this: We dive into devil's food cake with caramel foam for dessert, not that I've ever heard of caramel foam before. And coffee. Really, really, good, necessary, who-cares-if-you-sleep-tonight, coffee. I have worked through the inebriation and transcended to a different state of being: I am the twinkling light. Aunt Lucille looks completely contented; and Kevin Costner's dimple is lit up from all sides. Even the recorded music playing in the background doesn't bother me, though this seems like the kind of place that might have an ensemble, or a threesome, er, trio of violins. Scratch threesome, please.

I think maybe Aunt Lucille is right about everything.

"Happy Birthday to You!" I toast her with the coffee. She takes a little bow. Twinkle lights become her.

Kevin pays the check. "But we're splitting—" I say quietly, leaning over to him.

"We'll talk about that later," he says right into my mouth, as he's about an inch away. I'm not sure anyone has ever spoken *into* my mouth before. You'd think it'd be weird, but I can feel it down to my ankles. Probably down to my toes, if they weren't already asleep. We've been sitting awhile.

We talk more about traveling, wish lists, bucket lists. I have now had a lot of coffee. I have had more food and drink than in the last month, quite possibly.

We get up to walk to our cars, and I test my feet carefully.

I'm pretty much over the champagne. Eating several platefuls of hand-cut or other foods will do that to you, especially if like me, you get very drunk on four sips of wine. I still feel happy and twinkly, but I'm okay to drive. Aunt Lucille excuses herself noticeably and disappears, and Dentist Costner, DDS, and I stand together. It isn't cold, but there's a breeze, and he steps in.

"I'm so glad we did this," he says and if I didn't know better, I wouldn't be sure what he's referring to. Sobering up was a real good idea.

"I know," I say. "I'm really glad." I get real close. My mouth still tastes of caramel, so I'm feeling confident, ready. He's wearing a lavender silk tie that looks so soft I want to reach out and grab it, but it's not like we're in a romance novel or anything.

He kisses me. For longer than one kiss, but then, twinkle lights, you know.

It's a great kiss, a great lip-lock, and then, after a moment (maybe a minute, who's counting?) it's, well, it's not that great. It's just two (well, four) coldish lips with not enough suction or something. Like I'm kissing someone's kneecap, not that I've done this, but still it comes to mind. I try to replace the image with sweet red pandas, not to mention, um, young Kevin Costner. Still, nothing.

We break away. Kevin shrugs.

"I'd like to," he says, trailing off. I have to stop him. Like to what?

"I'm sorry," I say. "I just don't feel this way about you." I say it as gently as possible.

Kevin Costner sighs and looks down. "I don't feel it for you, either," he says. You're nice, though."

Yep, his champagne has worn off, too.

Ugh, harpoon through the heart. I'm nice? He's a dentist, and I'm the one who's nice? Aghh. I mean, it's good to be nice. Isn't that what everyone says? Do they mean it? Is it really? Okay, he's nice too, but I didn't say it out loud. And by the way, I'm not feeling nice right this minute, either.

He gives me his card. His DDS card. Which has smiling tooth characters on it. "But please, let's stay in touch."

I'm being rejected by a dentist who's handing me his business card. (Wait, is that Comic Sans?) I'm stunned, a little upset, and turning red. My mind is a blank. I know I don't feel it, but a little arguing wouldn't hurt my feelings, though another something in my brain says this is small of me. I want to be small. There are lights twinkling all around me. Something about the setting: It makes you want to be wanted. How can I fully appreciate twinkle lights without being adored by this man (okay, any man)? Yes, I have seen way too many movies. My feelings are hurt, and I may burst into tears. I told you romantic dinners never end well.

"Okay," I say, as I do often when my mind is a blank because if someone calls me on it later, I can just say I was at a loss for words and really didn't mean it at all. Or maybe I do. We just don't feel it the way Aunt Lucille wants us to. She returns from wherever she's been and looks at us with great hope, gratitude, and love. I hug her, feeling like a bad niece who couldn't even fall in love with her aunt's perfectly nice, cute, friendly, boring dentist (who doesn't love me, either). But the lights are still twinkling, and something in Aunt Lucille's eyes understands. She gives me a noisy kiss on the cheek, and we all say goodnight, caramel on our lips, something sweet to take with us.

I cry quietly in the car and lick my lips. They taste a little like the square butterscotch suckers I used to get as a child from See's. The ones that seemed to last such a long time. The tears wipe away the caramel taste too fast, and I hold tightly to my steering wheel surrounded by the Beetle, which, somewhat telepathically, drives home way more quietly than usual, without the slightest rattle and only a tiny bit of a reviving breeze in my face. My Beetle gets me.

18

Susan Hops to It

"At some point we're quickly approaching," Susan tells me, "we're going to be too old for job hunting."

I nod. "Although it is easier to search now," I say, though really, I've only ever worked at Kids Press and am grateful every single minute I can remember to be. As a SoCal girl, I should probably have a mantra for it, something to remind me of my incredibly good fortune, although I've found that just picturing Nelson's remarkably cheerful face, not to mention the extravagant lunches he often treats us to, does the trick.

"Easier is relative," Susan says. "Yes, we have all sorts of job searching sights on the Internet, but no, we have not all that many jobs for an art history graduate."

"You could teach..." I suggest.

"Teach other new art history majors that there are few jobs out there," Susan says, unusually downcast.

"That's no attitude," I say. "You need a readjust."

"Mom needs a café macchiato two shots of something," says

Libby from the backseat. She's right.

We're on a mini road trip today to check out a possible place of employment for Susan, and yes, we could all use a little shot of something but will settle for the drive-thru Starbucks in West Hollywood, which will then give us the fuel to hop on the freeway and head to a small town north of Pasadena called Altadena, which isn't known for much. We'll have to be careful with our drinks, though, as everyone who grew up here knows that the Pasadena freeway is—and has always been—incredibly bumpy, despite that they've been working on it since I was in my teens. Something about the freeway seems insurmountable, but as sunny Californians, we remain hopeful. Just be sure to secure your cup in the cup holder, or should you not have a cup holder, bring a friend with you. I don't think Starbucks ever intended to supply beverages to Pasadena freeway drivers.

We drink up. Susan drives a blue Prius hybrid with that little funny extra space in the back that extends the car slightly so you can add another bag of groceries from Ralph's or a large package of kitty litter and twelve cans of LaCroix, I happen to know. It's a Toyota, but it's so popular we often find a parking spot next to three identical vehicles. Same color and everything. We're part of something here, though yes, it is often hard to figure out which car in the lot belongs to Susan.

"The Bunny Museum," Libby begins to read a brochure from the backseat. She's the only one who can read in the car without barfing, which is not something you want to have happen on a job search, though this trip technically does not include an interview.

"I need details," I say to Susan. "How did you find this job?"

"Okay," Susan begins, fortified with caramel-based coffee. "I saw it on Indeed and then got another message from LinkedIn, and then five friends emailed it to me."

"Wow, you know how to network," I say.

"Again, just another reminder of how few jobs there are," she answers, heading onto the freeway. We all place our cups in their proper cup holders, of which the Prius is equipped with plenty.

"The Bunny Museum holds sixteen galleries in a 7,000-foot exhibition space that was previously an art gallery," reads Libby. I told you, she's an excellent reader. And no judgment in her voice whatsoever, which I know her mom appreciates.

"They're in need of a curator," Susan says, "and there would be fundraising involved of course, which is fine. I can branch out."

"So, we're talking real bunnies?"

"No," Susan says. "It's a collection of memorabilia celebrating the bunny in all of its forms."

"Huh," I say.

"No jokes, please," Susan adds. "No puns, no rhymes, no snide comments."

"I like bunnies," I say.

"I like bunnies," Libby says.

"You can bring that extra classy museum touch anywhere," I say. "Not that there's anything wrong with it as is. I hope."

"So, I applied, and they suggested I just drop by and take a look, wander around and get a feel for the place, then we'll talk another day. The owners aren't even there today, just a nephew of theirs running it on Saturdays."

"It has more than 40,000 bunny items," reads Libby from her brochure.

"That's a large number for you to read," I say, trying to

compliment Libby.

"We're counting into the Googleplex now," replies the first-grader. I hope I didn't insult her. I've always had trouble with numbers that need a comma and many zeroes. I still have to count the zeroes in threes after the comma to figure this out. Maybe I need to sit in on Libby's class even more often than I do.

"So, bunnies," Susan says.

"You like bunnies," her daughter reminds her. "And it says here that they do have a few real bunnies that you can feed. Did we bring carrots?"

"No," Susan says. "And we have to be careful not to touch the exhibits."

"And by we, you mean me, right?" Libby asks.

"I've been known to break the occasional tchotchke in a shop," I say. "Are we talking classical sculptures and artwork or cartoons and black velvet?"

"Yes," Susan says.

We get off the freeway and can resume holding our cup in one hand. It's that big of a difference. Freeway potholes are a thing here.

"I think that's it," Libby says. She has an excellent sense of direction for a child, but it also helps that there's a huge statue of a bunny covered in ivy out in front. He—or she, it's hard to tell and couldn't matter less—wears a painted-on multicolor jacket with orange pants, and yes, the pants are carrot colored. Bunny has pink circles around his eyes as if he/she is either tired or wearing a hip shade of eye shadow, and he/she smiles and looks ready to march or jog, whichever bunnies prefer for physical fitness, I guess.

"All purses go in the trunk," says Susan. "They're really

serious about keeping your hands tightly to your body."

"You are very, very brave," I tell Susan. She has an awfully serious face on, which I think means she agrees.

The building just behind Bunny looks like an older gift store, the kind that used to sell silver platters and crystal vases and glassware. The kind of place I also had to be careful what I brushed against.

I work in children's publishing in a room filled with toys. This could well be my kind of place, which is no doubt one of the reasons Susan has brought me along. Libby, appropriately, has a huge grin on her face.

"Go forth little bunnies!" I say as we all, well, hop out of the car.

"Happy Easter indeed," Susan whispers to me as we walk in. Because this place is bunny central. Floor to ceiling, but not in a bad way. If you loved bunnies (and you know you do), you'd love this place.

"Bunnies," Libby calls out to no one in particular.

Shelves lined with bunny figurines of every color and style, from realistic to way cute, cartoonish to google eyed to Bugs himself, though he's pictured dressed as a variety of famous women bunnies from the early motion picture days, like Veronica Lake Bugs, and Carmen Miranda Bugs, though I don't recognize the artwork from a movie or anything. You still can't not recognize what Bugs is up to, but it's hard to figure out why.

"Welcome don't touch," says the kid who must be the nephew. He wears big black glasses not too unlike what Susan wears with her curator uniform. The glasses tell us he's in charge, as does the Do Not Touch T-shirt he's wearing.

"Hi," Susan and I echo. She doesn't look inclined to tell this kid why we're here, possibly because he looks 16 and is wearing very expensive looking leather jeans, even though I think that kind of thing went out of style years ago. He doesn't introduce himself by name, so I shall forever refer to him as Outdated Leather Pants Guy.

"We don't allow touching of the artwork," he repeats.

"Says the Outdated Leather Pants Guy," I whisper to Susan. She nods. She got a look at the pants, too.

"But we can pet the real bunnies," Libby says, waving her printed brochure about the museum at him.

"Yes, the live animals are toward the back. Feel free," he says more warmly to Libby than to us, though this isn't really a place for kids. Still, she's no doubt closer to his age then we are.

"Well, I could work here," I tell Susan.

"You have dust allergies," she says. I do feel my eyes tickling a little.

"Well then," I say obnoxiously, "there must be dust bunnies."

Susan ignores me and takes the pamphlet from Libby. "The Bunny Museum began in 1998 as a private collection owned by a Pasadena couple," she begins reading.

"Solid footing, historic," I say.

"Huh. Says it's known as The Hoppiest Place in the World," Susan reads seriously, practicing her curator style. "Welcome to The Hoppiest Place in the World," she tries out in my direction.

"How's the salary?" I ask.

"Um, times are tough."

"It's a long drive out here," I say, though this isn't helpful. She nods and we look around.

"Bunnies!" Libby repeats. They must hear this a lot here.

There's a Hello Kitty that's a bunny, which isn't right at all, but I don't say anything.

"Oh," says Susan, "real ones!" We find Libby in an area called The Warden, petting two bunnies, one with each hand. These are big bunnies, white with brown spots, a little rodent-like but still cute in that bunnies are just cute and to think otherwise makes me feel bad. Like I'm breaking a rule that's important to me way deep down somewhere. Bunnies can only be cute. It's ingrained from childhood, I guess.

The thought of an ugly bunny just hurts me, somehow.

"Butterscotch and Jumper are Flemish Giants," reads Susan.

"Which is which?" asks Libby, but there's no way of telling, and leather pants guy is busy winding up music boxes in the front of the store, though I really think one music box wound up at a time is more than enough.

"Big bunnies," I say.

"Big bunnies, big hearts," Susan says, again with a brave face.

Bunny art lines the walls; bunny kitchen items fill a small room made up to be the kitchen, though it looks like the stove works, and I can smell cinnamon tea brewing. There's also a bathroom with an assortment of bunny object d'art if you like, including a little white bunny dressed in overalls holding a mini plunger. The art suits each room, kind of like at Chroma, Susan's color-based-rooms museum. But then, she's leaving that place.

"Oh!" Libby calls out. She's found an area where shelves along the wall hold what might be every bunny stuffed toy ever sewn, color coordinated, along with a plastic-covered couch with two real, purring cats on top of it. Libby slides onto the couch between them.

Susan reads from a small sign. "Poppy and Baby."

"They're real!" Libby exclaims. "I would so work here, Mom."

There's a large stuffed bunny riding a bejeweled child's bicycle hanging from the corner. I'll admit it's worth seeing and in its way is a real piece of art. I want to touch the baubles but as I said, it's hanging from the ceiling, which is way up there. This place is tall.

"Bling Bike by Art Romeo," reads Susan from another sign. "Decorated with eight pounds of vintage costume jewelry."

"Jewels," Libby says longingly, a large orange cat in her arms nuzzling Libby's chin.

Leather pants guy appears and admires the bike art with us. "One of a kind," he says, as if we couldn't figure that out. Though we all like it.

"Can we take a picture?" I ask. "Show it to Miralise? Great arts and crafts technique," I say, no insult at all meant to the artist.

"Photos from your camera are okay," says pants guy. "But don't let your child go in the back," he says, pointing to Libby.

"What's back there?" Susan asks, checking her printout.

"It's the Chamber of Hop Horrors," he says. "Rabbits' feet. Bunnies from horror films. Science experiments."

"God forbid," says Susan, directing Libby to stay in the couch area, where a TV set plays a nice bloodless Peter Rabbit cartoon.

"Not for the squeamish," he says, leaving us. Actually, he goes back there. We do not follow.

"It's like every museum has to have a dark side," Susan says.

"Is that a curatorial rule?" I ask. "Something in the mission statement?"

"Sounds like someone's bad idea," Susan says, taking in the whole of the place, the fuzzy, the feisty, the ferocious. A cat meows pleasantly and Libby laughs. There are worse places.

Susan looks toward that back room, then turns to me. We hear Vincent Price utter a scary warning and laugh in that Watch out! Shut your eyes! Don't look! Something bloody is about to happen kind of way that makes me really worry about the state of whatever bunny the movie's about to cut to.

Susan grabs Libby and almost runs for the door.

* * *

We return to Susan's house and switch gears, mostly because Susan looks like she has homicide on her mind, and we're none of us the violent type. She gives me a look, though, that those of us who have a best friend know: It says, Please get my daughter away from me now before I begin swearing something awful. Susan takes me aside.

"Please get my daughter out of here now before I begin swearing something awful," she says almost to the word. I told you, we go way back.

I, on the other hand, would like nothing better than time alone with my goddaughter. "Where would you like to go, just the two of us," I ask Libby.

She knows exactly where she wants to go since she's six, intelligent, and reads *Beach Living* magazine. And yes, she does look at the pictures. We all do.

"There's a new cat café," Libby says.

"Wow, decision made," I say.

Susan Googles the address and tells us she's going for a run.

"God help anyone who gets in my way," she says. But

it's Santa Monica. They all run fast here. I would so be in someone's way.

Libby and I jump in the Beetle and head for Washington Boulevard, a street just to the south of Venice Beach and a bit east, of course, as you can't really go west. This has always been this mishmash of a street, a wide boulevard filled with traffic to and from the beach and lined with shops, services, some really good restaurants you would never find if you didn't know about them, big-box stores, you name it. It's what's known as a main artery from east to west and is often packed post-beach trip by people trying to get on the freeway. People covered in sand in uncomfortable places, which could explain all the honking.

"This is new," I tell Libby. "I think it used to be a falafel shop."

"The one with the greasy potatoes?"

"Yeah."

"You just hate to see a place like that close," Libby says. Sure, health food stores are aplenty around here, but we value (occasional) really well-fried foods, too. Libby liked sucking the soft inner potato stuff from the skin, then Susan would eat the skins. It was a mother-daughter thing, but we'll have to make do.

"I thought they couldn't open a cat café because of health regulations," I say.

"Apparently," Libby says, "you can only open one of this side of the street," she says, pointing to the south side. "That side has different regulations."

"I think that's called red tape."

"Some adult's idea," Libby says with strong disdain in her voice, or like a six-year-old.

Beach City Kitties greets us. Gone is the old faded beige paint of the falafel shop, replaced by purple paint and pawprints on the outside. There's a door knocker shaped like a cat tail. I hold Libby up so she can knock it.

"Silly, but worth it," she says as I put her down.

We enter the small restaurant/shop to find a fun yellow and magenta checkered floor that you might not think would work but it totally does. We're surrounded by maybe seven small tables and chairs that look like they've been intentionally mismatched from thrift stores yet for some weird reason, you still wish you had them at home. One famous picture or poster of cats hangs on each wall around us—positioned just so, including that orange-y French Chat Noir one you see at every vet's office (but still appreciate).

"Oh, there's that poster!" I always say it. Doesn't matter where I am.

The women who work here wear pastel colored surgical scrubs featuring kitties all over them. Both turn to us and say "Meow!" in a really welcoming way.

"Here's how it works," says one whose badge reads Cat Mom/Angela. "You can get your tea and snacks out here, then you're allowed into the back kitty parlor for rest and relaxation with fuzzy cat toys and fuzzier kitties. You can take the tea back there, but not the food."

"Can we do it the other way," Libby asks immediately. "Cats first, snacks later?"

Libby has her priorities straight.

"Sure," says Cat Mom. "I like your style."

"Thank you," Libby replies.

"You know," says Cat Mom, "we're usually booked up but the party canceled. Must be your lucky day!"

Libby beams. I'm fairly pleased, too.

"Can I get you some chamomile tea?" asks Cat Mom. "With... milk?" she asks as the other two women all meow loudly at the word. I guess it's kind of like their way of saying "order up!"

Kitty café talk. It's good to know the lingo.

We head for the kitty parlor through the French doors in the back. The parlor looks out on a small garden I don't remember seeing at the falafel shop, neatly trimmed lawn and bird feeders, while inside the room roam a half dozen cats, some of them pawing the windows to try to attack the bird feeders, or maybe just the fat-cheeked birds gorging themselves.

"I love it," says Libby, though these are far from her first cats of the day. Libby loves all animals, but cats, well, she is my godchild after all. Libby's family has a bulldog named Harold. No one has ever explained it to me.

Libby practically throws herself on a cushion that's half chair, half floppy beanbag that makes a smoosh sound like there may be beans inside. Her attention is immediately caught by a white cat with a large dark circle above her eyes, a perfectly formed shape it would take most people ages to draw, not to mention at least a protractor or two.

My attention, on the other hand, is instantly caught by a guy sitting on the floor waving a feather tipped wand. As if wonders never cease.

"Hi, Girl in the '67 Beetle," Ben says.

"Hi, Ben," I say. I'd say he looks utterly out of place except for the weird fact that he doesn't. Even with the wand. The light blue T-shirt—no logo—over jeans says Saturday but also clean laundry. Funny how having no logo makes such a statement.

Libby is now covered in two white cats, one with the rectangle, the other with a heart shape over her butt, though this isn't the first thing you notice about her. A tortie cat eyes Libby like she could be of use someday, when the tortie is good and ready. Torties are like that, as many of you know.

"Libby," I say, "this is Ben. He's a mechanic and fixes up the Beetle." Among his other charms.

"Hey, Libby," Ben says. "Watch out for Morticia." He points out a small black cat that is about to jump on Libby's back in a way that might startle but still delight a six-year-old.

"All their nails are carefully trimmed," Ben says as Angela brings us tea. Angela is immediately attacked by cats but not at all fazed. I thank her and sit down not too far from Ben. Not too close you know, but not too far.

"Day off?" I ask Ben.

"Just an hour or two," he says. "Thought I'd spend some quality time." A fat gray tabby kitten chews on Ben's left pinkie. Ben lets it.

"That's Pugsly," Ben says, stroking the kitten's head with his free hand.

This could get serious, Amy. A roomful of cats, my goddaughter laughing, a guy practically nursing a kitten. Sometimes, it's worth taking a moment to appreciate where life has led you.

The tea is good, too, as if that matters.

"Gosh, come here often?" I ask. "We just found out about it."

"Great article," Libby says and one of the squirmy white cats climbs under her shirt. She's a pile of laughter at this point.

"It's new," Ben says. "Those are the owners out front. My

sisters."

"You're related to this place?" Libby asks, impressed, as a kitten pokes out from under the neck of her T-shirt.

"I am," Ben says proudly. Ben leans toward me and I can tell is about to whisper something that I really want to hear.

"Try the tuna sandwiches. These cat moms can cook." Ben turns to the tortie and yells, "tuna fish!" And I swear, the cat gives a low meow.

"Torties," he says. "Torties aren't afraid to voice an opinion when they're good and ready." I know just what he means but try not to let on too much. So I don't drool or anything. The guy knows his cats.

"Time for class," Ben says, handing me his wand and the nearly attached kitten. "Bye, Amy. Bye Libby. By Morticia." He bows to the cat. She's quite a little princess of a thing.

We wash our hands at the Kitty Clean Up station and return to the front room. I smile all the way through my tuna sandwich, which is grilled with red peppers, dill, and some kind of beyond-this-world yogurt-not-mayonnaise spread. Yogurt with benefits.

Yes, I'm thinking about the benefits.

Libby sips on a smoothie noisily, which as for most six-year-olds, means she's a happy camper. "I don't miss the potatoes one bit," she says. *Slurp, slurp.* "Oh—and yes, I do like that guy," she answers, as if I'd asked.

"Ben?" I ask? Though she was perfectly clear.

"The cats really liked him," she says.

I nod and listen to meowing from the back room.

But it's Ben I've been picturing in my mind since he left the shop. Images of him with and without a little gray cat. Both images are good.

19

It Feels Like Everything

I've spent the last week chin deep in fairy tale land. I get up, go to the office, work on Goldilocks, brainstorm, sketch. Go home, sketch, feed Lulu, sleep, dream of *Goldilocks in Space. Goldilocks Lost in Space, Goldilocks and the Final Frontier.* That's right, I don't have a working title. I hope no one writes it on my gravestone: *Never had a working title.* Yet, I persist.

It's been a week since the cat café encounter, and on Saturday morning, Ben calls and asks me if I want to take a walk on the beach. "Last minute. Nothing fancy." Oh, please don't put that on my gravestone: *Last minute. Nothing Fancy.* Not that I'll know what it says. Though I like being casual and spontaneous, really I do. Maybe that is the right thing for my gravestone. Maybe it's pure me, not an insult in the slightest. Maybe Ben senses this.

"I always want to walk on the beach, even when it's raining," I tell him, though I'm not sure why, as it hasn't rained in months. "I'm not afraid of mud," I add. I'm having a morning of brainstorming and seem to still be in that mind-set. Fairy tale land. Not quite reality. Stars in my eyes. I'm a little spacey, no pun intended. I've been working with a drawing pad, sketching Goldilocks in a jumpsuit, blue-and-white striped, non-gender specific. It's a handsome jumpsuit with patches and buttons that would no doubt appeal to any child, and yes, there's a penguin on one patch, for no particular reason other than I've never met anyone who doesn't like penguins, and I hope not to. A little oval over her heart reads "G. Locks" in the friendly way that a waitress' badge might. Or a mechanic's. Just saying.

"My car's running great," I tell him for no reason.

"I'm not surprised."

"Is this a date?" I am brave today. Brave enough to wear a blue-and-white jumpsuit, if only I had one. Brave enough to ask what this day holds. Brave enough to leave my routine and make new discoveries. Or maybe it's desperation. I've got to make some changes. Either way. I look at G. Locks' face on my desk; she seems to feel the same way. *Get out there,* her eyes tell me. *Discover.*

"Well, a walk on the beach, lunch, possibility of muddy feet," Ben says. "I've been on worse dates for sure."

As have I. My whole marriage was worse, and of course, Hooper whatshisface Tomlinson hated muddy feet. And sand. What was I ever thinking? How was I so taken in, and as Susan might ask, is that why I feel so afraid to move forward?

"What if I'd had plans," I ask Ben, semi obnoxiously. I don't have plans. You know I don't.

"Then I'd pretend I was asking for tomorrow. Then Monday. I'm flexible."

"Busy guy?"

"Never too busy for a walk on the beach, with the right company."

"Me, neither," I say completely truthfully, which feels nice.

Ben picks me up, and it's my first sighting of his car. I get that you can't judge a guy from his car, or maybe that you shouldn't. But you must know by now that I do. I judge everyone by his or her car. Maybe judge isn't the right word. If you have an old car—I actually admire that. Keeping old cars running gets extra points from me. It shows you care about something. Some might think you're just cheap, but as anyone who's tried to keep a classic car running knows, it's not a hobby for cheapskates. Probably costs less to buy a Ford Fiesta. Not that there's anything wrong with a Ford Fiesta. I'm sure it's fairly reliable and gets good mileage and has swell air conditioning. But if you care about old cars, well, it says something about you. Something I generally like. Call me a snob—I don't care. I also don't care if the car has a few dents or rust or a banged-up fender (though this might say something else about you, and I might not get in the car). Old cars have a place in my heart. That's all I'm saying. And my heart has been hurting a little lately.

Ben drives a T-Bird. Fifties-esque, maybe early sixties. Black with the top popped off. And Ben looks really good in it. Like it was made for him.

"I love it!" I gush. I can't help myself when it comes to extra cute classics. I have no control whatsoever.

Ben smiles behind his sunglasses. Yes, they're probably Ray-Bans, and they look old too, like maybe they're from the thrift store, a little banged up themselves. Maybe they came with the car. I have quite the imagination suddenly and am really stuck on this guy's car. Oh god, what if it's a borrowed car? No, this guy owns this car in every way.

"Why thank-you," he says with obvious fake modesty.

"Is it hard to keep running?"

"It's definitely a life choice," Ben says. "I've had to replace the radio."

"I hear ya," I say. The car is shiny and smooth. Yes, I'm touching his car in a possibly inappropriate way. And leaving fingerprints. Not that he's asked me to stop. It's just love at first sight. In fact, I feel like I know this car, and it knows me, and I've had nothing alcoholic to drink in a while so don't start wondering.

Old cars definitely get a reaction from me. Though this is a little extreme, even for me.

We drive to the beach not listening to said radio and not talking, just enjoying the vroom of the engine. I feel a little 1950s Grace Kelly-like, although I think I have the wrong make and model, if you know what I mean, and no head scarf on at all.

"Very cool," I say to the breeze. I'm smiling and don't even care what blows into my teeth. Though a scarf would have really helped, come to think of it.

Ben takes the long scenic route, which basically means he goes way out of the way so we can cruise because a car like this deserves it. And so do I. He finally parks carefully in a hidden lot I didn't know existed, in what looks like a special exhibition place for classic cars. Other men of various ages stand around admiring autos. They nod and wave to Ben, and approach to talk, then notice me and kind of turn right around, as if I'm something strange and off-limits. Ben laughs and points out a '63 black Beetle convertible.

"The guy brought it over when he moved from London," Ben

says.

"It looks like it could be my car's granddad. A classy distinguished granddad, with a sense of humor and candy in his pockets."

"It's the whitewalls," Ben says, and he's right.

We don't even have to pay to park. Maybe it's a club. There are a few women nearby, standing around a pink mustang from the sixties that looks like it would be any girl's favorite accessory. Women of assorted ages pose next to the car for pictures and as they say, laughter ensues. Two of the women wear old-fashioned 1960s style bikinis, pink ones. The men keep their distance, which doesn't feel wrong at all. The girls all wave to Ben, who looks at me and shrugs slightly.

"Just another day at the beach," he says.

We head for the sand. "So, where'd you learn about cars?" Ben asks.

"I guess I didn't realize I was learning anything, but Uncle Harry must have taught me a lot while I washed Aunt Lucille's Beetle from time to time," I say, remembering sudsing up the Beetle and drying it carefully with a thin cloth. "I was his assistant. I've always loved the Beetle."

"I think it knows that about you. It seems to smile a little when you're in it. If a car can do that. Which it can't, but yours tries."

"My car and I."

"You're in the right town," he says, gesturing around us at the people lovingly wiping imaginary dirt from their Camaros and Firebirds and one thing that looks like a truck reproduced with a VW.

"I'm not sure how I feel about *that*," I say, pointing.

"You're not alone in your ambivalence."

"Not your thing?"

"Can't beat a classic," this younger guy actually says to me.

We walk onto the beach, and I notice I'm not even worrying about tripping over indentations and mini hills of sand, which usually make me wave my arms around stupidly taking small steps. I seem light of foot, if that's a thing, and not a disease. I'm not really sure.

"My uncle once had a dune buggy," Ben shares.

"I loved those! Never got to ride in one."

"Then you've never experienced bumpy at its most wicked definition. It was like a Disneyland ride, but more intense. Maybe like a partially busted Disneyland ride."

I just nod, visualizing myself in a dune buggy, hanging on to some strap or metal bar or something. There's a big smile on my face, both in the pictures in my mind and, yes, probably on my face.

"What color?" I ask, still envisioning.

"Purple, of course."

"Oh, that's really good." We smile at each other. Ben's hand brushes mine. It's so L.A.: Talking about sweet old cars, walking on the beach. I've never felt I belonged to my city so much before. I may be a little clichéd. But I may have gotten past caring about it. And for some reason, my mind flashes on Ben's car again.

"Your T-Bird."

"Yep."

"There's something about it." I look at him—he's not laughing at me but listening closely, and I feel like I can confide a little more about my car craziness. "I feel like I knew your car in a previous life."

He smiles and yes, there's a dimple there just like on someone else I've seen recently but can't place at the moment. Am I nearsighted? Why does it take me so long to see things right in front of my face, not to mention on someone else's?

"You might not need to go that far back," he says. "It was your Uncle Harry's. He stopped driving it ages ago but couldn't part with it. He tucked it away in a garage and apparently went to visit it as often as he could. You've forgotten."

I'm stumped. Uncle Harry's T-Bird. I think he put it in storage years before he died, decided they didn't need to drive two cars, let alone park two cars in Santa Monica.

I stop walking and nearly fall over. "You bought Uncle Harry's car?"

"He sold it to me. He was very particular about who got it, I can tell you. A lengthy application process. Multiple choice and fill in the blank, plus a non-optional essay section."

"I do know that car," I admit to myself.

Yep." Ben leads me further to a spot on the beach screaming out for a picnic blanket, like, Pick me! Pick me! He drops his bag after pulling out a blanket to spread.

Quite a bit is screaming out at me right now. Or not screaming, just clarifying.

This is what people talk about sometimes, being in the moment. Feeling everything as it happens, and yet also realizing you're having one of those moments so you'd better stop to appreciate it. An epiphany, So-Cal style, but I am so not complaining.

Then it ends, as moments do, when I see a mirage of two people approaching me slowly but determinedly. My Beetle-like bubble of happiness pops, and I feel a sudden attack of sweatiness, which of course is really not at all normal for the Santa Monica beach.

I squint. The woman looks like a younger, blonder me, but blonde in a way that I never was, as in *Ha-ha, I'm blonde and I know it (and you're not, and you know it)*. Getting closer, she doesn't really look like me at all. It was just a momentary flash, almost a hallucination. She looks like a movie star. She looks like Barbie, not that I'm looking at her bustline. I'm not. (But, well, yeah.) I'm suddenly wishing for a world without Barbie. Once you've had one of those dolls, I don't think you ever feel right about yourself again. And in this particular moment, I don't feel right about anyone. Except maybe that group of twelve-year-old girls over there, sitting on towels, playing a no-doubt gender-free card game, completely and rightfully oblivious to the rest of the world. Oblivion is so underrated, if you ask me.

And it was such a nice day.

On closer look, it's not just that I see a living Barbie doll approaching me but that she's hand-in-hand with my ex-husband. When I get a better look, he's holding onto the manicured hand of a pregnant Barbie doll. Pregnant in a Barbie way, perfect all over with just a little bump in the front hidden under a tight swimsuit. Glowing skin, healthy hair, trendy bump. Looking around, I realize there is no graceful exit from the beach. Just tough-to-walk-in sand in all directions but one. Not that I'm above ducking into the waves. Just that I wait a second too long to veer westward.

"Hi, Amy," says Cooper, the ex, formerly known as Mr. Right, especially if you ask him.

"Hello," I say reluctantly because they have landed right in front of me. Are those highlights in his newly golden hair? Wait, which one of them is the Barbie here, anyway?

"Hey, guy," Hooper says to Ben as if he's trying to be cool

and not lawyerly at all. "Hoop Tomlinson," he introduces himself. Oh, and Hoop?

"Ben," Ben says. Ben doesn't give much away. Ben doesn't suffer fools gladly. Ben's hair is naturally dark and wonderful and seems to be lacking product in the way that all men's hair should.

"Amy," Hooper says, "I'd like you to meet Babe," he says, gesturing to the pregnant model dressed in a white tankini and a white shawl thing that whips around her in that *Vogue* way that doesn't happen in real life. "And it's her real name!"

Hooper you've gone over to the dark side, I think but don't say.

"I'm pregnant," Babe says, explaining away the bump as if no one here reads gossip magazines or Internet postings or has ever seen a fashionable pregnant woman before. (Okay, I've never seen one in real life.)

"We're expecting!" Hooper says. Hooper of the *I'm not sure I'd ever like to be a father* conversations from my past. Hooper, who I believe only recently mentioned something about a vasectomy. What is going on?

"I'd hoped to have a private conversation with you," Hooper continues, "but well, Kismet."

"Or something," Ben says, taking a cue from the look of astonishment and displeasure and who knows what else spreading across my face, which I can feel is turning red.

"Oh, Amy and I used to be married, but we were so young," Hooper says.

"Two years ago," I mumble under my breath. Wait, if we've been divorced a little over a year, is that one and a half years ago or more? Not that I could even tell you what day it is at the moment.

I should say congratulations. I know this. I won't.

"I had no idea," I say and mean about everything.

"Well, of course," says the new, lightened Hooper. *Hoop.* I can hear Susan saying it now. *Hooop.*

And can I say that the belly bump looks totally unreal. Can this be a hoax? You can get those things at prop stores, you know. It is L.A.

"Amy, could we talk? Would you guys mind? Just for a minute? Babe?"

Every time he says the name, I jump a little, even though thank God, Hooper never in his life referred to me as Babe. Or, now that I think of it, Honey, Sweetie, Dear, or any term of endearment. I have a startling memory of his once snapping his fingers at me to get my attention, although I might be hallucinating at the moment. Perhaps I'll wake up and find myself napping in my chair under Lulu as she purrs away. Or even under my chair. Or awake from a coma alone on a deserted island. Any of which would be better.

"Uh," I say.

Babe just smiles. Honestly and toothily, as if someone were about to take a picture, and she wanted them to. Then he touches her stomach, and I gag a little and feel like I might throw up.

"Or," Ben says, "we could just do it another time." Or not, his look tells me. He instantly does not like these people, I sense. His judgment is much better than mine.

"Right," I say, which makes Ben take my hand as if to steady me, but Hooper grabs my shoulder and seems to march me away from the shore, kind of like a lifeguard or policeman, telling me I've done something terribly wrong on the beach, like thrown a sand crab in someone's face or attacked a pelican. And all I was doing was gliding along happily. I would never hurt a pelican. I still feel sick to my stomach, which might explain why I let Hooper take me aside. It rings through my head: *He's taking me aside.* I always hated that phrase.

Which wakes me up.

"What do you want, Hooper?" I say in a not nice way, although not as meanly as I probably should.

"I know, I know. You must be so confused."

"Ickkk." It's all that comes out of my mouth, but I think you know what I mean.

"I met Babe. I'm still so amazed that someone like that would come into my life," he says. "I had the vasectomy reversed. And you know, it's all so long ago, that I'm not even sure if you wanted children."

Now, my mouth is just open. I did. I said I did. Okay, I wasn't 100 percent sure because I wanted someone to be married to me who wanted to have kids with me, too. So, I'm mouth agape, and I can feel my face wrinkling up, and wasn't this supposed to be a nice day at the beach with someone who likes me?

"I do know I didn't want to," Hooper says factually, ever the lawyer. A point he needs to check off a list.

"Go away, Hooper," I say. "Because I feel like if I were some kind of wild animal, a snake maybe, I'd spit at you right now. Or worse," I say.

I would grab him with my teeth and spit him out. Disgustedly. Then stomp on him with my sharp pointy feet (if I had them) or cover him with slime—either way. I wonder how you verbalize this. I could draw it for sure, and it would be scratchy lines and painful expressions and blood and gore. And I illustrate little kids' books, so this would be a departure. I can feel my hands wanting to grab something and make really heavy charcoal-like drawings. Venomous ones.

"All right, all right," he says. "But I have a subsidiary plan to make it up to you."

"A subsidiary plan?" I'll bet he never says the word *subsidiary* to Babe. And no, I do not believe that is her real name. Barbara or Babette or Bernice. I'm rooting for Bernice. I begin to walk away, and Hooper actually places his a hand on each of my shoulders, which I now realize are getting sunburned despite the sunscreen because sometimes, you just cannot protect yourself even though you tried, didn't you, you did try.

"I'd like to draw up a contract. I've thought about it," he says legalese-y again. "I'd be willing to impregnate you, given no further obligation, as laid out in a binding agreement that I'd be happy to have your lawyer review. I feel I owe you, and this would be payment in kind."

I laugh suddenly and loudly. I mean it—I crack up! If I had a mouthful of water, I could so drench him right now (and spit like an animal after all). It's one of those laughs that feels like it's not going to end soon, like I'm going to have to lie down, or bend over to contain myself, and that I'm going to cry with glee and run out of breath and then start coughing, but then start up again laughing just hearing the words reverberate in my mind. I am ha-ha-ha-ing all over the place. Then I take a deep breath to say something and yes, start coughing, waving away help, thoughts, cares, concerns. I'm engulfed in hilarity and I don't care.

Ben comes over. "Are you okay?"

I can't answer. I am laughter. Look me up in the dictionary.

Babe steps in. "This is bad for the baby," she says, and I double over, then kneel down in the sand, hysterical and no doubt unattractively so, but still in a really good way. Ben pulls out a bottle of water for me from his pack. Oh good, maybe I really will get to spit at Hooper.

"Maybe another time, Amy," Hooper says, then nods at Ben, who really just stares back. Another time, what? Impregnate me another time? (No strings, though.) Talk another time? No turkey baster required?

I sip water and calm down a little, but I'm still just over-whelmingly having a good time now. I feel happy, fully capable of seeing that the universe has a perverse but very enabling sense of humor. And it's telling me to enjoy my day at the beach. Opportunities like this come so rarely.

The happy couple recede down the beach probably in search of lunch and a prenup.

"Babe?" I say. I can see her white wrap trailing her in the breeze, but not in the Isadora Duncan kind of way I might hope for. Everything about her screams Condé Nast. But then, I'm in publishing.

I look at Ben, who is unpacking some cheese and apple slices—ruggedly sliced apples, not the kind in the bag from Trader Joe's. Which means he cares, it strikes me. Someone cares enough to cut apples for me. I might cry.

"I can't begin to explain that," I say. Plus, Ben's brought the really good cheese from Switzerland that I can never remember the name of.

"Old Hoop and Babe?" Ben says, shaking it off. "Just another form of exotic marine life."

I nod and inhale deeply. I know there's pollution and stuff, but it's beach air. It feels so good.

"No judgment," Ben says, "but he drives a BMW, doesn't he."

"Judgment," I say. "Totally deserved judgment."

"You know," Ben says, "I don't think that's a particularly

good guy."

"I'm getting that."

"I hope I'm not the first to mention this, not that it's my business." Ben hands me half a kiwi, the most adorable of all fruit. I pet the sides of it and pick up a small dainty spoon Ben has packed. How many guys out there pack little spoons? Ask yourself sometime.

"I think I may have had some kind of learning disability when it came to that person. Or maybe a little stroke. But I've made great strides overcoming it." I'm just figuring this out. But having Ben and Hooper on the same beach, well, the expression clear as day couldn't be more, well, clear.

"Glad to hear it. Gotta keep learning." Then he brings out little pastel French macarons, the kind that are (almost) too pretty to eat. And I feel a tear slide down the right side of my face because they're pink and green and mine, and no one has ever presented me with French macarons before. And of course—of course—they taste even better than they look, gently crumbling around my smiling mouth. And Ben's. If you're the type of person waiting around for a sign, you could do a lot worse than a pink macaron melting on your tongue and leaving delicate crumbs on your face, plus the face of the attractive guy across from you.

Ben leans over and gently kisses the crumbs around my mouth. (No tongue: I actually don't want someone licking crumbs off my face, though no offense if it's anyone else's thing.) Eventually, he lands directly on my mouth, and we press in equally, no one in any hurry, no one taking any kind of ownership role, the voices on the beach silencing, the Santa Monica version of mini waves making their little light rhapsody behind us. It's just the best. Plus, there are two packs of macarons. It's not everything. But it feels like everything.

20

A Buzz in the Air

"It is time for me to say good-bye to Chester."

"Wait, which one is he again? I get confused." Susan says. "Let's put it in terms even a child could understand," she says, though we both look around her house to make sure Libby isn't around. Not that Libby wouldn't understand. More like the six-year-old would probably offer some sincerely wise advice, or worse, make fun of us for being so dense.

"Chester is the older fellow with the groovy Volvo."

"Why does Volvo always sound dirty?"

"You know why," I say. We all know why. I have no problem saying the names of body parts out loud if needed. I just don't feel the need to at the moment.

"Okay, he's the one that's too old," Susan continues. We're drinking pink lemonade at her patio table like six-year-olds, come to think of it. But it's Trader Joe's pink lemonade from a pretty bottle, so there's that. "And Ben's the one that's too young, right?"

"Ben," I say, then quickly slurp lemonade so I don't have to say more. Ben.

"And the dentist guy is just right, numerically speaking."

"Jeremy. He's my age, if that's what you're saying."

"You know what I'm saying," Susan says. "Just sayin'."

"Jeremy's not right despite being just right. There are many factors to consider."

"Sing out, Goldilocks."

I twirl my hair for her. I've had it lightened (naturally, they say) and though I sound like a shampoo ad or something, I feel lighter everywhere. I sort of hate it a little bit that I have this response to how my hair looks, but I do. Getting a haircut makes me feel like I'm evolving, growing, and not just my hair. A little color? I'm not above such things. I don't need it, and I'd fight anyone who insisted that I do it. (I even fought Hooper about this, well, a little. I'd have preferred it to be my idea, not someone else's idea of what I should look like.) Now, I just like it. I'm not doing it for anyone else. Okay, I am sounding all Clairol now. I hate how commercials limit how we think about ourselves. I'm just doing it, and it's not hurting anyone, especially since it's the natural coloring with no multisyllabic petroleum products. I hope.

And yet.

"So, Mr. Right just isn't right," Susan says. "Welcome to the real world. There is no Mr. Right."

"Correct. But maybe I can get Mr. Right for Me," I say. "I can take in all the data of all the people, or in my Scientist Goldi model, all the planets. Facts, features, personalities, kindnesses. Compare and contrast. Look for what feels right, what I need, what I want, plus that little extra something—"

"That gives a little extra kick."

"Yeah."

"And Ben has that kick?"

"Yeah," I say quietly. Oh yeah.

She raises her lemonade glass. We're using wine glasses, but you probably could have guessed that. We clink. We clink our pink drinks, says the badly rhyming children's writer inside of me, so you can see why I'm really more of a designer. If I illustrated this scene, I wouldn't hesitate to put cheerful smiles on our faces and a few lines around our eyes (and just beneath my mouth on the left side). Because we're celebrating, which I'm afraid we too often fail to do, probably like most women. Let's celebrate everything we can, every day, every minute we can remember to. Lemonade is always a good idea.

* * *

Chester. Have I described Chester properly? Yes, he's older than me, with graying streaks in otherwise light brown hair with no particular cut to it, just not too long, but maybe a little longer than you'd think. Chester's a little short as these things go, maybe five foot eight, not that I'm good at numbers. I'm not too tall myself, so it doesn't really matter. He dresses grayish, professorish, which he is (semiretired). Sometimes he wears these smallish glasses. He's cute, maybe a little elfish, like your endearing absent-minded professor of yore who drops things. Likable. Nice. Funny. Perfect? Well, who's that, anyway.

We haven't been completely out of touch, just not in so much touch physically. Sometimes, we chat on the phone, Chester telling me what he's been reading, which is often something esoteric about philosophy, and sometimes even something

Tantra related, though not the sex part. (Who knew there was more?)

Chester and I meet at Montana Natural health food store, at a table outside. We're sipping healthy protein drinks because that's what people do now. At least they aren't green, so I count my blessings. The day, in case you couldn't guess, is magnificent, sunny, not too hot, not too, well, you know the rest by now.

"You look healthy. Very centered," he says.

"Well, that's good. You too," I say. I don't know what it means, but he doesn't look uncentered, so I'm sticking with it.

"I brought you these," Chester says, handing me a small box that's sort of decoupaged with purple and pink papers, although I don't know if decoupage is still a thing.

"Oh, you don't have to."

"I do! Look inside," Chester says proudly. *Don't be jewelry. Don't be jewelry*—I think.

Inside are several rocks. Or maybe stones, which sounds nicer. Purple, pink, a green, a deep blue. The purple may be a crystal—I don't know the geological difference between rock, stone, crystal, and just glass. I don't mean anything derogatory by calling them rocks, either. I like rocks. Despite the Charlie Brown "I got a rock" connotation.

"Thank you." I run my index finger over each. Smooth. Alluring even.

"Here," Chester says, handing me a little card with printing on it. "You can see the properties of each to know which to carry based on what your body—and spirit—need at any particular moment."

"That's very thoughtful," I say. I mean it. I'm no snob about new-agey stuff. I need all the help I can get. I may not be a believer, but they're nice rocks and would go well in a little dish or something by the couch.

"Let's both touch the amethyst one, together," Chester suggests in a way that's not quite dirty but still suggestive and kind of, well, strange.

"Oh, I don't know," I say. "I don't know."

"Okay, maybe later," Chester says. "Amy," Chester says. "I've found a retreat. It's just outside of Sedona. Special tribal experiences, aromatherapy treatments, time for reflection. For two. Intensive mud massages. Open-air bathing, clothing-optional chanting, guided meditation. The works. Let's go together, and see where it leads us. I think it's time. What do you think?"

Okay, it's not the worst offer. (Oh, that would be Hooper's offer of insemination. Yes, that's my worst offer so far and hopefully, ever.) I'd like to see Sedona. I like Chester. I'm game for guided meditation. I'm nowhere near ready for open-air bathing and clothing-optional anything. But the fact is, I'm not going to be with Chester. He's somehow both too old and too experimental, spiritually I guess, not that age is what it's about. It's just a number. Chester's so much more than his age. More adventurous or adventurous in a different way. No one's ever given me rocks before, and I like that, but intensive mud massages? It's just not right, not for me anyway. Plus, you know, Ben. Ben of the macaron kisses. Focus, Amy.

"Chester, I really like being with you," I say. And I mean it. I get such a kick out of Chester and his ideas and creativity, a real love for life. I could use a little more of all of that. "But I don't think I feel the way you might want me to, and I don't think it's going to happen. I'm sorry, I really am."

"I'm not looking for forever or everything. Just someone to

take on a spiritual if not spiritually physical journey. We could try Sedona," he says.

Would I rather do Sedona with Ben? Is that what I'm thinking? No, I don't see Ben doing clothing-optional chanting, although I like picturing him this way, if you know what I mean.

"I don't think it's what I'm looking for. I don't see myself going this way, exactly." I offer him back the stones.

"No, you absolutely keep those," he says. "The psychic at the rock shop helped me pick them out for you. They won't work for just anyone."

"Thank you," I say. The words *parting gift* roll through my mind, sadly. If I were on a game show, I know I'd feel like I lost something of potential value, but the parting gift is still very nice and kind of comforting, like a Barcalounger but way cooler, and easier to fit into your apartment.

We sip our thick, sweet protein drinks and split gluten-free apricot-date rolls that look like candy but aren't. "I think you should go to the Sedona retreat, though," I tell him. "It sounds like a wonderful opportunity." *Really unique,* I think, even though I know that phrase is grammatically incorrect and just plain-old redundant. It still feels appropriate.

"It does sound like me, doesn't it," Chester says with a shrug, perking up a bit. "But what about you? What about your spiritual journey?"

"I think I'm getting there," I say. "Getting somewhere, anyway."

"Finding your planetary station," he says, reminding me of Dr. Goldi's search for celestial well-being and a place we can all call home, if need be. Hoping to find a place (or person?) that's just right for the future, or maybe just for a few decades, if not millenniums. Keep your expectations reasonable, but hope for the best. The scientific way. I was an English major, so I'm guessing here. But that's what my scientist Goldilocks book is going to be about. Wisely choosing the best possibility that appears in front of you, often unexpectedly, and maybe even being thrilled with your discovery. Not that you weren't looking, just that you didn't realize how great what (who) you find might be. Making a discovery beyond your wildest dreams.

Chester grabs a game of Masala off the sideboard, and we play with the little stones fairly happily, somewhat hopefully, drinking not-quite-perfectly-blended juice that sticks slightly to our tongues, a somewhat loving sensation that lets you know you are alive at this moment, at the very least, albeit drinking something weird.

* * *

On Monday, I drive to work, where nothing at all seems normal.

"It's the day of reckoning," Hannah tells us when we're all collected.

"Bible, right?" Nelson our boss asks. "Or is it from *Ulysses*?"

"*Valley of the Dolls*," Chris says softly. "Classic."

"It's my last day and my last field trip. Line up, please," Hannah says, and I swear she motions girls on one side and boys on the other. Chris is hopping between lines because he would and thinks it's cute. None of us really knows what to expect, but it is Hannah's show today—her last one. On a Monday, which strikes me as strange for a last day. But then what isn't strange about Kids Press and our stern manager, Hannah?

"We're headed to the beach. Feel free to bring your work,"

she says. We're only a few blocks from the beach as is, but not one of us says anything.

"Play day at the beach!" says Nelson, who I suspect knows where we're going, as does his assistant, Kelly, who always knows everything. Plus, she has two clipboards, which is a little much even for her.

"We're you a Boy Scout?" Chris pokes Kelly. "Always prepared."

Kelly hits Chris over the head with one of the boards. Not hard, but hard enough to make a clunk sound the rest of us can appreciate. Chris winces.

"Girl Scout," Kelly says.

"Aren't they all just scouts now?" asks Nelson. "Like you're not allowed to attach a gender-related adjective?"

"Boys sell Christmas trees; girls sell thin-mints," Chris says.

"That's what makes this country great," Nelson says. "Or it's what makes this country something or other," Nelson says.

"Thin mints alone make the country great," Chris says. "And, they're nondenominational."

"But it takes a Girl Scout to raise a village," says Kelly, who whacks Chris on the head again, a little more gently. I sort of get what she means and appreciate the ferocity with which she says it, even if her metaphors are mixed up.

I take Hannah's suggestion/warning seriously and grab a few mock-ups of my Goldilocks project. I got ambitious last night and felt inspired by genius—or it could have been the Frappuccino I splurged on after leaving Chester. I know sugar is bad for me and that I should cut down. I plan to. After 40. Like a prize for reaching middle age, if middle age is now 40. I'm guessing it is—and just thinking about it makes me wonder how I'll ever give up Frapuccinos. Maybe cutting back will be

255

enough. Or maybe 50 is the new middle age, which works just fine for me, too.

Prize might not be the right word for turning 40 in several years, but I'm sticking with it for now.

Dr. Goldi has come a long way in the deep-dark productive hours of the night. Gone is any semblance of long ringlets, I'm happy to say. Dr. G has slightly blonde brown hair in a no-nonsense, age-appropriate, shoulder-length shag cut with slight waves that can be pulled back into a scientifically inclined ponytail or brushed a little for a fun, happy, take-me-as-I-am look fit for any social (or antisocial, hey, no judgment) situation. In fact, as I've drawn her, a good shake of the head will make this haircut work for the professional woman on the go, whether she's going to outer space or not.

I like her. She's not me, exactly. She's cool. She's cool without trying, scientist-cool, coolest girl in the room because she's smart, and smart enough not to need to fuss with an overly trendy, fussy haircut. She has places to be, people to see, planets to discover. (No nail polish, either, although I know I'll get in trouble with someone about this, possibly Libby.)

Every time I think of Dr. G, I have to fight the urge to shake my head a little over our shared haircut glee. But why fight it, Goldi, I mean Amy?

Dr. G dresses cool. Kind of like Libby, actually. When Dr. G wears a skirt, she's got pants underneath, and boots that look a little like those old moon boots—soft and squishy and comfortable. Another sketch has her in roomy pants and what used to be called Wallabees, I think, topped with a sweater that says I Heart Science, with a cute little pic of a heart, the atrial kind. And very, very groovy in-your-face black glasses over butterscotch-colored eyes. Let butterscotch be the new blue, say I. Let's abolish this blue-eyed priority thing altogether. Maybe Dr. G's eye color should change every page. Maybe her irises should sparkle different colors with every discovery. Or not. Maybe eye color is just that, nothing more, although maybe I'm overly optimistic. Amy Shepherd, changing stereotypes, one eye color at a time.

No eye makeup. She knows who she is: a scientist. She knows what she wants: to discover the best possible planet to be a friend to Earth. These are the voyages of Dr. Goldi. To certainly go where no man has gone before. Screw Maybelline.

Dr. Goldi is a scientist. She has no doubt taken some kind of oath—even if it's just one in her mind—to serve as a discover for the greater good, a woman of the planet, a believer in the powers of math and science above all. She has a fondness for machinery, binoculars, telescopes, scopes and such that measures down to a mili-something, if not smaller. (Okay I need to read more *Science Digest*.) She is our hero, our savior, our girl in the field, so the fact that she has a cool, individualistic, I-like-it-like-that style in the way she dresses is completely secondary, though it makes life easier for the illustrator and girl-behind-the-Goldi, me.

And if we were to see her on the road, she'd drive a '67 Beetle, light blue, with or without a really adorable mechanic beside her. And she'd always be in the driver's seat.

I just love her.

* * *

We find ourselves at the MyBug guys' offices again. We walk into their shiny building in Marina Del Rey, but it's altogether different inside now, more inviting. Instead of vast walls of white and cold-looking tables of wood and metal, it's like a dream cottage come true. Everything you'd want. The walls are colorful, splashed with periwinkle and lavender colors; posters of kids playing, birds playing, musicians playing, puppies playing.

"Puppies," Kelly says, but you know we're all thinking it.

"Hmm," Hannah says, far less critically though than you might think.

"Welcome," says the tall, cute Swiss guy, who goes right for Kelly, but I think he means all of us.

"Hey ya!" the one called Paul yells. I think it's a greeting, at least. Hannah glares at him, and he pretends he was going a different direction. And who can blame him?

"What's happened here?" Chris asks me. I just shrug. The room looks as if Libby had her way with it, with pretty canopies here and there over worktables stacked with actual artists' materials, paintbrushes and paper (that's right, real paper), easels to one side. It's possible it reminds me of Libby because, well, there is Libby, my godchild, standing to the side of this area doing the Carol Merrill move, the ta-da gesture of talk shows and show and tell.

Libby's whole class is here with their teacher, Miralise.

And Hannah is smiling, and god knows when that happened last. And Susan is here. I'm having a *This Is Your Life* moment, but in a good way.

Because throughout the room, we see Nelson's old toys displayed. There's an area for wind-up toys (I notice some of the more expensive ones are in cases), but you can play with many, too, and kids are. A cacophony of wind-up toys with animals making noises and cranks making motors run. An area of dolls by sizes. Susan hangs some old children's artwork.

Why is Susan here? Not that I'm not glad to see her.

"Cool," say Gabriella and Jefferson together, admiring an ancient How High Can You Hit hammering type machine you might have found at a kids' fair in the '60s. Or '50s.

"I love it," Nelson screams. "I smell cotton candy!"

"I smell it too," Chris says, though I'm worried that it's our imagination.

"I didn't realize these toys had a scent before," Kelly says.

"It's one of those scents you can taste," I say, imaginary pink sugar melting onto my tongue.

But no, we're not imagining: There's a little cotton candy area to the side, where you can get snacks, along with a small, mandatory clean-up sink for washing your hands. I sense it's mandatory because of the enormous You Must Clean-Up! sign overhead. In neon lights, which fits the theme really well.

"Welcome to the Children's Art Museum of the Marina," says Susan, the former curator of the Colorful Museum that was, or maybe still is. Not that we'll be visiting, I imagine.

Nelson applauds. Hannah looks guiltily pleased if not just plain responsible.

"Well done," Nelson says to Hannah, as he goes over to shake Susan's hand. I seem to be one of the few not in the know here. Even my six-year-old godchild knows more about what's going on than I do. But maybe she always has.

"Libby," says Chris, reading my mind yet again, "Could you please tell us what's going on?"

We turn our attention to Libby, who is wearing the kind of headband that could serve as a tiara, if you were royally inclined, or British, I guess. She turns from side to side to show it off. It's sparkly.

"Very nice," I tell her.

"So is my new job title," she says.

"Princess of the toys?" Chris guesses. Libby grimaces.

"Vice President of Children's Creativity," Libby says. Her mom, Susan, joins us.

"Accept nothing less than vice president, I say," says Susan.

"And you are here because—" I ask

"Isn't it right that I be here for Libby's promotion?"

"Yes," I say, "but there's something about the design of the room that screams you had something to do with this. That, and you're wearing a name tag that says you're a vice president, too." I can't quite make it out.

"Always the vice president," Chris says, "never the—"

"Yeah, yeah," Susan interrupts him, "you want to stop right there."

"I can't read it," I say, reaching for her name tag on a lanyard. A Hello Kitty lanyard.

She reads the name tag to us. "Vice President in Charge of Everything."

"I like it," I say.

"Long," Chris says, "not to mention overwhelming and intimidating."

"And accurate, I'll bet," I add. Susan looks really happy. Everyone in the room looks really happy. Libby shows off a series of jack-in-the-boxes that feature creatures who aren't Jack. One has Cecil from *Beanie and Cecil.* I'm not sure how I know this.

"Surprise," Susan says with no surprise in her voice at all. Major deadpan. "I found a new job," she continues.

"And it found you," Nelson comes up to Susan. They look like they're in love. With the museum, of course.

"All my toys have found a home," Nelson says. He's pretty

giddy, actually.

"Where'd the offices go? Are we all working here now?" I'm alarmed and yet: I notice a selection of Raggedy Anns I'd like to check out, and wait, isn't that doll a Goldilocks?

"We all work upstairs," the serious Swiss boy/man says. He and Libby mirror more game show host/hostess moves, inviting us up a newly installed fun-looking stainless-steel stairway. The kind that makes that great stomping noise when you step, as if you're at a playground. We stomp our way up.

"That's right; that's right," says the nervous one, Paul, behind us, herding us up like sheep, if sheep were to somehow walk on steel steps (which I doubt). "Right this way; right this way," Paul says, barker style. Then he gives Libby a fist bump and I suddenly think the world of him. Funny what a gesture can do.

"Here we are," says the nice tall guy, Joel. "Your offices await."

And yes, it's nice. Lots of artwork on the walls—some done by kids, maybe, some from films, some blown-up book covers. The desk space is open—no modular walls for us, thankfully, but spaced far apart enough to be somewhat private. Plants on desks. Mugs shaped like Felix the Cat holding brightly colored pens. A troll doll with colorful hair on each desk.

"New chairs!" Gabriella and Jefferson say together again, grabbing one each and spinning around. High art chairs in powder blue pleather (I'm assuming). All of our chairs are colorful. All of our workspaces are a pretty light gray with splashes of color: chartreuse magnets, peacock blue pencils.

"And new computers," Hannah says.

"I'll handle that!" Paul runs over and begins turning each one on, happily humming a tune that sounds like it's from a

1960s race movie. He practically buzzes. The whole place does, really.

"Welcome to the new It's Your Bug Publishers," says the Swiss Michael. Kelly is right next to him. He hands her a big office key that's decorated with je wels. Barbie would dig it. Kelly kind of likes it, too, and blushes.

"It's really hard to say just who the princess is here," Chris whispers to me.

I guess hearing us, Joel grabs a box, then begins passing around golden crowns for each of us. Susan shows me to my desk, where a small Goldilocks fairy beams beside my lamp. Holding a magic wand. Paul turns on my computer, grabs the doll and taps the wand on the large screen (we're talking super large, here), then hands her to me.

"Vice President of Astonishment," Chris reads the placard on my desk to me, and I feel my own face get hot. Then he runs to the next desk—clearly his because there are Bobby figures next to his computer (the Bobby with a broken leg and the Bobby with a chipped tooth). He picks up his placard and reads.

"Vice President of Imagination and Childlike Play," he reads.

"And yes, there's a raise," Hannah says.

Someone turns on '80s music for dancing. As if the day could get better.

21

The Universe Conspires

The event tonight screams out Goldilocks! but not in a way that would frighten small children, say. It's the premiere for my new book, the night of my book reading here at the new-and-improved It's Your Bug Publishers—IYB for short because it's all about the acronym, Paul tells me. It's taken us months to get it all together, but tonight is for festivities. It's a party scene. A children's party. Balloons, party hats, finger-size foods, plastic cups with lids, which, let's face it, are appropriate at any age. Ask anyone who frequents Starbucks. They're just giving you the adult-sized sippy cup you know you've always wanted. Why would anyone ever not want a cover on their cup?

The office/museum is alive with banners, pictures of my new Dr. Goldi Locks. Chris did pitch the surname Lox, and I liked it, but somehow it got voted down—I guess some people are afraid to stray too far from tradition. I suspect it was the Swiss guy, though he's helpful in every other way.

So okay, in case you'd already figured it out, Dr. Locks does look a lot like me. Oval face, hair tinted a little blonde, or maybe she just hangs out (sun-screened) in the sun, which is healthy in small doses even for a picture book character, I suspect. This Goldi has her vitamin D down. My own hair is now kind of tousled—I've given up blow drying because, well, why not, and what took me so long? Like Dr. Locks (okay, kids can call her Dr. Goldi, again because we need to work our way off tradition one surname at a time), I'm sporting some fun dark frames I found on the boardwalk (where she got hers I happen to know, since I'm not just the illustrator but the writer as well). I had them filled with my prescription and tossed my contact lenses, which were old anyhow, so I didn't feel like I was being wasteful—just plain brave. Everyone loves my frames, and I feel kind of groovy, if that's still a word anyone uses. I use it proudly and suspect I always will, especially in these frames.

The Dr. Goldi book, *Dr. Goldi Locks Searches for the Perfect Planet (or at Least One That's Just Right)*, is out in all the stores. You can buy a version for your MyBug (also new and improved, and somehow, not quite as creepy as the earlier versions) and change the endings and add new (female) physicist assistants, as well as kittens and puppies. Kelly suggested the kittens, and I let her draw a few for the prototype—several of which I used. She even has a credit as Kitten Illustrator—apparently, she's been harboring a desire to contribute but was too shy to ask. She's good, which I do not hesitate to tell her every single day.

In the book, Dr. Goldi discovers a series of new planet possibilities and calculates why each one might be a little too big, a little too small, or just right, along with other qualities, like too bright, too purple, too infested with ladybugs. Though I still question whether you can ever have too many ladybugs. But Dr. Goldi fears it might be too distracting to get any work done at all if you're surrounded by ladybugs, and as her author, I had to let her speak. Does a hexagonal planet present too many problems for humans? The answer: depends on the gravity situation. I actually found a physicist, Dr. Jill Yesko, who helped with some of the science, though most of it was beyond me in every way. She felt strongly that a hexagonal planet without sufficient gravity would be more trouble than it was worth, no matter the number of attractive insects and flowers. She's also credited in the book as Scientist in Chief and duly thanked.

You just know she wears big black glasses.

The planets run the gamut from beautiful to really scary. Kind of Tim Burton scary. For this, I asked Chris to contribute. He was all over the idea of a frosty, midnight blue, forbidden planet, though he admitted he still found it a little attractive and wouldn't hesitate to check it out if he were an astronaut. I believe he's seen too many space movies. Most of the kids I've shown the planet to do shriek appropriately, though some just nod and say Cool.

You can do some interesting things on the MyBug with that Forbidden Planet—just imagine the creatures you can make crawl around, and should you desire, eat one another. This story arc is not for the squeamish, but you know, something for everyone.

Okay, Libby calls it the boys' planet.

You can play with the other planets, too, make flowers grow, use little scientific formulas (thanks, Dr. Jill) to increase the temperature or length of day, or just change Dr. Goldi's glasses should that be your thing. (There's an excellent illustration of a pair of Oliver People's glasses in a light tortoiseshell color that I've always wanted—just saying.)

The options are nearly endless, although I suspect you can't find your own planet without the PhD. But otherwise, the MyBug guys have developed the capability to lose yourself for hours changing things around, adding elements to space (the endless frontier, indeed), and even doing some math problems, should that be your thing—they're well hidden within riddles, and I can't answer some of them, which doesn't bother me too much. But a little.

You can also create short stories about the planets, add to Dr. Goldi's log/journal of planetary and personal notes, and create haikus about the space system by rearranging a whole bunch of space-age terms, and include your own. Both halves of the brain can be completely occupied by the story. The toy and book are approved for ages five to a zillion, the packaging says.

And nowhere does anyone ask Dr. Goldi if she has a boyfriend or is married. Or divorced. Or if she has a lot cats. It's not part of the story. There are quite a few female physicists and only a couple that are male, and no one says a thing about it. And even by using the MyBug, you cannot change this at all.

Although some of the kids I showed the rough draft to (in Libby's class) did want to know if they could use the MyBug to make some of the scientists marry one another, so they could throw a big wedding and dress them up, then have the ladybugs fly around, but I told them no. Not in this storybook. That's not what our story is about.

Though in the second round of MyBug development, marriage may just be an option. I'll be the judge of that.

After I read part of the book to our crowd of virtually everyone I know—mostly first-graders—we gather for punch, which is the same purple color that I've used in the book for the universe, or at least the punch color is as close as parent-approved natural grape food coloring will allow. My book isn't pastel girly; it's more a kaleidoscope of colors, embracing the wacky, wild, and unknown I think this Goldi Locks gravitates toward. (Okay, I also have a new bedspread this color. I believe I've earned it.) The kids move past the punch bowl to check out a large sculpture of a telescope, patchworked together of various metals, different colors, and a few odds and ends (yes buttons and playing cards and rubber balls; not anything sharp or scary). The artist? Well, you might know him.

It's Ben, my mechanic (though this phrase means so much more and I don't mean anything dirty by it at all, really I don't). Ben has welded together this elaborate, five-foot-tall, hippie/steampunk/just-plain-fun telescope. And it works. Seems he welds, and well. Not that this should surprise anyone in the entire universe.

"Step right up," he says to me, wanting me to have the first look. It's pointed out the window, but just in case it's cloudy out, we've hung a few planets—Jefferson a nd Gabriella's designs that will be sold with the book. They are cute and educational, and the MyBug sales guy was into it.

You can also play a game on the MyBug with Goldi and her planets, with lots of different moon boots to choose from. Libby insisted.

Let me just say that after months of hanging out together, I love Ben. Though I really sensed it much sooner. But it's new to me so maybe I had trouble deciphering it: love without the pain and anguish part—something way closer to just right. I'm taking it slow, being careful, and feel really happy almost every single minute—whether he's around or not. You might think it's impossible to really be happy almost every single minute, but I've sat with a watch and timed it. Susan has held the watch. Okay, there might have been fermented grape–filled drinks involved in sitting there with the watch, but there's nothing wrong with that. It beats drinking alone and miserable, not to mention drinking because you're alone and miserable.

The thing I want to stress about Ben is that I love how devoted he is to cars. I love how interested he is in learning new things—he's taking a class in hydroponics, specifically about growing plants in water for third world usage—and I like hearing about it. About whatever topic strikes him. And as I was working on this project, he looked over and saw my telescope drawing, and mentioned he'd like to weld one for the kids to play with in the office/museum (which we call the office-slash-museum, though Chris has taken to calling it Kidsville, USA).

"You can weld a telescope?" I asked Ben.

"I can weld almost anything, though four-legged creatures come out a little wobbly," he said.

I just want it to be clear that I respect Ben for who he is. I have no illusions or hopes he'll turn into someone else. He doesn't have to become a great artist, a fine welder, or even a save-the-world hydroponics specialist in his spare time. If he wants to, I'm all for it. But I've come to love the smell of the mechanics garage, which is the smell of Ben, five or six days a week. It reminds me of Uncle Harry, of the Beetle, the old T-Bird. It's probably like walking into a kitchen that smells of cooking herbs and lasagna for some people, or maybe roasted chicken. To each her own. I go for the smell of grit and American automobiles from the modern age, and I don't care who knows it.

* * *

Aunt Lucille walks in beaming, wrapped in a color let's call galaxy blue for the occasion. The man on her arm, escorting her through planets of pink and green, is Chester. Chester of the rounded Volvo and adult board games and creative dating scene. And he looks not just pleased but smitten. And it doesn't hurt a bit.

"Aunt Lucille?" I say raising my voice at the end as well as my eyebrows. "Don't you look wonderful!"

"I'm so glad you and Chester got a chance to know each other," she says, only a little bit creepily but still approvingly. Chester beams.

"She was always my favorite piano teacher," says Chester, dreamily. Chester, it's clear, is madly in love with Aunt Lucille. And maybe always has been. But who isn't? I like him with her. He's a younger man for her, which somehow feels, let's face it, just right.

"Plus," Aunt Lucille says, "we're going to move in together." It's only a little shocking because Chester looks kind of mischievous at the moment and of course, I had no idea whatsoever.

"I'm finally adding on to my old house. Your aunt will have her own studio for art, meditation, everything!"

"So, you can stay at the condo," my aunt says, then takes a good look at Ben. "For now."

Both Aunt Lucille and I have ended up with younger men. I think I might use this in a sequel for Dr. Goldi Locks, if she's ever into dating. Or maybe another children's book entirely. It could be a whole new area to explore. Maybe poor little Bobby, of the divorce and illnesses and injury book series, could use a little bit older girl falling for him. A babysitter maybe. Imagine what it could do for his self-image.

Although it sounds like I'm branching out into young adult books, if not flat-out risqué romance. Still, I can't picture Bobby on the cover with his shirt off Fabio style. I don't think anyone should have to picture this.

I may be thinking a little too much about work at the moment. Digressing from life. Which I'm happy to get back to, as this room pretty much incorporates my entire world, if not universe.

Hannah, our former director and Nelson's right-hand woman, steps up to Aunt Lucille, and they embrace, which is a surprise to me. Then again, Aunt Lucille does know everyone in town. One big happy family, it turns out.

But Hannah never seemed particularly huggy to me. "What are you doing here," I ask. I thought she and her husband were moving away somewhere.

"Hannah is taking over the column for me," Aunt Lucille explains.

"I'm going to whip readers into shape," says Hannah a little too literally, I think. She may be the opposite of Aunt Lucille's warm and fuzzy advice columnist, but maybe it will grow on her. Or maybe it really is a whole new world and we should get ready to take on some more serious issues.

"I thought your husband's job was moving away?" I ask.

Hannah shrugs in a way that indicates she still holds a lot of sway. "I talked him into retiring instead," she says. For a second, I think maybe she winks at me.

Ben steps up to my side. He and Chester shake hands in a way that's friendly and nice. Aunt Lucille watches, one eyebrow only slightly raised in amusement and approval.

"Aunt Lucille, you're giving up your column?"

"For now. We're going to travel!"

"I've found a salsa cruise to take your aunt on," says Chester.

"Salsa the food or salsa the dance?" I ask.

"Both!" Chester says excitedly. I can kind of see it.

I smile at Ben. I don't think I need to explain any of this, which is a big relief. It just is. It's okay with him, his smile tells me back.

Susan passes by dragging our boss, Nelson. Or is Susan now his boss? Just like Nelson's relationship with our editorial director Hannah, it's kind of hard to tell. Nelson needs a strong hand. Susan needs a job she can feel passionate about, involving art and kids and producing something you can be proud of. Having her curate the toy museum is so win-win. All of which I understand so completely it makes me want to cry a little. Because my best friend and I have come to a happy ending, for this chapter of our lives at least.

Neither she nor I have mentioned bunnies ever again.

Ben takes my hand but is interrupted by Libby, who asks him to come back to the telescope.

"You're needed for science," she tells him in an official manner. It's clear that someday, we'll all work for six-year-old Libby, anyway. Well, she'll always seem six to me.

"Excuse me," Ben says, following his small boss. I watch him walk off, and I know I'm smiling, so it's not like anyone feels the need to embarrass me further by pointing it out or commenting on the nature of my extremely wide and goofy smile. Though I can see Susan is trying hard to keep some comment to herself, as she seems to be physically pressing her lips together to suppress something.

Instead, I watch Ben direct the kids' gazes toward the stars out the window. There's a planet out there with Goldilocks' name on it, so to speak. A whole universe to explore.

I join Ben at the telescope anyway.

He turns to me. "Did I mention I saw this adorable kitten at the farmers' market rescue group?" Ben asks me, fake innocently.

When Lulu, who is not the touchy-feely love-at-first-sight type, met Ben, she scratched him hard on his right hand. But he held it right back out for her to sniff, blood dripping on his jeans and everything, and I swear that within ten minutes, she was hooked. She has always shown impeccable judgment. Although I'm not sure she wants a kitten in the picture, I'm ready to make the next commitment.

And let my universe expand, albeit gently.

The End

Thank-Yous

Thank you to my medium-size boatload of friends near and far who've come with me on this fun journey. Special thanks to Cindy Lambert for her more than 25-year-long conversation; Jill Yesko for all things Yesko and Lenhoff; Jane Rosenberg LaForge for motivating and understanding emails (and occasional visits); and Jennifer Ball, Linda Childers, Jinny Chun, Marissa Commins, Cindy McDonald, Lynn Muradian, Vicky Norton, Keri Northcott, and Christina Pitcher for years of friendship and support. Angioline Loredo and Rick Mumma: Neither of you is in this book (this time), sorry. And I'm sending major love to my baby cousin, Corinne Karr—I'm going to give you such a big hug when it's safe. Jackie Garcia: Thank you for teaching me how to use Canva. Thank you times infinity.

Many thanks to Mandy Miller for her close reading and suggestions for "the Beetle book."

Super thanks and lots of love to the Everitt clan, all the way down to the tiniest new additions. And my deepest thanks and love to Michael and Casey Everitt for being my family and sharing our little stories.

And thank you to Lulu and her fuzzy kind.

About the Author

Linda Lenhoff's first two novels, *Life a la Mode* and *Latte Lessons*, were published in 2005 and 2008. *Life a la Mode* served as her thesis for an MFA in Creative Writing and has been translated into four languages. It was also a Literary Guild selection. An upcoming novel, **Your Actual Life May Vary*, was recently named a finalist for the SFWP Publication prize and the Galileo Press prize, and will appear in 2022 or 2023. Linda works as a writer and editor in the San Francisco Bay Area, where she lives with her husband and daughter. She writes about books, travel, and the little things that get us through the day.

Author photo by Haley Nelson.

You can connect with me on:
- https://lindalattelessons.wordpress.com
- https://twitter.com/LindaLatte

Subscribe to my newsletter:
- http://lindalattelessons.wordpress.com

Also by Linda Lenhoff

Don't miss Linda's first two rom-coms, *Latte Lessons* and *Life a la Mode.*

Latte Lessons

Claire Duncan seems perfectly happy at her copywriting job for a small advertising agency in Venice, California. But it's a big surprise when she begins working with a new band of boy singers. Is the band's young leader becoming infatuated with her? What does this mean for Claire's relationship with Dennis, the other copywriter in the agency, with whom she shares an office space, allowing her to spend time guessing just how and when he'll spill his next cup of latte? Claire would be happier if her recently widowed mom would stop taking her along on double dates. Claire's pal Jackie has a few dating suggestions, including lists of eligible men to choose from. Can Claire deal with sudden success, not to mention the jealousy of her boss? Can she figure out what's going on with her therapist, who seems to be getting a little too friendly with the men in Claire's life? Join Claire as she takes control and learns a few important latte lessons.

Life a la Mode

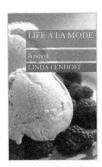

What do you do when your little sister has been engaged six times, your mother is dating a sixty-five-year-old man obsessed with fish, your father has run off from a family reunion with a woman who claims to be a distant cousin, and your ex-husband keeps stopping by with little gift-wrapped parcels of spicy food? Holly Philips doesn't really know what to do next. Holly's pharmacist friend Maria has some of the answers, and a few cold capsules just in case. And Holly's officemate and fellow production editor Tom has a few ideas he'd like to share with Holly, if only he can bring himself to speak around her, and only when their mocking boss, Monique, isn't too close by. Will Tom ask Holly out, and will it be for more than lunch at The Jelly Deli across from their Greenwich Village office? Holly's about to find out about Tom, about her sister Janie's passion for all things bridal, about Maria's weak spot for men who get their hands dirty, about her mother's intended four-month-long African safari, about her ex-husband's plans for their future, and about long-lost Dad, who may not be so lost after all. *A Literary Guild Featured Alternate.*

Made in the USA
Monee, IL
24 September 2021